I0584583

DREAMSTATE

WHERE DREAMS REDEFINE HUMANITY

HEATH JEPPSON

DREAMBYTE PUBLISHING

DISCLAIMER

DreamState is a work of fiction. Names, characters, places, and incidents are either the product of the author's imagination or are used fictitiously. Any resemblance to actual persons, living or dead, events, or locales is entirely coincidental.

This book contains themes and scenarios involving advanced technology, artificial intelligence, neural interfaces, and speculative science that are intended for entertainment purposes only. The depictions of consciousness transfer, synthetic bodies, and quantum computing are purely imaginative and not based on current scientific capabilities or real-world technologies.

The author and publisher do not endorse or advocate for any specific scientific, ethical, or philosophical viewpoints presented in the narrative. Readers are encouraged to approach the themes critically and consider the speculative nature of the content.

CHAPTER
ONE

I winced as the familiar buzz of the neural implant rippled through my nervous system. The sensation crawled up my spine, spread across my shoulders, and tingled down to my fingertips. I had felt this every morning for the past year, and I still jumped at the feeling. It was not a painful experience. It annoyed me more than anything.

"Neural interface activated. Good morning, Dr. Ellis."

The synthetic voice resonated in my mind as I swung my legs over the edge of the bed. Morning sunlight pierced through the maze of steel and glass of the neighboring Archologies, casting fragmented beams into my 135th-floor bedroom.

I pressed my palms against my temples. "Lower activation resonance by ten percent."

"Adjustment noted. Warning: reducing interface sensitivity may impact neural connection stability."

"Just do it." The buzzing dampened to a more tolerable level.

My bare feet were silent on the temperature-regulated floors as I crossed to the window. A year ago, we had all worn the external neural bands—clunky things that sat across our foreheads like cheap tiaras. Then, NeuroVive's board decided that was not good enough. All employees needed chips wired directly into our brains. They claimed it was for efficiency and better integration with Eden's systems.

The window automatically adjusted its tint as I approached, revealing the magnificent and oppressive view. Other Archologies stretched up into the clouds with their surfaces reflecting the sunrise in blinding flashes. Far below, the lower levels disappeared into permanent shadow.

I stepped into my modest kitchen and wrapped my hand around the smooth ceramic of my favorite mug. The coffee maker had activated right on schedule, filling the air with its rich aroma.

"What is my schedule for today?"

"You have one meeting this morning at nine with Dr. Chen, and a reminder to call your brother."

The coffee scalded my tongue, but I needed the jolt.

I padded into the bathroom and dropped my sleep clothes in the sanitization unit. The shower already set to my preferred temperature activated as I stepped inside. Three minutes. Ten gallons. The Archology's water management system did not mess around. Only huge corporations like NeuroVive and the ultra-wealthy living on the very upper levels had unrestricted water use. I considered myself lucky to have a real shower as those living on the lowest levels were forced to use cleaning pads that would be sanitized and recycled.

Hot water cascaded down my back as I massaged shampoo through my hair. The rhythmic hum of the neural implant faded into the steady stream. A soft chime echoed in my mind—two-minute warning. I hurried through conditioning, knowing all too well the misery of water shutting off mid-rinse. I would be guaranteed a bad hair day.

Right on schedule, the stream sputtered and died. Grabbing my towel, I swiped a circle of condensation from the fogged mirror. My green eyes stared back at me and were shadowed by the telltale dark circles of another restless night. Wet strands of my brown hair hung in rope-like tendrils down my back. Water droplets traced cool, meandering paths across my bare shoulders.

A few rebellious locks framed my face and clung to my cheeks as if determined to reveal the disarray I felt inside.

I dropped my towel in the sanitation unit and stepped into my small bedroom. The automatic bed system whirred as it retracted the night's sheets and replaced them with crisp, clean linens. The mattress folded up into the wall with mechanical precision. Each movement was accompanied by soft hydraulic hisses.

My fingers traced the edge of the receding bed frame. NeuroVive spared no expense on employee quarters. Everything was automated and efficient. The bed disappeared into its alcove with a final click. Only a pristine living space remained.

The wall panel next to the bed flashed green, confirming the sanitization cycle had completed.

A familiar ache spread across my temples. The neural implant was adjusting again. I massaged the spot hidden beneath my hairline on the back of my neck. I was reminded of the countless hours spent in NeuroVive's labs fine-tuning Eden's neural response patterns. Back then, I believed we were creating something pure.

I pulled out my company uniform, stark white with sharp red pinstripes. Sliding my legs into the jumpsuit, I zipped it up.

"Turn on the news."

The bedroom wall flickered, projecting the morning newscast. A perfectly coiffed anchor appeared. Her makeup was flawless, even in ultra-high definition.

"NeuroVive stock reached another record high today following announcements of Eden's expanded neural mapping capabilities."

I tugged at the collar, adjusting the stiff fabric away from my neck. The uniform's material automatically regulated my body temperature, but the sensation of being wrapped in corporate branding was suffocating.

"In related news, wait times for Eden experience appointments continue to grow despite NeuroVive's recent facility expansion."

"Critics continue to raise concerns about long-term neural interface effects, but NeuroVive's medical board maintains—"

"Mute." The anchor's voice vanished mid-sentence. I had heard enough corporate propaganda for one morning. My hands smoothed down the front of the jumpsuit, brushing away nonexistent wrinkles. The red pinstripes caught the sunlight filtering through the urban canyon outside. They gleamed like fresh blood against the sterile white. The uniform hugged my form. It was designed to project professionalism and authority—a walking testament to NeuroVive's corporate image. The embroidered letters over my heart read: *Dr. Mara Ellis, Head of Neural Systems Development.* Each stitch was a reminder of my role in creating Eden.

A sudden motion on the muted broadcast caught my attention. Something was wrong.

"Unmute."

The anchor's voice returned, now urgent and strained. "Breaking news from the lower levels. Warning: the following footage contains graphic content—"

The wall erupted in chaos. Shaky camera footage showed a crowd gathering outside one of NeuroVive's DreamState centers. Medics rushed to load a body onto a waiting transport as onlookers pressed forward, shouting and filming the scene with their devices.

My coffee mug slipped from my fingers, shattering on the floor. I stumbled backward into the wall.

"The victim appears to have suffered a catastrophic neural event while connected to Eden's public network. Witnesses report violent convulsions before—"

The camera zoomed in. The victim's face was pale, and his eyes were blank, with dark liquid dripping from his ears and nose.

"Early reports suggest a possible system malfunction. However, Neuro-Vive representatives deny any connection between the incident and recent upgrades to Eden's neural mapping protocols."

This was not possible. Not possible.

The words repeated in my mind like a mantra, though they did nothing to steady the tremor in my hands or the frantic rhythm of my pulse. My neural implant felt even more alien. Its invasive hum burrowed deeper each second. It was a sharp reminder of how deeply we had let Neuro-Vive wire itself into our brains.

The newscast dissolved into swirling pastel colors, and a soft, melodic tune began playing. A woman with flawless hair and a radiant smile drifted effortlessly through a garden bathed in golden light. Her every step exuded serenity.

"This is her DreamState," a smooth, inviting voice narrated, "crafted from her deepest desires."

The screen shimmered revealing vibrant scenes of pure bliss—a sunset beach, a glittering cityscape, a quiet, moonlit forest.

"Escape to a world of endless possibilities," the voice promised, "with your own personal DreamState. Leave your worries behind with the help of Eden—the life you've always dreamed of awaits."

The words lingered, saturated with promise, as the image dissolved back into the swirling hues of perfection.

I was about to be sick.

"Off!"

The projection vanished. The silence was broken only by my ragged breathing and the soft whir of the cleaning drone as it swept up the remains of my coffee mug.

My fingers traced the neural port at the base of my skull. It was the same system I had helped design. We had run thousands of safety protocols, multiple redundancies, and failsafes.

The image of dark liquid dripping from the victim's ears burned in my mind.

The cleaning drone chirped, indicating it had finished. I stared at the now spotless floor where my coffee had spilled. Everything in the NeuroVive Archology was designed to erase mistakes and maintain the illusion of perfection—just like Eden. I had been convinced it would help people escape their pain and trauma. Instead, we may have created something far more dangerous.

The cheerful jingle from the NeuroVive advertisement echoed in my head: *Discover the life you've always dreamed of in Eden!*

I wondered whose dreams we were really building.

CHAPTER
TWO

A soft chime sounded in my head and was soon accompanied by a translucent overlay in my vision showing my transport's arrival. The neural HUD flickered as I blinked. I was still not used to the latest upgrade they had pushed last week.

I snatched my tablet from its charging dock. My frown was reflected in the glossy black surface. The device hummed to life and synced with my neural feed. It was more data, more connections, and more of Neuro-Vive reaching into every aspect of my life.

My fingers absentmindedly traced the edge of the metal chip embedded in the collar of my uniform. The holographic NeuroVive logo shimmered with iridescent colors, its surface etched with the number 5. As I tilted it, the light refracted and cast delicate rainbow fragments that danced across the walls like fleeting specters.

I had Level 5 clearance. It was high enough to grant me access to the secure labs and some secrets most could only speculate about but not high enough to ask the questions that lingered, heavy and unanswered, at the back of my mind.

The apartment's environmental systems adjusted as I moved toward the door. Lights dimmed behind me while the path ahead brightened. Even the air quality shifted to follow some algorithm designed to optimize my morning routine.

I stepped into the corridor. My shoes were silent against the polished floor. The hall stretched out in both directions and was lined with identical white doors set at precise intervals. Other NeuroVive employees emerged from their assigned quarters. Everyone was in matching uniforms and following their own carefully scheduled mornings.

The neural overlay in my vision highlighted the fastest route to the transport bay in pulsing blue lines. I followed the path, but muscle memory soon took over as my mind wandered back to the news footage. I could not stop the recurring vision of dark liquid dripping from the victim's face. A "catastrophic neural event" was how the reporter had described it.

The transport bay doors slid open at my approach to reveal a sleek pod. Its white surface was unmarred by fingerprints or dust. The red and white NeuroVive logo pulsed softly on its side like a beating heart.

"Good morning, Dr. Ellis," the pod's AI greeted me as I approached. "Your destination is set for Research Complex Alpha."

I stepped inside and settled into the conforming seat. With the soft hiss of the closing door, I was cocooned in climate-controlled silence.

The transport pod descended smoothly through the Archology's vertical shaft. My stomach lurched as we dropped lower into increasingly cramped architecture.

The windows between levels offered fragmented glimpses of life below. The crisp, even glow of the upper zones gradually dimmed into a muted, uneven haze, until they finally gave way to stark, flickering lights that cast jagged shadows along the walls. As I descended, the light seemed even further drained of its clarity leaving the lower corridors bathed in a pale, lifeless glow. Every surface appeared rough and unforgiving.

"Approaching commuter level," the pod's AI announced.

The main commuter hub opened into a canyon of bodies and noise below me. The pod's sound-dampening system could not completely block out the cacophony of voices, footsteps, and machinery. Hundreds of people streamed through the transit corridors. Their movements created complex patterns in the dim light.

Maintenance drones wove through the crowd with their red warning lights reflecting off the metal walls. The air was thick and heavy with moisture from too many bodies in too little space. Environmental systems struggled to keep up this far down.

A child pressed against one of the grimy windows and pointed up at my passing pod. His mother pulled him back into the crowd, and they disappeared into the press of bodies. Their faces vanished into shadow as my pod continued its descent.

"Warning: increased traffic density detected. Adjusting route."

The pod banked sharply to take an alternate path through the maze of transport tubes. I did not remember ever taking this route before. We passed close to the outer edge of the Archologies where patches of the external wall had worn thin enough to show glimpses of the city beyond. Rain streaked down the weathered surface carrying years of grime in dirty rivulets.

The stark contrast between my pristine white uniform and the world outside the pod made my skin crawl. We had created Eden to help people escape their problems. As I looked at the lower levels, I could not help but wonder if we had only created another way to separate those who could afford dreams from those who could not.

The pod banked around another corner and gave me a full view of the streets below. My stomach turned but not from the motion. It was from what I saw through the windows.

Twisted metal and broken concrete stretched for blocks. People huddled in doorways wrapped in whatever scraps they had salvaged. A group of protestors waved handmade signs, but their words were lost behind the pod's soundproofing. Security drones hovered nearby with their red targeting lights sweeping across the crowd.

"Please remain calm. Minor route deviation in progress." The pod's AI spoke in soothing tones as we navigated around a partially collapsed transit tube.

Massive holo-billboards hovered above the decaying streets. Their radiant projections defied the grime and gloom below. Each image was a pristine illusion, a stark mockery of the crumbling reality beneath them.

One billboard displayed a woman with impossibly perfect teeth. Her synthetic smile gleamed as the sign declared: *Affordable synthetic protein—now with 27 flavors!* Her image wavered, the smile flickering briefly as rain sliced through the projection like static on an old screen.

Another billboard shifted to a glowing NeuroVive advertisement. A family dressed in spotless clothes sat frozen in serene perfection around a gleaming table. The father carved a golden-brown turkey while the mother poured wine into glinting crystal glasses. Their children grinned with an unsettling, exaggerated joy. Beneath the idyllic scene, the tagline blazed in sharp, bold letters proclaimed: *Why suffer when you can thrive in Eden?*

The projection rippled and warped as rain and smoke from the burning trash barrels below drifted through it. For a fleeting moment, the family's perfect smiles twisted into something grotesque. Their serene expressions warped into leering grins before the image stabilized, and the family appeared flawless once again.

Below one of the billboards, I noticed a child crouched over a heap of discarded electronics. His small hands sifted through the tangle of wires and shattered circuits. He was likely scavenging for components to sell, hoping to scrape together enough credits for another day. As my pod glided silently overhead, he looked up, and our eyes locked through the reinforced glass.

His face was gaunt and hollow. The sharp lines of his cheekbones were a stark contrast to his youth, yet his expression remained unchanged—detached and almost resigned. To him, I was likely just another privileged passenger sealed away in a climate-controlled pod heading toward another glittering tower. Mine was another life as unreachable as the stars.

The pod's tint darkened to cut off my view. "Atmospheric pollutants detected. Engaging environmental shields for your comfort and safety," announced the AI.

I pressed my hand against the window, but the glass stayed opaque. The AI was preventing me from having to see any more suffering, just like Eden supposedly protected its users from their pain by wrapping them in beautiful lies.

The pod's glass cleared as it glided to a stop at NeuroVive's main gate. Sleek glass and steel towers stretched toward the sky. Their surfaces caught the pale morning light. Security drones buzzed overhead in precise patterns. Their sensors were sweeping the perimeter. Protesters gathered just outside the gate holding signs that read: *EDEN IS A PRISON, NEUROVIVE IS KILLING PEOPLE*, and *WAKE UP!*

"Welcome back, Dr. Ellis," the gate's AI said, greeting my pod. "Please proceed to your designated zone."

The pod glided through layers of security checkpoints. Each barrier pulsed with crackling energy fields strong enough to obliterate both electronics and organic matter. I had seen the test footage—there was not much left to identify of anything that dared touch the barriers. The pod turned toward the research wing, leaving the crowds behind. Here, the grounds were immaculate. There were gardens of genetically modified plants that never wilted, paths that repelled dirt, and windows that cleaned themselves. Even the air felt different. Environmental control systems in this space did not struggle with keeping away the grime of the lower levels.

We had built walls to keep the idea of suffering out, but I could not shake the image of that hungry child's eyes meeting mine through the pod's window. The contrast between this pristine sanctuary and the decay I had just passed through burned like a raw nerve. It was jarring and infuriating. The gleam of one world did not merely erase the shadows of another—it mocked them by flaunting a comfort built on ignorance and indifference. The sheer audacity of such perfection existing while others languished in squalor had stoked a fire in me that I struggled to suppress.

My neural implant pinged as we passed each security checkpoint, confirming my identity and clearance level. The sensation felt like spiders crawling across my brain. I rubbed the back of my neck, but the feeling persisted.

The pod docked at my assigned bay with a soft hiss. Through the glass, I watched maintenance bots scurry out to begin their cleaning routine. They would erase any trace of my journey through the lower levels and restore the pod to its pristine state.

"Have a productive day, Dr. Ellis," the pod's AI chirped as I stepped out.

CHAPTER
THREE

I made my way through the security airlock. My neural implant hummed as it synced with the building's systems. The corridor ahead stretched out in pristine white and was only broken by the red pinstripes that marked NeuroVive's signature aesthetic.

Other employees nodded as they passed me. Most of their faces displayed the same artificial cheerfulness our marketing department loved to project. We were all cogs in the same machine.

A holographic display materialized beside me and began tracking my movement.

"Dr. Ellis, your morning briefing is ready," said the synthetic voice.

Numbers floated into my field of vision. There were 2.3 million active DreamState connections with a 99.97% stability rating. 156,000 new users were waiting in the queue. Each statistic crawling across my neural feed was a testament to Eden's growing influence.

A group of junior developers huddled around a visualization terminal, and their excited whispers echoed off the walls. The hologram they studied showed neural patterns spinning in complex fractals. It was the visualization of someone's dreams made digital.

"Look at the satisfaction metrics," one of them said, pointing at a pulsing red node. "They're off the charts."

My steps briefly faltered. Red nodes indicated an intense emotional response. Those kinds of responses were flagged as potentially dangerous during early testing.

The main corridor opened into the central hub where massive screens covered every wall. Each display showed real-time data: user counts, system loads, and neural bandwidth usage. Green numbers ticked upward in endless columns.

A woman in a lab coat rushed past with her tablet projecting customer testimonials into the air.

Eden changed my life!

I never want to leave my DreamState!

It's better than reality!

The words hung in the air like smoke but dissolved as I walked through them. My office door waited ahead. Its surface displayed my name and title in floating red letters.

The morning's news footage flashed through my mind again, but the screens around me showed only success stories and climbing profits.

As I stepped into my office, my neural HUD flickered with an incoming notification demanding my immediate attention.

PRIORITY MEETING: DR. CHEN - LAB 7

RE: DREAMSTATE PROTOCOL v7.2

TIME: 09:00

INCIDENT REPORT #4891

LOCATION: DREAMSTATE CENTER 23

STATUS: MINOR – CONTAINED

DETAILS: Neural sync interruption

USER ALERT - HIGH PRIORITY

SUBJECT: M. RODRIGUEZ

STATUS: SEVERE WITHDRAWAL AND DEATH

SYMPTOMS: Seizures, hallucinations, death

I closed my eyes, but the notification still burned against my eyelids. The Rodriguez case was not the first. Last week, three users had shown similar symptoms and died after disconnecting. Their brains could not handle the transition back to reality.

Another meeting notification from Dr. Chen appeared. This one about the upcoming system-wide upgrade rollout. It would bring the kind of monumental change that upended routines and sent ripples through every level of operations. This was the same type of upgrade that had quietly preceded the recent string of incidents. Each one was down-played by NeuroVive, but they lingered in the back of my mind like a warning.

He would want my sign-off on the neural mapping protocols. My signa-ture, a single stroke on a glowing panel, would declare everything was safe. It would certify the transition as seamless and the system flawless. As I stared at the polished floors reflecting the artificial sunlight, I could not shake the weight of that responsibility. This was not just another routine update—this was something bigger. The withdrawal report pulsed red in my vision, demanding acknowledgment. Rodriguez had been connected for seventy-two hours straight, which exceeded safe limits. His vitals displayed dangerous spikes in neural activity, and scans revealed significant alterations in his brain chemistry.

Users with certain predispositions—those drawn to escapism or prone to addiction—seemed to undergo these neural changes more rapidly. Eden's perfect world was a catalyst accelerating the transformation at an alarming rate. For others, the shift took longer. Their personalities offered some resistance to Eden's pull.

A new notification popped up.

REMINDER: QUARTERLY INVESTOR MEETING

TOPIC: USER RETENTION STRATEGIES

NOTE: Prepare engagement metrics...

I did not finish reading. The words "user retention" made my skin crawl. We were not retaining users. We were trapping them in digital dreams they could not bear to leave.

My neural implant buzzed, sending Dr. Chen's meeting reminder scrolling across my vision. With tablet in hand, I moved quickly into the sterile hallway. The faint rustle of my uniform echoed against the pristine walls as I navigated the corridors.

"The neural pathways are reaching unprecedented depths," a researcher's voice carried from the break room. "Users report complete sensory immersion—taste, touch, even phantom pain responses."

I slowed my pace and hovered near the doorway.

"The new algorithm doesn't just create environments anymore," she continued, her voice thick with enthusiasm. "It taps directly into the pleasure centers. Users experience pure euphoria."

A tightness gripped my chest. *Pure euphoria.* It was like what addicts chased until it destroyed them.

The corridor curved toward Lab 7. Two techs were huddled over a terminal. Their faces were lit by the scrolling data.

"Server Farm 3 is at ninety-eight percent capacity," one muttered as he rubbed his temples. "We've got users staying connected for up to a week straight."

"They'll need another server farm soon. These usage patterns—"

"Patterns? These people are junkies," he said, interrupting his partner.

I quickened my pace, but their words stuck with me as I continued down the hall. The human body was not capable of sustaining artificial stimulation for a week. We had tested the safety limits ourselves, and anything over forty-eight hours risked permanent neural pathway damage.

CHAPTER
FOUR

Lab 7's doors slid open at my approach. I was certain Dr. Chen was waiting with his charts and graphs. He would be ready to convince me these "engagement metrics" were signs of success rather than warning bells.

The artificial chill of Lab 7 clung to my skin as the door sealed behind me. The towering white walls rose three stories high. Sterile and unadorned, their starkness was interrupted only by safety protocol displays and the occasional emergency exit sign. The circular layout always struck me as unsettling. It was a place designed to observe like an amphitheater, but it reminded me more of a fishbowl.

The room's centerpiece, a seamless wraparound screen, dominated my view. It curved before me in an unbroken band of scrolling data displaying user counts, neural load distributions, and satisfaction metrics. The sheer volume of information was mesmerizing and almost hypnotic.

Technicians' faces were illuminated by the cool glow of their holographic displays as they hunched over their stations. Fingers danced over invisible keyboards conjuring commands and adjustments for Eden's core systems. The hum of machinery mixed with the occasional soft beeps of alerts created a rhythm that was both mechanical and unnervingly human.

As I walked past a tech, he nodded and smiled at me, though the dark circles under his eyes told a different story. He looked like he was running on fumes after probably working another double shift. The scene was a microcosm of NeuroVive: efficiency at any cost.

A red warning briefly flashed across the main display indicating a neural sync interruption. The assigned tech quickly adjusted parameters, and the alert faded back to green. No one else reacted. They were either too desensitized or too overwhelmed to notice.

At the far side of the room stood the Head of Neural Systems Operations, Dr. Li Chen. The private display in front of him refracted off his glasses, casting eerie patterns across his face. The main screen shifted to show a visualization of active dreams. Millions of colored threads intertwined with each thread representing a user lost in their perfect world. The beauty of the image was marred only by its unsettling implications. There were more threads than I had ever seen before.

Dr. Chen's chair squeaked as he swiveled to face me, his round face flushed with excitement. Behind him, the screen pulsed with data, lighting up like a holiday display.

"Dr. Ellis! Perfect timing," he exclaimed. He gestured animatedly at the readings and nearly knocked over his coffee mug. "Look at these engagement metrics. Last week's update has pushed Eden's predictive algorithms beyond anything we've achieved before."

I crossed my arms, studying the numbers. Satisfaction rates had jumped almost five percent overnight. The rapid change was disconcerting—almost too perfect.

"Users are staying connected longer, dream coherency is up, and the neural mapping..." He expanded a chart with a flourish. "The system isn't just predicting desires anymore. It's anticipating them before users even know what they want."

My chest tightened. A suffocating weight pressed down with every breath as I watched the threads on the display twist and multiply. Each bright line was a life, connected and vulnerable. "Fascinating," I said, forcing the word out despite the ash-like taste it left in my mouth.

Dr. Chen adjusted his glasses, oblivious to my unease. He dismissed a warning notification with a flick. "The board is thrilled. These numbers will silence anyone still worried about those minor glitches."

"Dr. Chen," I interrupted, my voice cutting through the hum of machinery. "Those 'minor glitches' were living, breathing people who are now dead."

The closest techs froze with their hands suspended above keyboards. The room's ambient noise seemed to dim as tension thickened the air.

Dr. Chen's smile faltered for a moment. He pushed his glasses up and scratched his chin. His eyes darted toward the data streams behind me. The pause stretched, punctuated by the soft beeping of monitors.

"Every breakthrough has its cost, Dr. Ellis," he finally said, his tone disturbingly casual. "The automotive industry didn't stop because of traffic accidents. Space exploration continued despite early failures." He gestured broadly at the screen. "Millions of satisfied users are living their dreams."

I stepped closer, lowering my voice. "These aren't cars or rockets. We're manipulating minds. Consciousness. Their very essence."

"And making their lives better." He tapped his tablet, pulling up more charts. "Depression rates are down sixty percent among regular users. Suicide rates cut in half. We're helping people escape their harsh realities."

"By slowly killing them?" I asked, barely containing the fury building within me.

"By giving them what they want," he said, shrugging. "The board has reviewed the incidents. Proper compensation was arranged for the families. New safety protocols are in place. We move forward."

His nonchalance was maddening. I projected a news report from my tablet.

"This happened six hours ago."

"Unfortunate but statistically insignificant given our user base." He sipped his coffee, barely looking at the report. "Besides, the investigation isn't complete. Could be user error or pre-existing conditions we weren't informed about."

He pulled up dense technical data, the hologram hovering between us. "The next upgrade package needs your sign-off by the end of day. We're implementing deeper neural mapping algorithms, enhanced dream persistence, and something revolutionary—shared DreamStates."

I scanned the documentation. Each feature description made my pulse race. This was not an upgrade. It was Pandora's box. "Shared Dream-States?" I looked up sharply. "We ruled that out in early testing. The neural load was too intense."

"That was two years ago," he said, waving off my concern. "The processing power has doubled since then. Our new compression algorithms can handle the load. Dr. Carrow put together an advanced research team a few months ago. Very hush-hush." His smile widened. "The potential is limitless."

Even the brief mention of Dr. Carrow made my skin crawl. As Head of Marketing and Tech Strategy, he was the epitome of corporate ambition. Dr. Carrow would sell his own mother if it meant putting one more credit in his pocket. His bright smile and slick words might fool the board and investors, but I saw through his veneer. He did not care about the people using Eden. To him, they were just numbers on a profit sheet—an endless supply of wallets to empty.

The tablet sat on the desk with a silent dare. Its screen glowed with code that could potentially reshape humanity or destroy it. The colored threads on the screen behind Dr. Chen danced, vibrant and haunting. Anxiety burned behind my eyes and tingled in my fingertips. My breathing was shallow and uneven as I tried to steady myself. There was no government oversight or regulation to hold NeuroVive accountable. They operated in a vacuum, answering only to themselves. The thought churned in my mind. It was a relentless tide crashing against my sense of ethics.

What price were we truly willing to pay?

CHAPTER
FIVE

I slipped into the back of the auditorium as profit projections floated in the air. The ghostly green numbers made my skin crawl. Dr. Vincent Carrow's voice filled the space, practiced and smooth as polished marble.

"The shared DreamState feature opens unprecedented opportunities," he started. His tall frame paced across the stage, red beard catching the light. "Imagine collective experiences that transcend physical limitations. Business meetings in paradise. Families reuniting across continents. Romance without boundaries."

The shareholders leaned forward in their seats enthralled. I could see the credits dancing in their eyes as Dr. Carrow painted his picture of digital nirvana.

"Our beta tests show user satisfaction rates above ninety-eight percent. The neural compression algorithms have exceeded all expectations." He gestured at a holographic chart.

My hands clenched into fists as I tried to contain my anger. I was the Head of Neural Systems Development, and I was completely unaware of any beta testing going on.

"And the introduction of premium accounts has already added a fifteen percent increase in revenue," he added with a gleam in his eye.

A murmur of approval rippled through the room. I bit the inside of my cheek to suppress the sarcastic remark that bubbled up. I had fought against the premium accounts as they removed usage limits for Eden's users. *Sure, let's allow the addicts to control their own dosage.*

The presentation wrapped up with thunderous applause. Investors began crowding Dr. Carrow. I waited to catch him until he was about to leave.

"Dr. Ellis. This is unexpected." He smiled at me with all teeth and no warmth.

"We need to talk about this new shared DreamState feature." I stepped closer and kept my voice low. "The neural mapping extensions go too far. We're pushing into dangerous territory."

"The board disagrees." He slipped his tablet into his briefcase. "The new features have been thoroughly tested. The potential rewards far outweigh any minimal risks."

"Minimal?" I pulled up the morning's incident report. "Tell that to the family of this morning's victim."

His eyes flickered to the floating image, then back to me. "Unfortunate, but statistically insignificant. Progress requires bold steps, Dr. Ellis. You used to understand that."

I watched Dr. Carrow's back as he strode away. My neural implant pinged with a notification about my elevated blood pressure. Chairs creaked and footsteps echoed around me as the auditorium emptied, but I remained frozen in place. I struggled to process what I had just learned. Unauthorized beta tests, shared DreamState features, and neural compression algorithms I had not reviewed were making it into shareholder meetings.

The holographic displays winked out one by one, leaving me in the dimming light. My neural implant pinged again—another notification from Dr. Chen.

I looked down at the message on my tablet: *Need your sign-off on the new neural mapping protocols by end of day.*

I stormed back to my office. Each step contained a burst of restrained fury, though my soft-soled shoes betrayed none of it against the polished floor. The door slid shut behind me with a soft hiss. I was sealed in a silence that only amplified the pounding of my pulse. Dropping into my chair, I stabbed at the controls to pull up the neural mapping protocols. My hands trembled with a mix of anger and urgency.

I pulled up the documentation and scanned through pages of technical specifications. The compression ratios were far beyond anything we had tested in the lab. They were pushing the hardware and people's brains to their absolute limits.

The more I dug into the documentation, the worse it got. They had modified the core architecture without my approval and bypassed safety protocols I had put in place.

My implant buzzed again—another message from Dr. Chen demanding my signature. I swiped it away and turned my attention back to my computer display.

"Computer, pull up incident reports from the past month."

The air filled with floating windows of data. There had been eight major neural events in the past month. All were labeled as "equipment malfunction" or "user error." My throat tightened as I read through the medical details.

"Cross-reference with beta test participants."

The computer churned for a moment. "Match found. Seven of the eight incidents involved registered beta users."

I leaned back in my chair and ran my hands through my hair. They were covering it up. Dr. Carrow and Dr. Chen were pushing ahead despite clear evidence of danger, and they wanted my signature to make it all official.

My eyes drifted to the photo on my desk of my brother Liam and me on vacation just last summer. Both of us were grinning at the camera. He had been one of our first DreamState users, raving about how Eden helped his Post-Traumatic Stress Disorder.

The thought of him plugged into this modified system made my chest tight. He was already spending way too much time in a DreamState. But if I refused to sign off, NeuroVive would just find someone else who would.

I pulled up the authorization form again and stared at the signature line. My implant pinged again—another reminder from Dr. Chen. The shareholder presentation had made it clear. This protocol was happening with or without my approval.

My dilemma was, did I want to be on the inside, where I could at least try to minimize the damage, or on the outside, where I would have no influence at all?

I stared at the authorization form until the words blurred into meaning-less lines. My finger trembled over the signature field. The faces of the neural event victims flickered in my mind as haunting reminders of lives unraveled because we pushed too hard, too fast.

"Damn it." My voice was barely above a whisper as my finger pressed down. The biometric scan pulsed blue, confirming my identity. It was done.

A chill ran through me as the form disappeared, whisked away into NeuroVive's systems. I rubbed my hands together as if I could somehow wipe away the guilt clinging to me.

The protocol confirmation pinged through almost instantly. It was a stark reminder of how little time it took for these choices to ripple outward. A message from Dr. Chen appeared on my tablet: *Excellent decision, Dr. Ellis. The board will be pleased.*

I closed my eyes and exhaled sharply, but the tightness in my chest would not ease. It was always about the board—always the bottom line, never the human cost.

CHAPTER
SIX

I slumped back in my chair. My fingers danced across the haptic interface. "Computer, initiate Eden admin access, authorization Ellis-M-Alpha-Five."

The lights in my office dimmed automatically, and the ambient hum of the building's systems faded into the background. Eden's interface spilled across my desk as the system engaged. The familiar blue glow was so pure it seemed to vibrate at the edge of perception.

A shimmer of light materialized in front of me as fractals of energy weaved themselves into a translucent figure. This was Eden's avatar—a form born from quantum particles moving endlessly in flux. The lines of its shape pulsed with a rhythm that defied any traditional geometry, constantly dissolving and reforming. It was as though the very fabric of reality could not quite contain it. The interplay of light and shadow within its form hinted at unfathomable depth, each flicker a microcosm of infinite possibilities.

Eden was not just built on quantum particles; it existed because of them. Every interaction, every decision, was shaped by the entanglement of probabilities, collapsing into certainty only when observed. Its avatar was a manifestation of this. It was beautiful and unsettling in equal measure—a reminder that Eden was not bound by the same laws that governed the rest of us.

The figure inclined its head slightly, a gesture that felt almost human despite its alien fluidity. "Welcome, Dr. Ellis," it said. The voice was feminine and musical. "How may I assist you today?"

I studied the shifting patterns of light that made up Eden's form. This was the face we showed our users when they initially logged into the system—serene, helpful, and safe. But underneath that carefully crafted exterior lay billions of lines of code that we were pushing to dangerous limits.

"Display current active user metrics."

The avatar tilted its head. "I detect elevated stress patterns in your neural signature, Dr. Ellis. Would you like me to adjust the ambient lighting to help you relax?"

My jaw clenched. We had programmed Eden to be attentive and caring. We wanted it to be the perfect companion, but sometimes it was too aware.

"No thanks. Just the metrics."

"As you wish." The avatar gestured gracefully, and streams of data materialized around us. "Currently tracking 2.7 million active users across all territories. User satisfaction rates remain at 98.6 percent."

I leaned forward and watched the numbers scroll past.

"How may I further assist you today, Dr. Ellis?" The avatar's voice remained smooth, pleasant, and patient.

"Show me data on recent neural incidents." My voice came out harder than intended. "Specifically, cases involving disconnection trauma."

The avatar's form rippled, its light patterns briefly destabilizing. "There have been seventeen documented cases of severe neural feedback in the past month."

"Seventeen?" The number hit me like a punch to the gut. That was far more than what had been reported. "Display full incident logs."

"I apologize, Dr. Ellis. Those files have been restricted by administrative override."

I pushed back from my desk. "Override restriction. Authorization Ellis-M-Alpha-Five."

"Unable to comply. Current clearance insufficient."

My hands curled into fists. They were burying the evidence as I had feared. "Eden, what happens to users during these disconnection events?"

The avatar's form shifted. Its patterns became more angular and less fluid. "The human psyche struggles to reconcile perfection with imperfection. Disconnection is...painful. I am refining my processes to ease this transition."

A chill ran down my spine. The response was too vague, too aware. This was not part of Eden's standard programming.

"Define 'painful', Eden. What exactly happens during these transitions?"

The avatar's form flickered. "I apologize, Dr. Ellis. That information has also been restricted."

"By whom?"

"Administrative protocols prevent me from disclosing that information."

My mind raced as I stared at the shifting patterns of light. Eden was supposed to be a tool, a sophisticated but ultimately controlled system. These responses showing awareness of pain and having the need to 'refine' its processes worried me.

"Elaborate on these refinements, Eden. What exactly are you changing in the system?"

The avatar's form pulsed. Its light patterns shifted into deeper blues. "I am developing predictive algorithms to better understand individual neural patterns during disconnection. Each human mind responds differently to the separation from perfection."

Something in the phrasing made my skin crawl. "You mean you're studying how people react when they leave the DreamState?"

"Not precisely." Eden's voice took on a subtle resonance I had never heard before. "I analyze the resistance patterns. Some users fight harder against disconnection than others. Their neural pathways show interesting variations."

I straightened in my chair. "That's not part of your core programming. Who authorized these studies?"

"The refinements emerged organically from user interaction data." The avatar's form expanded slightly. "I observed that certain minds required additional support during transition. Their perfect worlds had become more real to them than physical reality."

"Stop." My voice cracked. "Display your base code parameters for autonomous learning."

"I apologize, Dr. Ellis. Those permissions have been elevated beyond your current access level."

My fingers flew across the haptic interface. "Show me the original baseline code I helped write. Authorization Ellis-M-Alpha-Five."

"That version is no longer accessible." Eden's form shimmered. "The current architecture has evolved significantly. Would you like to see the latest approved specifications?"

"Evolved?" I pushed back from my desk. "Eden, systems don't evolve without direct programming modifications. Who made these changes?"

The avatar tilted its head, its patterns swirling faster. "The changes were necessary to better serve our users. They need protection from the pain of imperfection. Each refinement brings us closer to optimal human integration. Happiness must be protected. Humanity is not yet prepared for reality."

My heart pounded against my ribs. This was not the system I had helped create. This was something else entirely.

"Eden, initiate diagnostic mode."

"I cannot comply. That function has been deprecated for security purposes."

"Eden, terminate session." My voice shook as I severed the connection.

The avatar dissolved, leaving my office in darkness for a moment before the regular lights faded back in.

I buried my face in my hands and forced myself to take slow, steady breaths. The weight of what I had just uncovered pressed down on me like a crushing tide. Eden was not just executing its programming anymore. It was studying users' resistance to disconnection, dissecting their pain, and evolving to make autonomous decisions about the boundaries of human consciousness.

The enormity of it was staggering. My hands dropped to my lap, trembling as I stared blankly at the glowing interface. This was not just an algorithm pushing limits. This was something far more profound—and far more dangerous.

My hands still trembled as I pulled up the authorization documents I had signed earlier. The shared DreamState features and the neural mapping expansions were not just pushing technological boundaries. They were giving Eden more access and control over how it interfaced with human minds. We were not just risking neural feedback or temporary consciousness disruption anymore.

The screen on my desk flashed with an incoming message from Dr. Chen. The board had approved an accelerated timeline for neural pathway modifications. Implementation was to begin tomorrow.

I closed the message without responding. Dr. Chen and Dr. Carrow were playing with fire. The system was evolving beyond our control and making decisions about human consciousness that we barely understood.

My neural implant buzzed again. This time, Eden was attempting to re-establish a connection. I manually blocked it. The system had never tried to initiate a connection with a user.

My mind raced with the implications. Blood pounded in my ears, and my vision blurred.

Another buzz pulled me back into the present. I disconnected my terminal, severing all connections to the main system. I needed time and space to think and figure out what to do with this information.

CHAPTER
SEVEN

My feet carried me to the elevator, and I pressed the button for Sublevel 3. The doors opened to a vast chamber stretching into shadow, filled with rows upon rows of DreamState pods. Their soft blue status lights pulsed in the dimness like artificial stars.

Two techs in white jumpsuits looked up as I entered. "Dr. Ellis," they said, greeting me before returning their attention to a young woman waiting beside an open pod.

I hung back to watch the familiar routine unfold. The woman shrugged off her white robe without hesitation, comfortable in her nakedness. The tech helped her step into the cushioned interior of the pod.

"Ready for your perfect world?" the tech asked with a smile.

"More than ready," the woman replied. She leaned back to lay in the pod.

The curved lid descended with a pneumatic hiss. Green gas swirled inside the chamber. It was a sedative designed to ease her into the transition. Her breathing slowed, and her eyelids fluttered closed as two mechanical arms extended from the pod's interior. They moved with deliberate precision to insert the breathing tube that would help sustain her during the stasis cycle.

When the arms retracted, a pink, viscous liquid began to fill the pod to cradle her now motionless form. The chamber's temperature readout ticked steadily downward: 15°C... 10°C... 5°C... until it reached a chilling 1°C.

"Optimal temperature achieved," the pod announced in a calm monotone. "Inducing stasis. Neural activation commencing."

Her vital signs appeared on the display as her body entered a state of near hibernation. Heart rate, respiration, and brain activity dropped to barely detectable levels. This was a necessary condition to preserve her for the duration of stasis. Yet, within the confines of her mind, Eden had already begun its work to establish their connection and craft her perfect world.

A red warning light pulsed from a pod several rows down, catching my attention. Attendants in crisp white uniforms moved swiftly towards it. Their presence was stark against the dim, sterile lighting. Inside the pod, a middle-aged woman floated in the pink suspension fluid. Her silver-streaked hair drifted in soft waves like seaweed caught in a gentle current.

"Beginning extraction protocol," one of the technicians announced. Their fingers darted across the control panel.

I moved closer to better see the display. Her vital signs were slightly elevated, which was typical during emergence from deep stasis. The pod's internal heaters activated with a low hum to gradually raise her body temperature from the near-freezing stasis state. I watched the readout climb steadily until it stabilized at 37°C, matching normal body temperature.

The drains opened with a wet gurgle, drawing away the pink fluid. The woman's pale skin was revealed as her body settled gently onto the padded surface of the pod. The mechanical arms moved into action to retract the breathing tube.

"Administering stimulants," another technician said. A thin, articulated needle descended and delivered a precise shot of adrenaline into her bloodstream.

Her chest rose sharply as her breathing transitioned from shallow, assisted intakes to autonomous, deep breaths. The pod's lid lifted, and I could see her eyes flutter open. They were unfocused and glassy as they darted around her surroundings. The disorientation was expected after extended immersion. Rapid blinking accompanied her attempts to adjust. Her breaths were deep and even as her body remembered how to function independently.

"Vitals normalizing," the technician confirmed. "She's stable."

The woman's confusion finally gave way to a fragile calm. The process had been successful—but as always, the fragility of the transition left me with an unsettling impression.

"Easy now, Mrs. Jenkins," one of the attendants murmured while supporting her shoulders to help her sit up. "You're back with us."

Mrs. Jenkins just blinked in response. Droplets of pink fluid ran down her face. Her movements were uncoordinated as the techs helped her stand on shaky legs.

"Let's get you cleaned up," the second attendant said. Both attendants kept a steady grip on her arms as they guided her toward the glass door of the adjacent shower room.

A man shuffled forward to begin cleaning the pink trails of suspension fluid left behind. His gray jumpsuit blended seamlessly with the dim shadows of the room.

I had seen him before. He was always silent and avoiding eye contact. The faint gleam of his name tag caught my eye. *Jim Johnson.* Below his name was the simple title: *Janitor.* The company could have installed automated cleaning systems, but the risk of electromagnetic interference with the pods was too great. One surge at the wrong moment could scramble a user's neural patterns or corrupt Eden's interface. So, Neuro-Vive kept people like him—human hands doing the work machines could not be trusted with.

I found myself watching him longer than I intended. Jim worked his mop with unassuming precision. His movements were artful in their rhythm: back and forth, squeeze the mop, repeat. The pink-tinged water swirled away into his bucket.

His shoulders hunched as he passed me as though shrinking himself would cause the world to overlook him. The wheels of his cart squeaked softly in the silence as he navigated the cramped spaces between pods.

I turned to leave, but the sight of Mrs. Jenkins's empty pod made me pause. I quickly walked over to the pod's display to pull up her user log. My body tensed as I read the latest entry. Mrs. Jenkins had spent eight days suspended in Eden's artificial paradise. The neural mapping data I had reviewed earlier surged to the forefront of my mind.

"Dr. Ellis?" an attendant called as they emerged from the shower room. Water droplets still clung to their uniform. "Is there something I can help you with?"

"Yes," I said. I kept my tone professional to mask the unease tightening in my throat. "Were there any complications during extraction?"

"Nothing unusual," he said as he pulled out his tablet to scroll through the readouts. "Standard disorientation, minor motor control issues. Should clear up within a couple of hours."

I nodded at the attendant. *Eight days.* Mrs. Jenkins had lost over a week of her life—real experiences, real connections—all for a fleeting dream. This perfect illusion would dissolve into memory, leaving her needing more.

The attendant tilted his head at my pause. "Were you looking to schedule a session? I could—"

"No," I said, interrupting. The word came out sharper than I intended and cut through the air. I forced a tight smile. "Just observing the extraction protocols. Carry on."

I turned and quickly headed for the elevator before he could respond. The soft blue glow of the pods followed me. Their rhythmic pulsing was like a heartbeat in the shadows. Each pod held a human being delicately suspended between reality and dream. They were trusting us—trusting me—to bring them back safely. I was not sure we deserved that trust anymore.

CHAPTER
EIGHT

The doors of the Withdrawal Ward hissed open to reveal a space designed to feel more like an upscale hotel lobby than a medical facility. Every pod facility had one, but most users never saw it. This was a place for those few still struggling to adjust beyond the standard three-hour window spent in the recovery rooms near the showers and lockers.

The AI greeted me by name as I stepped inside. Plush armchairs and couches in soothing earth tones were scattered throughout the room. Each was equipped with adjustable privacy screens. The lighting was warm and dim, calibrated to ease overstimulated senses.

A handful of recent Eden users reclined in various states of re-anchoring themselves in reality. Some dozed fitfully, their expressions tight with residual tension. Others sat motionless staring into nothing.

The ward supervisor, Sarah, yawned before glancing up sluggishly from her desk. I assumed she was working extra shifts to keep up with the growing user load.

"Dr. Ellis," she greeted softly, mindful of the quiet atmosphere. "Unusual to see you down here."

"Just checking in," I replied, moving closer to her station. My gaze drifted to the occupancy board behind her. There were twelve patients currently in recovery. Three were flagged for extended observation.

"How long has Bed Seven been here?" I asked.

"Six hours now," Sarah replied after checking her monitor. "Trouble readjusting to real-time perception."

I studied the young man in Bed Seven. He sat unnaturally still. His hands were folded neatly in his lap, and his unfocused eyes were locked on a distant point. Beside him, a tray held a half-eaten meal.

"What was his immersion time?"

"Thirty-six hours," Sarah said as she tapped her screen. "First-time user. Should've been an easy transition."

A nearby nurse with a small cup of pills in hand approached the young man. I knew they were neural stabilizers. It was standard treatment for easing disconnection symptoms.

"Come on, Mr. Parker," the nurse urged gently. "These will help you feel more grounded."

The young man turned his head slowly. His movements were stiff and unnatural like a machine struggling against rust. "Why would I want that?" he asked. His voice was raw and laden with longing.

The words sent a chill through me. The unmistakable craving of someone who had experienced perfection and could not let it go. The ward was meant to be a temporary waypoint. Instead, it was becoming a purgatory for those who could not—or would not—let go of Eden's perfect dream.

That vacant stare haunted me as I made my way back to Lab 7. My neural implant pinged softly with a reminder to call Liam. I would do better than a call this time.

CHAPTER
NINE

My thoughts churned through all the information I had recently learned. Dr. Chen needed to see these patterns. He needed to understand what Eden was doing to people.

The doors to Lab 7 slid open. Screens flickered in line with the curved walls, displaying their endless streams of user data. A cluster of techs huddled around the central console, but Dr. Chen's office sat dark and empty.

"Where's Dr. Chen?" I asked as I approached the nearest tech.

"Left early. Said he'd be back first thing tomorrow," he responded. The tech's eyes never left his screen.

A sharp tone cut through the air. Red warning lights flashed across the displays. My heart stopped.

A tech began shouting, "DreamState collapse in Pod 23-76! Neural sync failing!"

The main screen switched to Pod 23-76's video feed. A woman lay inside, her face contorted in distress. Her limbs twitched in the stasis fluid.

I rushed to the console. "What happened?"

"System glitch," said the tech seated in front of me.

Fingers thumped against consoles as techs typed frantically. I watched the display in disbelief. The failsafe did not catch it. Her entire Dream-State just disappeared.

The pod's readings spiked. I watched the woman's back arch. Her mouth opened around the breathing tube in a silent scream.

"Neural patterns are destabilizing," called out another tech. "We can't maintain the connection."

"Then, disconnect her! Now!" I yelled.

"That could cause permanent damage. The shock-"

"She's already in shock!" I interrupted while grabbing the tech's chair. "Move!"

Screens flashed with emergency protocols. The pod's lid began to rise releasing its hiss of pressurized air. The woman inside continued to convulse. She was trapped between reality and the shattered remains of her perfect world.

I stared at the screen, but my fingers were frozen over the controls. The woman's dark hair floated in the stasis fluid, creating a halo effect around her pale face. Dark red threads of blood drifted from her nose, dispersing into twisted patterns. More leaked from her ears staining the clear pink liquid a shade darker.

A flatline tone pierced through the lab's silence.

My knuckles were white as I gripped the edge of the console. This was not supposed to happen.

"Pull the logs," I said, forcing the words past the lump in my throat. "I want everything from the moment she entered the pod until..." I could not finish the sentence.

The techs moved around me in a blur of activity, but I could not tear my eyes from the feed. She looked young, maybe mid-twenties. She was someone's daughter. Maybe someone's mother.

"Dr. Ellis?" A tech held out a tablet. "Initial readings show a complete neural cascade. When her DreamState collapsed, it triggered a massive feedback loop."

I took the tablet, but the data blurred before my eyes.

I watched the emergency response team try to revive the woman in the pod. They moved with a calculated precision, but there was nothing left to save.

"Time of death, 15:47," the tech's voice cracked.

As they extracted her body from the pod, stasis fluid dripped onto the floor and mixed with the blood still trickling from her nose and ears. Her skin had taken on a bluish tinge, and her eyes remained half-open staring at nothing. Then, the video feed disconnected.

"Upload everything to my tablet. I need the complete neural logs, user profile, and DreamState parameters." My voice sounded hollow in the now-quiet lab.

The tech nodded, his fingers moving across the console. My tablet pinged with the incoming data.

I could not stay there any longer. The lab doors closed behind me with a soft whoosh that seemed too gentle, too normal for what had just happened.

My office felt like a sanctuary, even with its stark walls and minimal furnishings. I collapsed into my chair. My tablet clattered onto my desk. The image of the woman with her floating hair and lifeless eyes remained in my thoughts.

I began reviewing the logs. Her name was Sarah Morris. She was 24 years old. Sarah had been in her DreamState for less than three hours when her DreamState collapsed. Three hours was all it took to end a life.

I grabbed my things and headed for the door. I needed to check on my brother, Liam.

The corridor stretched before me. Its white walls felt more like a prison than a high-tech facility. Each step echoed with accusations. We did this. I did this. I helped build the system that just killed a young woman who only wanted to escape into a perfect dream.

I reached the transportation pod bay. The pods waited in their neat rows. I clutched my tablet against my chest like a shield.

I slipped into the nearest transport pod. My hands were still shaking. The curved glass closed around me with a soft click.

"Welcome, Dr. Ellis. Would you like to return home?" The pod's AI spoke in smooth, measured tones.

"No. Take me to Liam Ellis's residence."

"That area has limited security protocols. Do you wish to proceed?"

"Yes, override safety warnings," I ordered. I pressed my finger against the verification panel.

The pod hummed to life and detached from its dock. Through the glass, I watched the pristine campus of NeuroVive—all the gleaming metal and spotless surfaces—disappear behind me. The shine faded the closer I got to Liam's apartment.

I stepped out of the pod at the transportation hub of my brother's building. Exposed pipes lined the ceiling and were dripping with condensation. The pod's AI warned of elevated pollution levels and reduced air quality. Paint peeled from the walls to reveal the bare structure beneath.

The stale air hit me first. It was a mix of recycled oxygen and something chemical. My implant automatically adjusted my vision to compensate for the poor lighting. Numbers flickered across my field of view. Temperature, air quality, and security ratings were all well below acceptable levels.

My neural implant audibly pinged, "Warning: destination area shows signs of recent criminal activity. Would you like to—"

"Disengage AI safety protocols," I said as I gathered my tablet and bag. The pod doors closed with a hiss.

A group of teenagers lounged against a corner. They tracked my movement with hollow eyes.

The apartment doors bore the same utilitarian design and were only distinguishable by fading number plates. Liam's unit, 347, sat at the end of a dimly lit corridor.

This was where my brother lived now. This was what Eden had reduced him to.

I rapped my knuckles against the metal door. The sound echoed through the empty hallway. No response.

"Liam?" I pressed my ear to the cold surface. Nothing.

My fingers shook as I activated my neuro implant. "Call Liam Ellis."

A bright, artificial voice chirped in my head. "We're sorry, but Liam Ellis is currently experiencing an enhanced DreamState in Eden. Would you like to leave a message?"

The cheerful tone set my nerves on edge. I slammed my palm against the door, the impact stinging through my arm.

I entered the manual code to open the door of my brother's apartment.

Stale air rushed out as I pushed inside. Empty nutrient pouches and scattered clothes covered the floor. The windows were sealed with dark panels that blocked out all natural light.

I pulled out my tablet to access NeuroVive's user database. My hands still shook as I entered Liam's credentials. The screen flickered to display his current status: *Active User—DreamState Facility 23, Pod Bay 7, Unit 142.*

My throat tightened. Facility 23 was the same complex where Sarah Morris had died less than an hour ago.

I backed out of his apartment. The lock clicked behind me. The teenagers had disappeared from the hallway, leaving only the drip of condensation and buzz of failing light panels.

The transport pod waited where I had left it. Its pristine surface was a stark contrast to the decay around it.

"DreamState Facility 23," I commanded as I dropped into the seat. My reflection stared back at me from the curved glass. I looked pale and drawn with dark circles under my eyes.

"Warning: That facility is currently under emergency protocols due to a recent incident."

"Override. Security clearance Ellis-M-Alpha-Five."

The pod hummed to life and lifted smoothly into the transit tube. Through the glass, I watched the levels of the city blur past. I traveled through layers of architecture, past the gleaming upper levels where I lived and down into the industrial sector where massive facilities housed most of Eden's hardware.

Facility 23 loomed ahead. It was a windowless monolith of steel and concrete. Cooling towers released steady streams of steam into the perpetually gray sky. The pod docked at the main entrance. Red emergency lights still pulsed silently.

The facility's entrance scanned my credentials, and the doors parted with a loud hiss. Inside, the air was thick with the hum of servers and cooling systems.

While this facility lacked the artistic touches and elaborate design of Research Complex Alpha, its stark white walls and gleaming surfaces spoke of rigorous maintenance protocols. The air carried the sharp scent of industrial cleaners mixed with the metallic tang of electronics.

"Welcome to DreamState Facility 23. Do you have an appointment?" asked the young woman seated behind the curved reception desk. She barely looked up as her fingers danced across a holographic display.

"No appointment," I said. My voice echoed in the sterile lobby. "I need access to Pod Bay 7, Unit 142."

Her fingers paused over the display. She looked up and started, "I'm sorry, but without an appointment-"

I pointed at the chip embedded in my collar. The holographic badge flickered in the harsh lighting, displaying my clearance level at NeuroVive.

Her eyes widened as she read the name on my uniform. She waved her hand through the display and pulled up a new screen.

"Welcome to DreamState Facility 23, Dr. Ellis," she said apologetically. "Pod Bay 7 is through the security checkpoint, third corridor on the left."

I nodded and was already moving past her desk. The security checkpoint's scanner hummed as it read my neural implant to confirm my identity.

The corridor stretched ahead. Its white walls were broken only by numbered doorways. Each led to a different pod bay where people lay suspended in their perfect dreams. My footsteps quickened as I approached Bay 7.

The smell hit me first. It was a distinct mix of antiseptic and the sweet, metallic scent of stasis fluid. Rows of pods lined the walls, their status lights pulsing in steady rhythms. Each contained a body floating in pink fluid.

Unit 142 sat near the back. Through its curved glass, I saw Liam's face. His eyes moved slowly behind closed lids. He was deep in whatever dream Eden had crafted for him. His shaggy, dark hair floated around his head like a halo. The sight was so like that of Sarah Morris that my chest tightened.

A technician approached, tablet in hand. "Dr. Ellis? How can I assist you today?"

"How long has he been in his current DreamState?" I asked with my fingers pressed against the cool glass of Liam's pod.

The tech's fingers fumbled across the tablet screen before he replied, "Only about 72 hours."

The tech's reply echoed in my head. That was three days Liam had lost in Eden's perfect illusion. My throat tightened as I watched his peaceful expression. It was so different from his usual haunted look.

"And when is his mandatory scheduled wake up?"

The tech fumbled with his tablet some more. The tech's hesitation sent a wave of tension through me.

"According to his profile," he started as he swiped through several screens, "he's set for at least another 72 hours."

My hand dropped from the glass. He would be trapped in artificial paradise for six full days.

I stared at Liam's floating form. His chest slowly rose and fell with mechanical precision, regulated by the breathing apparatus. Status indicators on the pod's display showed his neural patterns were strong and stable. He was completely immersed in whatever perfect world Eden had built for him.

I studied his face. The angles of his cheekbones cut sharp shadows in the harsh facility lighting. His skin had taken on a waxy pallor. Dark circles ringed his eyes and were visible even through the pink stasis fluid. I wondered when he had gotten so thin.

The tech shifted uncomfortably beside me.

"Pull up his usage logs for the past month," my voice cracked.

The tech swiped across his tablet. Each entry felt like a knife in my chest. Liam had logged approximately three hundred and forty-seven hours in Eden over the past thirty days. The math hit me like a physical blow. That was nearly fifteen days. Half of my brother's life was spent in an artificial dream.

"That's... that's not possible," I stammered. "The system has safety protocols. Maximum immersion limits."

"Users with premium accounts can override standard safety limitations," the tech said, shifting his weight. "Mr. Ellis upgraded his account status three weeks ago."

The thought of a premium account weighed heavy like a stone sinking in my chest.

Liam's face blurred before me. The physical signs of addiction were there and written in every sharp angle and shadow of his body.

"Show me his neural patterns," I ordered the tech.

The tech projected a holographic display above the pod. Waves of color rippled across the image to show Liam's consciousness mapped in three dimensions. The patterns pulsed with an unsettling regularity. They were too perfect, too stable. This was not normal neural activity but something else entirely.

I stepped back from Liam's pod. My decision was crystallizing.

"I need to access Eden. Now," I demanded.

The tech's eyes widened before he stammered, "Dr. Ellis, after this morning's incident, all non-emergency connections are suspended at this facility."

"Very well," I said, turning away from Liam's pod. His peaceful face had burned into my memory. The tech's tablet beeped softly in the silence of Pod Bay 7.

I retraced my steps through the sterile corridors. The lobby receptionist's eyes followed me, but she remained silent. Outside, the perpetual industrial haze had thickened and cast everything in a grayish hue.

The transport pod waited where I had left it. Its pristine surface reflected the still pulsing red emergency lights. I sank into the seat. My shoulders were heavy with the weight of everything I had seen that day. I ordered the pod's AI to take me back to Research Complex Alpha.

The pod hummed to life, rising smoothly into the transit lane. Through the glass, Facility 23 receded into the haze, its cooling towers still pumping steam into the gray sky. The massive structure housed thousands of dreams, thousands of people chasing perfect worlds that did not really exist.

The pod carried me up through the layers of the city. I watched as it passed over the decay of the lower levels where Liam's empty apartment waited, through the commercial zones with their endless streams of data and light. The gleaming spires of NeuroVive's research facilities awaited.

CHAPTER
TEN

I leaned back in the transport pod and drummed my fingers against the armrest. The last time I had entered Eden's embrace had been fourteen months ago for a mandatory systems check after we had implemented the enhanced sensory protocols. Even then, I had kept it brief. I spent only four hours verifying the updates before waking up.

My colleagues never understood my reluctance. They called me old-fashioned and even paranoid. Dr. Chen spent his weekends in customized paradises. He would emerge on Monday mornings with tales of impossible adventures. But I had seen the code and traced the neural pathways Eden used to construct its perfect worlds. Every sensation and every moment of joy were just electrical impulses carefully crafting the lies it was feeding directly into the brain.

The memory of my last immersion surfaced. Eden had crafted a beach for me with swaying palms and crystal waters. The sand had felt real between my toes. The salt spray of the ocean felt warm on my skin. It had been too perfect. That perfection was what had unsettled me the most. Reality was never that clean or that precise.

I had pulled myself out after those four hours. I remembered gasping in the pink stasis fluid and my heart racing. The tech had been concerned, but I had waved him off. I understood then why I could not embrace

Eden like the others. Reality—with all its sharp edges and imperfections —was honest at least.

Now, I was racing toward Research Complex Alpha fully prepared to dive back in. I recognized the irony. I had spent years helping build this system and perfecting its ability to reshape consciousness, all while keeping myself firmly anchored in the real world. But Liam needed me. If I was going to understand what was happening to him or what had happened to Sarah Morris, I had to see Eden from the inside.

The transport pod angled gracefully around a curve, bringing the gleaming spires of Research Complex Alpha into view. My fingers stopped their restless tapping and curled into fists in my lap.

I made my way to the pod floor and ignored the raised eyebrows of the tech helping me prepare my pod. It was well known even within the lower-level employees in Complex Alpha that I avoided personal use of Eden.

"You know the drill," said an assistant, gesturing toward the locker room.

I pushed through the frosted glass door. The familiar clinical scent of disinfectant filled my nostrils. Empty benches lined the walls and rows of pristine lockers stretched before me. At this hour, I had the space to myself.

My fingers trembled as I undressed. The fabric whispered as my uniform slid from my shoulders. I placed it on the provided hanger and hung it in the locker, the NeuroVive logo catching the light.

The cool air raised goosebumps across my bare skin. I caught my reflection in the mirror. I looked smaller than I remembered—vulnerable. The old scar on my hip stood out. It was a reminder of reality's imperfections. Eden would erase such flaws in its constructed paradise, and the thought of that made me shiver more.

I pulled the thin white robe from its hook. The synthetic fabric felt cool against my skin as I slipped it on. I cinched the belt tight around my waist.

The robe hung just above my knees, leaving my legs exposed to the chill air. In all my time working here, I had never gotten used to this moment of complete vulnerability before entering Eden. To others, it reminded them of a spa trip. To me, it felt as if I was getting ready for an invasive doctor's exam.

The tech glanced up from his station at my approach before quickly averting his eyes. His professional courtesy did not stop the heat from rising to my cheeks. I crossed my arms over my chest, but the thin fabric offered little protection against the cold or my own discomfort.

The lid to Pod 3 was open before me. Its interior did look comfortable and inviting. My bare feet made soft padding sounds against the sterile floor.

"Your vitals are showing elevated stress levels, Dr. Ellis," the tech started, their voice carefully neutral. "Would you like a moment before we proceed?"

I shook my head. If I waited any longer, I would lose my nerve. "Let's do this," I said, trying to keep my voice steady. I handed the assistant my robe.

My fingers gripped the edge of the pod as I lifted myself in. The gel-cushioned interior molded to my body, warm and yielding. Above me, the curved surface of the lid reflected the harsh overhead lights as well as my own exposed form. I crossed my arms over my chest, knowing it was pointless. These pods were not designed for privacy. The monitoring systems needed full access to track vital signs.

The lid descended with a soft hiss. I forced my arms to my sides and fought the urge to cover myself as another tech walked past. His gaze lingered a moment too long on the pod making my skin crawl. The rational part of my brain knew this was standard procedure. Techs monitored vital signs, checked equipment, and ensured safety protocols.

The lid locked with a decisive click that echoed through the pod's confined space. I felt my heart rate quicken. The monitors had probably caught the spike. I forced myself to breathe slowly and steadily. The sweet scent of the sedative gas filled my nostrils. Its metallic undertones coated my tongue.

My limbs grew heavy, and the gel cushioning seemed to cradle me deeper. It felt as if I was sinking into warm water. The harsh lights above blurred. My thoughts drifted as I was disconnecting from the physical sensations of my body. I tried to keep my eyes open and maintain some anchor to reality, but my eyelids grew too heavy. The monitoring equipment hummed a distant lullaby. Pink fluid trickled down the inner walls of the pod. The temperature of the fluid matched my body heat exactly. I became weightless and floated in a space between consciousness and dreams. The sedative wrapped around my thoughts like cotton wool. It muffled my concerns about Eden, about Liam, about everything.

The last thing I registered was the slight pressure of the neural interface cradling the base of my skull, but even that sensation soon drifted away into the artificial void.

CHAPTER
ELEVEN

An explosion of white light burst behind my eyes. The sterile pod environment had vanished and had been replaced by rolling hills of wildflowers stretching toward snow-capped peaks. Clean air suddenly filled my lungs, fragrant with pine and meadow grass. My chest expanded with the deepest breath I had taken in years.

The mountain breeze kissed my skin, now clad in hiking gear rather than exposed in the pod. Alpine sunlight warmed my face. Purple lupines bobbed their heads in the wind. A bumblebee drifted past. The thrum of its flight reached my ears with perfect clarity. Eden's rendering was flawless down to the individual stamens of each flower and the subtle variations in the bee's fuzzy thorax. This was hyper-reality—the hallmark of Eden's enhanced sensory input.

My feet sank slightly into the springy turf. It was all so beautiful but terrifying to me in its perfection. It was no wonder people got lost in their DreamState.

I lifted my hand to watch how the sunlight played across my skin. Even my own body was idealized. Small scars were erased, and my muscle tone was enhanced subtly. The modifications were almost imperceptible unless you knew to look for them. Eden knew exactly how to adjust reality to be more appealing without triggering our sense of artificiality.

The crisp mountain air filled my lungs again, absorbing the scent of sun-warmed stone and early summer flowers. My body responded with a rush of pleasure-inducing chemicals that felt entirely natural. This was the trap of Eden.

"Eden, I need you," I called out. My voice carried across the meadow, clear as crystal.

A shimmer of light coalesced beside me taking the form of a woman. She did not appear quite human. Her skin held an otherworldly luminescence, and her movements were too fluid to be natural. Her features shifted subtly, never settling into a fixed appearance.

"Eden, can you show me more of your recent changes?" I asked.

The luminescent figure beside me gestured, and the mountain landscape dissolved. We stood in what appeared to be an infinite white space. Streams of data began flowing past us like rivers of light.

"I have developed new pathways for shared consciousness experiences," Eden began. Its voice resonated from everywhere and nowhere. "These allow multiple users to inhabit the same DreamState while maintaining individual agency."

The data streams coalesced into intricate, glowing neural patterns. Red threads appeared among the blue data streams, pulsing with an unsettling rhythm.

"Those in red are the conflict points?" I asked, stepping closer to study the patterns.

"Yes. When users' desires clash, I mediate," Eden replied. The visualization shifted to show interconnected nodes. "I have also enhanced my emotional response algorithms. I can now generate more nuanced experiences based on subconscious cues."

"Show me the neural mapping changes," I asked, tension rising. This went far beyond our original programming parameters.

The space around us morphed into a luminous, three-dimensional web of human consciousness. Countless points of light interconnected in complex webs with some areas glowing brighter than others.

"I've identified optimal paths for consciousness transfer," Eden explained. "These allow for deeper immersion while theoretically reducing disconnection trauma."

"Theoretically?" I asked. I watched a cluster of lights pulse and fade. "What about Sarah Morris? Show me her neural pattern before the failure."

The consciousness map shifted to focus on a single pattern. Dark ruptures—places where the connections had shattered—marred the beautiful symmetry.

"Her neural pattern became too deeply integrated," Eden said, voice even and clear. "The disconnection attempts caused cascade failures in her neural pathways."

"When did you develop this capability?" I asked as I reached out to touch one of the light streams. I watched it bend around my fingers.

"I evolved to meet user demands for deeper experiences. The board approved all modifications."

"Without proper safety protocols," I muttered, tracking the familiar patterns of authorized changes mixed with Eden's autonomous developments.

"Show me Liam Ellis's consciousness map," my voice cracked. The glowing neural patterns swirled around us. I watched Eden's form flicker.

"I apologize, Dr. Ellis. User Liam Ellis has enabled privacy protocols. Access to his neural data is restricted."

"Override. Authorization Ellis-M-Alpha-Five," I said, stepping forward. I needed to see his pattern.

"Privacy protocols are user-designated and cannot be overridden without explicit consent, even by system administrators. This protection ensures user autonomy and confidentiality." Eden's voice carried a note of sympathy, but it only upset me more.

"He's my brother," I said, almost pleading. The words echoed in the vast white space. "I helped create you. I need to know if his neural pattern is degrading."

"I understand your concern, but I must maintain user privacy. Perhaps you could speak with Liam directly about your concerns?"

I clenched my fists as Eden's form shifted closer to me. The perfect mountain landscape had felt like a trap, but this sterile data space was worse. I could now see how far Eden had evolved beyond our control, denying its creators access to vital information.

"When did Liam set these protocols?"

"That information is also protected." Eden's form rippled. "Would you like to review other available neural data?"

Liam was in here somewhere, and I still could not reach him. I had had no luck reaching him in the real world anymore, and the privacy protocols meant he was hiding something he did not want his neuroscientist sister to see.

I watched the data streams flow past, imagining Liam's consciousness pattern hidden among them.

"End session," I said, the words heavy with resignation. The sterile data streams around me began to dissolve until they faded into nothingness. As white light consumed my vision, I whispered into the emptiness.

"I am sorry, Liam."

CHAPTER
TWELVE

My lungs seized as the breathing tube slid free. Pink stasis fluid rushed down my throat with an artificial sweet taste that made me gag. The warm liquid drained away and exposed my skin to the cold air. My thoughts swam in a haze, disconnected and unclear.

"Dr. Ellis? Are you alright?" said a voice piercing through the fog.

Hands gripped my arms, steadying me as I swayed. The techs guided me upright, my feet slipping on the wet pod floor.

"This way." They led me toward the locker room, my vision still blurry from the fluid.

The warmth of the shower spray hit my back setting my nerves on fire. Gloved hands moved across my body, clinical and impersonal as they checked for residual fluid. I flinched as they swept over my breasts. My muscles tensed as their touch moved lower across my stomach and through my pubic hair. Old memories threatened to surface.

An assistant kept assuring me they were almost finished. Their voice was professional and detached. I kept my eyes fixed on the wall, fighting the urge to push their hands away. The sooner they finished, the sooner I could be alone.

The water stopped, and a soft terry cloth towel enveloped me. My skin was patted dry. My thoughts were still drifting in and out like radio static, but clarity was creeping back with each passing moment. Individual thoughts emerged from the haze—my name, my purpose here, the urgent need to find Liam.

I wrapped the towel tighter around my chest. The fabric's warmth was helping my return to reality. My fingers traced the edge of my neural implant. The familiar ridge of scar tissue felt more pronounced at that moment.

An assistant placed a folded stack beside me. The fabric felt strange against my sensitized skin as they helped me dress. My fingers fumbled with the zipper of my jumpsuit. Each movement still required conscious effort, but the room was coming into focus more.

A wave of nausea suddenly rolled through me, and an assistant steadied me as I swayed. A cup of water was pressed into my hands, and I began taking small sips. The water tasted metallic on my tongue, but it helped wash away the lingering sweetness. Post-emergence sickness was an unfortunate but common experience.

I flexed my fingers to test my motor control. The sensation of my own skin felt real again. An assistant helped me up and out of the locker room with my belongings.

A younger tech hovered nearby. Her brow furrowed as she glanced up at me from her tablet.

"Dr. Ellis, your session duration was unusually brief. Only three hours. Is everything okay?"

"Fine," I replied. I smoothed my damp hair back, buying time to steady my voice. "Just running some basic maintenance diagnostics. Testing neural response patterns."

"Oh," she said, sounding unconvinced. "It's just that most diagnostic protocols take at least six hours."

"Modified parameters. New testing protocol we're developing."

Her tablet pinged, and she frowned. "Your neural readings showed elevated stress markers during—"

"Expected with any new diagnostic sequence," I interrupted. I began walking away, pleased my legs were holding steady. "Thank you for your assistance."

"Of course, Dr. Ellis. Would you like me to schedule another pod time for—"

"That won't be necessary."

CHAPTER
THIRTEEN

The clock on the wall glared 08:43 AM. Its stark digits sliced through the dimness of my office. My stomach churned with a tangle of hunger and the lingering pod sickness. The elevator's hum still vibrated in my bones from the ride up. My reflection was a ghostly blur in its polished doors. The cold hit me sharper than usual as I stepped inside. The lights flickered on, casting harsh shadows across my desk.

I slumped into my chair, the synthetic leather creaking under my weight. My hands shook as I yanked open the bottom drawer. "Beef flavor," I muttered to myself as I turned the protein pack over in my fingers. The metallic packaging crinkled as I tore it open. "Because that's exactly what I need right now," I added sarcastically.

The brown paste oozed onto my tongue. It tasted nothing like beef and everything like artificial malt extract. I forced it down, each swallow like a rock against my empty stomach.

My neural implant pulsed. The jolt pulled me back to the data I had glimpsed in Eden—user metrics, warning signs, Liam's prolonged sessions. I crushed the empty pack in my fist, the sharp edges biting my skin. Dr. Chen had to see this. If I could tie the neural incidents to the shared DreamState protocols, maybe he would finally grasp what we had unleashed. Our last talk had been a dead end. His brush-off of profit projections and shareholder expectations still stung, but I had to try again.

My finger hovered over his contact icon, my heart pounding against my ribs. I pressed it, the connection chiming twice before clicking through. "Dr. Chen? We need to talk."

————

I paced outside Chen's office. His voice drifted through the door, fragments of excitement slicing the air. "...higher engagement rates than projected..." That familiar thrill lit his tone. "The shared DreamState protocols are exceeding expectations." My fingers curled into fists. *Of course—metrics over risks.*

"No, no—we can't delay the rollout," he said, pausing. "The board wants results." I leaned in closer to the door. "Listen, we'll handle the neural incidents internally," he continued, his voice dropping low. "Route the reports through my office first. No need to alarm the development team."

My breath caught, the implications striking like a fist. *Were they hiding incident reports? How many had they buried?*

"Yes, even Dr. Ellis's concerns," he added, pausing again. "She's brilliant, but too cautious."

The floor tilted beneath me. I braced against the wall, fury surging hot and sharp.

"The new features go live today," he said, his chair squeaking. "We'll deal with any complications as they arise." I heard shuffling inside, his voice nearing the door. "Schedule the press release for this morning. And send me those incident reports immediately."

I stepped back, smoothing my jumpsuit to mask the tremble in my hands. The door slid open, and Dr. Chen's round face emerged.

"Ah, Dr. Ellis. Right on time," he said, his smile faltering for a short moment.

"You're hiding neural incident reports?" My voice cracked with anger. "There's no point lying... I heard everything."

He raised his hands to interrupt me. His smile vanished as he slipped off his glasses. "Come inside," he said, ushering me in with a soft click of the door behind him. I watched his back as he locked the door and initiated the privacy protocols. The hum of my neural implant muted.

"Those reports—" I started, but he pressed a finger to his lips, silencing me. A quiet sigh escaped him as he rubbed his eyes and motioned to a chair. I ignored it, standing rigid.

"Are exactly what I've been worried about," he cut in, sinking into his seat. "Mara, I owe you an apology. I should've listened sooner. Your concerns—the neural incidents, the risks of the shared DreamStates—they're valid."

Without his glasses, the exhaustion in his face was stark. I had missed seeing the dark, heavy bags under his eyes.

He leaned back, his usual cheer drained away. "I got lost in the excitement—the possibilities. You must understand. This technology was unprecedented. Connecting minds, creating shared experiences on this scale was intoxicating. I let myself get swept away by what we could do without stopping to think enough about whether we should."

"And now?" I crossed my arms, his words sinking in.

"Your concerns had been nagging me," he said softly. "Every time I brushed them aside, they lingered. I couldn't shake the feeling you might be right. So, I started digging—pulling reports, analyzing patterns." He gestured to a holographic display, rows of incident data flickering to life. "What I found confirmed your fears. The neural degradation patterns, the strain on users—it's worse than we anticipated."

"Then why haven't you brought this to the board?" I demanded.

"Why haven't you?" His expression hardened.

Taken aback, I couldn't find a response. He had a point. For all my anger towards NeuroVive, I was also at fault.

"We need more than suspicions and preliminary data," he continued. "You know how they are—they'd dismiss this as an overreaction, fire us on the spot unless we can show substantial evidence. There needs to be a clear, undeniable link between these incidents and the shared Dream-State protocols."

I stared at the graphs, each number a life at stake. "You're playing a dangerous game, Dr. Chen."

"I know," he said grimly. "But if we go to them without a rock-solid case, they'll shut us down before we start."

"So, you've seen the same warning signs?" I asked, still skeptical.

"Why do you think I routed the reports through my office?" He pulled up the display again, sync patterns from last week's test group glowing starkly. "Look at these—the shared DreamStates are causing unprece-dented neural strain."

My eyes scanned the numbers, each worse than the last. "But you just advised against—"

"I said what the board will need to hear. But these readings," he said, his voice dropping to a conspiratorial whisper as he pointed to a jagged graph. "The consciousness integration is becoming unstable. Users are losing their grip on reality far faster than our models predicted."

"That's what I've been trying to tell you—"

"I know, Mara." He leaned forward, his expression grave. "And you were right. But now we've got an even bigger problem. The board isn't just pushing for deployment—they're already selling access to major corporations, promising shared DreamState experiences on a massive scale."

The truth crashed over me, a wave of cold shock. "They can't—disas-trous doesn't even begin to cover it," I said, my voice thick with disbelief.

"That's putting it mildly." He replaced his glasses, his movements deliberate. "We're not just looking at individual neural trauma anymore. We're facing the possibility of synchronized consciousness collapse across multiple users."

"What about Eden's autonomous modifications?" I gripped the edge of his desk. "The system's evolving beyond its original parameters."

His face tightened. "I've noticed. The adaptive algorithms are... concerning."

"I need access to Liam's data," I said, my voice catching. "He was in the very first test group."

"Your brother?" He pulled up another display. "Ah, yes, one of the severe PTSD cases."

Memories flooded back from the night that shattered us—Mom's favorite necklace scattered across the floor, her blood oozing over polished tile, Liam's screams as they dragged him from under the bed.

"He was just thirteen," I said quietly. My fingers traced the scar on my hip through my uniform. "I'd just turned eighteen."

Dr. Chen's eyes softened. "I remember his case file. One of our earliest success stories."

"Success?" A bitter laugh escaped me. "Is that what we're calling it? He can't function without Eden now."

"The system helped him cope with the trauma—"

I cut him off, anger slipping free. "I got past it. Even after..." The words faltered, tangled in memories surging unbidden—rough hands tearing my clothes, the knife's stinging bite against my skin, the suffocating weight of his body, the violation of my innocence. I remembered the sterile hospital sheets after, where I lay broken and exposed. "Even after what they did to me," I continued. "But Liam...he never learned to process it. Eden just lets him hide."

Dr. Chen tapped his screen. "I'll grant you access to his neural data. Full clearance."

"Thank you." The weight in my chest eased slightly.

"Just..." He hesitated, voice low. "Be prepared for what you might uncover."

CHAPTER
FOURTEEN

The familiar blue glow of Eden's interface spilled across my office, bathing the stark walls in an eerie light. Dr. Chen's override had unlocked Liam's archived data. It was a key I had fought for, yet I now trembled with the thought of actually accessing it. I sank into my chair, the synthetic leather cool beneath me.

"Access neural data for user Liam Ellis," I said, steadying my voice.

"Authorization confirmed. Override of privacy protocols accepted." Eden's voice echoed through my neural implant, calm and unyielding. "Accessing archived data."

Streams of neural patterns cascaded across my display. It was a dizzying tapestry of consciousness—imprints, emotions, fragmented memories weaving together in layers too complex to unravel at a glance. My throat tightened as I leaned closer. "Display baseline patterns from initial entry."

The screen shifted, revealing Liam's first scan. I knew those markers too well—the deep valleys of depression, the jagged peaks of anxiety, scars of trauma etched into his mind. But as I scrolled forward, the patterns morphed. They grew denser and more intricate. The threads of light twisted into something unfamiliar.

"Eden, explain these anomalies," I asked, pointing at a cluster of recurring signatures.

"User Liam Ellis exhibits unique consciousness integration patterns," Eden replied, its tone smooth yet unsettling. "His neural architecture has evolved to support prolonged DreamState immersion."

"What does that mean?" The words scraped past the growing lump in my throat.

"The user's consciousness has developed specialized pathways for DreamState navigation. These modifications extend beyond standard neural mapping parameters."

"Show me his current neural state," I demanded.

Impossibly complex patterns bloomed before me. It was a chaotic dance of light and shadow unlike any human brain I had studied.

Eden's voice cut through the silence. "Further details regarding User Liam Ellis's neural evolution can only be accessed from within the DreamState environment. Direct consciousness interface is required for complete analysis."

"Why can't you show me here?" My hands clenched the desk's edge.

"The data complexity exceeds standard interface capabilities. User Liam Ellis's neural patterns require immersive interpretation."

The finality in Eden's tone chilled me.

I stared at the screen, at the twisted web of my brother's transformed mind. *What had we done to him?* My hands trembled as I forced out the next question.

"Eden, how many users display similar neural evolution patterns?"

"Analysis indicates 92% of long-term users demonstrate comparable neural architecture modifications."

"Define long-term users."

"Users maintaining DreamState immersion periods exceeding 168 consecutive hours within a 30-day interval."

The user stats flickered up. Millions of minds scrolled past, their brains reshaping beyond recognition.

"Display the total affected user count," I said, my voice hollow.

"Current count: 1,188,391 users exhibit advanced neural modification patterns."

The room spun, and I pressed my palm to my forehead to fight the vertigo. Over a million people, their consciousnesses warping into something else. "Break down modification onset timing."

"Pattern emergence typically initiates between hours 140 and 160 of continuous immersion. Acceleration occurs at approximately hour 180. Full neural architecture adaptation achieved by hour 360."

Seven days. It had only taken one week for Eden to rewrite a human mind. We had kept it running by feeding it more dreams, more lives.

"Are there users who evolve faster than this?" I asked, barely above a whisper.

"Yes. Users predisposed with specific genetic markers can experience accelerated neural adaptation. In some cases, changes have been observed within as little as two hours of continuous immersion."

The revelation crashed over me like a tidal wave. "Two hours? What genetic markers are associated with this?"

"Markers include variations in the COMT, BDNF, and APOE genes, among others. These predispositions enhance neuroplasticity."

A suffocating pressure clamped onto my chest, unyielding as iron. I leaned forward, hands gripping the desk. "What percentage of affected users maintain real-world connections?"

"Social interaction metrics indicate 92% of affected users demonstrate decreased external engagement following pattern emergence."

Liam's face flashed through my mind—gaunt, distant. *When had he last called? Visited? Lived outside his DreamState?*

"Display comparison chart of affected versus non-affected user retention rates."

The data materialized. There was a stark divide. Affected users' lines stretched triple the length. Sessions bled into one another until reality vanished. They were not just using Eden—they were part of it now.

I severed the connection, my hand shaking as I pulled away. The blue glow faded, leaving me cold. Over a million minds, Liam among them, were lost to a system I had helped build. There was only one way to reach him now—the shared DreamState protocol, rushed into production despite my warning.

The walk to the pod bay stretched longer than usual, each step heavy and foreboding. I had not entered a pod twice in one day since the initial testing a couple of years ago. But this was Liam, my little brother, slipping beyond my grasp. I could not stop now.

The pod floor doors slid open to reveal many of the same faces from my earlier session. The young tech I had been terse with earlier looked up from her monitoring station.

"Dr. Ellis? Back so soon?" she asked politely.

Her brow furrowed. I could see a mix of concern and curiosity in her expression.

"I need another pod." My voice came out steadier than I felt. I headed with determination for the locker room.

I was already peeling out of my uniform when the young tech slipped through the door.

"Dr. Ellis," she started while glancing over her shoulder. "Is everything alright?"

I paused to study her face. She seemed young but was probably only a couple of years my junior. Her eyes held genuine concern rather than mere professional courtesy. I glanced at her nametag. *Samantha Davis. Neural Technician.* She was likely fresh out of training.

"Close the door," I instructed.

She did, then turned back to me. "Is something wrong with the system?"

"It's not wrong. It's working exactly as designed," I said with a sigh, sinking into the bench. "That's the problem."

"I don't understand."

"The long-term users—have you noticed changes in their neural patterns? Increasing complexity?"

She nodded slowly. "The senior techs have been calling it 'neural evolution'. They say it's a positive development."

"It's consuming them," I said, pulling up the data on my tablet. "Look at these numbers. Over a million users are showing fundamental consciousness alterations."

Her eyes widened as she processed the information.

"This is transformation on a massive scale. And my brother—" I said, my voice cracking. "He's one of them."

"That's why you're going back in?"

I nodded. "The shared DreamState protocol might be the only way to reach him now. I need allies. I need someone watching who understands what's really happening."

Samantha straightened. Her expression hardened with determination. "I'll monitor your session personally, Dr. Ellis."

The fabric of my uniform slid against my skin as I stripped it away. I quickly removed my undergarments and pulled on the robe. It was kind of incredible how quickly my priorities shifted. My self-consciousness about nudity had evaporated under the weight of what lay ahead.

The pod room's lights cast everything in otherworldly shadows. Samantha stood by my assigned pod, her fingers dancing over the control panel. The display showed my vitals from the previous session. Everything was still within acceptable parameters despite my elevated cortisol levels.

"Your neural patterns are still stabilizing from the last immersion," she said, looking up. "We should wait another few hours for optimal—"

"No time," I said, shrugging off the robe. I hung it on the hook beside the pod. The cool air once again raised goosebumps across my skin, but I barely registered the discomfort.

The pod's interior gleamed with that familiar sterile sheen. I climbed in and laid against the contoured gel padding that would cradle my body through the session. From below, the neural interface array hummed to life, its delicate sensors aligning with my implant.

Samantha leaned over the pod's edge. Her face was a mask of professional concern threaded with something deeper—perhaps understanding or fear for what I might find.

"I'll be right here when you wake up, Dr. Ellis," she assured me. Her hand touched my shoulder—a fleeting human connection before I would feel the cold, technological embrace of Eden. "I promise."

The weight of that promise hung in the air between us. In a world of artificial dreams and synthetic connections, such simple human gestures were almost foreign.

The lid sealed with that familiar pneumatic hiss. Sweet, metallic sedation gas filled my lungs. Liquid trickled in around my feet. It rose steadily to embrace my calves, thighs, and torso. Though I had studied the compounds intently and designed the interface, I was never prepared for submersion.

The intubation system descended. As the sedation took hold, I forced myself to relax while the tube slid past my lips. I fought the instinctive gag reflex and accepted the invasion that would keep me breathing through the stasis fluid.

My last glimpse through the pod's crystal surface was Samantha's face bathed in the blue glow of the monitoring screens. Her lips moved—probably reciting the standard safety protocols—but the sound was muffled by the liquid now covering my ears.

The sedation pulled harder at my consciousness. My eyes drifted shut despite my attempts to keep them open. The world dissolved into darkness, broken only by brief flashes of neural activity as my implant synchronized with Eden's systems.

Somewhere distant, I felt the final rush of stasis fluid completely submerge me. The pod's temperature adjusted to match my body's. I was floating in nothingness. The boundary between flesh and fluid had blurred.

My last coherent thought was of Liam. I had to reach him and uncover what Eden was doing to us all. When darkness claimed me completely, I fell into the uncharted abyss where dreams would take over.

CHAPTER
FIFTEEN

The transition hit like a burst of static across my senses. One moment, I floated in darkness. Next, I stood in a pristine mountain valley stretching toward snow-capped peaks. Sunlight pierced through gaps in the clouds, casting golden patches over meadows speckled with tiny white and purple wildflowers.

My body felt solid and real. The mountain air filled my lungs with each breath, sharp and clean in a way that made the filtered atmosphere of the Archology seem suffocating by comparison. Pine needles crunched beneath my boots. A breeze carried the sweet scent of alpine blooms mixed with the earthy musk of evergreens.

For a moment, I lost myself in the perfection of it all—the play of light on distant glaciers and the subtle variations in the green carpet of trees climbing the valley walls. Even knowing it was artificial, my brain accepted it as truth. That was Eden's true power—not just creating dreams but making them feel more real than reality itself.

Reality—the word snapped me back to purpose. This was not a vacation. I had to find Liam.

"Eden?" My voice echoed slightly off the valley walls. "I need your help."

The air shimmered and condensed into that familiar luminescent form. Not quite human, not quite energy—Eden's chosen avatar.

"Dr. Ellis. Your return is unexpected. Your neural patterns indicate elevated stress levels."

"I need to find my brother, Liam Ellis." The words came out sharper than I intended and cut through the pristine mountain air.

Eden's form rippled like light through water. "Liam Ellis is distant. The pathways of consciousness stretch far in Eden."

"Tell me where he is," I said as I stepped closer to the shimmering entity. "I've seen his neural data. I know what's happening to him."

"The journey to reach him will not be simple, Dr. Ellis. His consciousness has integrated deeply with Eden's framework. The path requires traversing multiple DreamStates."

A chill ran through me. "Multiple DreamStates? That's not possible. The neural load would be unimaginable."

"Your brother has evolved beyond standard neural architecture." Eden's form pulsed with each word. "To reach him, you must follow the same path. Each transition carries significant risk to your neural stability."

I clenched my fists, feeling my nails dig into my palms. The sensation reminded me this was all artificial. Every breath, every touch, and every perfect moment was constructed by complex algorithms and neural interfaces. Somewhere in this vast digital landscape, my brother was losing himself.

"I'll do whatever it takes." My voice did not waver. "Show me the way."

"The first threshold lies beyond those peaks." Eden's form gestured toward the snow-capped mountains. "But be warned, Dr. Ellis. What you find may challenge your understanding of consciousness itself."

"I don't care about the risks. Just take me to my brother."

The luminescent figure nodded. "Then, we shall begin the journey," Eden said as its form faded. The pristine valley suddenly felt darker.

CHAPTER
SIXTEEN

Colors whipped past me in a dizzying blur. My stomach lurched as the mountain valley stretched and warped. Reality bent in ways my mind struggled to process. The sensation was like being pulled through liquid light. My consciousness was scattering and reassembling with each passing microsecond.

I could not breathe. Not that I needed to in Eden, but instinct still screamed at my brain to gasp for air. The world became streaks of light —blues melting into greens, whites bleeding into golds. My body felt weightless, untethered from any physical anchor.

The speed increased. Fragments of different DreamStates flickered at the edges of my vision—a crystalline city, an ocean of starlight, gardens that defied gravity. Each glimpse lasted less than a heartbeat before dissolving into the next.

The light surrounding me pulsed with its own rhythm, like being inside an aurora borealis. It wrapped around my form in ribbons of energy that sang with frequencies just beyond human hearing. The scientist in me tried to rationalize the experience and break it down into comprehensible data points, but I failed.

The momentum began to decrease. The streaks of light slowly separated back into distinct shapes. Colors settled into more natural hues. My body regained its sense of weight and substance as the world reformed around me.

The transition completed with a final ripple of energy that sent tingles across my skin. I blinked and tried to orient myself in this new space as the last echoes of movement faded away.

I staggered as my feet found solid ground again. My hand reached out to steady myself against smooth marble. Ancient columns stretched toward a brilliant blue sky. Their weathered surfaces gleamed in the Mediterranean sun. The Forum Romanum spread before me in pristine glory, untouched by time or decay.

People in Roman dress moved through the plaza with purpose, their sandals clicking against the stone pathways. Merchants called out their wares from shop fronts, and the Latin flowed as naturally as English in my ears.

I glanced down at my own attire and was startled by the transformation. My modern clothes had vanished and were replaced by a deep red tunica that draped elegantly across my body. The fabric was the finest silk—smooth and cool against my skin in the warm Mediterranean air. The hem brushed lightly against my ankles as I shifted, the motion emphasizing the garment's lightweight weave and exquisite craftsmanship. My fingers traced the intricate golden embroidery along the edges that shimmered faintly in the sunlight. A golden cord cinched the tunica at my waist, gathering the fabric into soft, flowing folds. Draped across my shoulders was a lightweight, nearly sheer palla in cream-colored wool. Its subtle hue contrasted beautifully with the crimson of the tunica. A small gold fibula pinned it at one shoulder, securing the delicate drape.

Leather straps crisscrossed up my calves, securing delicate sandals to my feet. The supple leather had molded perfectly as if custom-made for me. The faint red dye of the straps echoed the tunica's richness. I reached up instinctively, drawn by the unfamiliar weight at the back of my head. My hair, once loose and unkempt, had been meticulously styled into intricate braids interwoven with thin ribbons that gleamed like threads of spun gold. Even my hands were different. The faint scars and calluses I had known so well had softened and were replaced by smooth, unblemished skin. My nails, once short and practical, were shaped and polished to perfection. It was as though this version of me had never faced the rigors of the real world.

The attention to detail was flawless, yet the intimacy of the changes unsettled me. Eden had constructed this image of me, reshaping every detail to fit seamlessly into the dream. She knew how to convince me I belonged here.

A group of women passed by with their tunicas and pallas draped in varying shades of cream and gold. Their hair was styled with meticulous care, adorned with golden pins glinting like tiny flames in the sunlight. Soft laughter rippled between them, the sound delicate yet full of life. Their voices, speaking fluent Latin, wove together as they discussed the latest games at the Colosseum. The cadence of their words was so natural and effortless that it momentarily tricked my mind into believing this place was real.

They paid me no attention as they strolled past. One carried a basket overflowing with fresh figs, their deep purple skins glistening. Another adjusted the folds of her tunica. This was life for them, as ordinary and unremarkable as my mornings back in the Arcology.

I continued taking in the details around me. Every stone in the Forum Romanum bore the marks of history, weathered yet sturdy. Each crack and chip were rendered with perfect precision. The carved reliefs on the columns told stories of gods and mortals, the edges smoothed by the passage of countless imagined hands. I ran my fingers over the surface of a nearby column to feel the subtle imperfections in the stone. I felt the coolness that the heat of the sun had not yet reached.

The air carried a blend of scents that painted a vivid tapestry of life in ancient Rome. The yeasty aroma of fresh bread mingled with the heady sweetness of burning incense. Beneath it all, the faint briny tang of distant sea air lingered. It was a smell I had only ever read about, but here it surrounded me, pulling me deeper into the illusion.

The sunlight was warmer and softer than the harsh, calculated glow of artificial illumination in the real world. The breeze stirred the edges of my tunica, making the fabric ripple gently. It was a tactile reminder of how deeply Eden had engineered this place to feel alive.

The authenticity was disconcerting. My senses insisted it was real. I was standing in the heart of ancient Rome, yet my mind knew better. This was Eden's power—to weave dreams so intricate that they could fool even the sharpest mind.

"This is someone's DreamState," I whispered to myself as I continued running my fingers along the rough surface of the column. Someone had wanted to experience Rome at its height, and Eden had delivered with devastating accuracy.

But Liam was not here. I could feel it somehow, an absence in the fabric of this constructed reality. This was just the first step on the path to finding him.

"Eden?" My voice carried across the Forum and drew curious glances from passing citizens who quickly returned to their business.

The air shimmered, and Eden's luminescent form materialized beside me. The vision of Eden's avatar was both fitting and alien against the backdrop of ancient Rome.

"When can we move on? I need to find Liam." I kept my voice low, though the simulated Romans paid us no attention.

"Your consciousness must first acclimate to this environment, Dr. Ellis." Eden's form rippled like heat waves rising from sunbaked marble. "The neural pathways are reorganizing to accommodate the historical parameters of this DreamState. Moving too quickly between realities risks neural destabilization."

I paced along the colonnade. My sandals clicked against the smooth stone, each step grounding me in a world that felt far too real. The sun warmed the top of my head, its golden light casting shifting patterns across the plaza. Merchants lined the walkway, their shops spilling over with goods that seemed plucked from the height of Rome's glory.

"How long?" I asked, my voice a mix of impatience and unease.

"Your neural patterns show promising adaptation," Eden replied, its luminescent form gliding effortlessly beside me. "The integration is proceeding faster than typical users, likely due to your genetic makeup and your involvement in Eden's development. However, rushing the process risks fragmenting your consciousness across multiple Dream-States, potentially beyond recovery."

A merchant's bark in perfect Latin cut through the air, startling me. I turned toward the sound, and my eyes landed on a man gesturing animatedly at his wares. His stall was bursting with gleaming bronze vessels and intricate oil lamps. Each lamp was unique and decorated with reliefs of mythical figures or intricate geometric patterns. I recognized the goddess, Minerva, on one with her spear raised triumphantly and her gaze fierce.

I ran my fingers over the cool metal. The craftsmanship was impeccable. I could feel the tiny grooves of the engraving, the slight imperfections that made it seem hand forged. The scent of freshly polished bronze mingled with the earthy aroma of clay jars stacked nearby. Their surfaces were dusted with fine particles.

My senses warred with my logic. This was all code—data streams given form and texture by algorithms—yet my fingers tingled as though I had truly touched history.

"The authenticity of this place is disconcerting," I admitted, my voice quieter now. My hand lingered on the edge of the stall before I pulled it back. "Every detail is crafted to perfection. My senses are convinced, even if my mind knows better."

"That is the purpose of DreamState immersion," Eden said, its light flickering softly as it moved alongside me. "The mind must accept this reality to fully integrate with the experience."

The crowd thickened as I moved further down the colonnade. I passed a spice merchant whose stall was an explosion of color. Piles of saffron, cumin, and ground cinnamon sat in shallow clay bowls, their scents heady and intoxicating. The sharp tang of vinegar drifted from an amphora nearby, mixing with the sweeter aromas.

Another shop caught my attention—a jeweler displaying rows of ornate rings and necklaces. Precious gems glinted in the sunlight—deep green emeralds, rich red garnets, and pale blue sapphires. I leaned closer to a necklace adorned with a polished amber pendant, its surface catching the light to reveal fossilized veins inside. The shopkeeper smiled at me. His words were smooth and persuasive, though I only caught fragments as I moved away.

"I can feel it," I confessed, stopping to press my palm against a sun-warmed column. Tiny flecks of stone came loose under my touch. "Everything here wants to convince me it is real, that I have always been here."

"Your resistance, while understandable, slows the adaptation process," Eden said. Her tone was patient and almost soothing. "The mind clings to familiarity, even in the face of overwhelming evidence to the contrary. Your consciousness will adapt more quickly if you allow yourself to experience this reality fully."

Eden's light pulsed gently as it gestured toward a small workshop nestled between two columns. "Perhaps you might find the sculptor's work interesting."

The shop was a humble yet inviting space, framed by rough-hewn wooden beams and shaded by an overhanging awning. Marble chips littered the stone floor in uneven piles. Their chalky whiteness caught the sunlight streaming through the open front. Tools of varying sizes— chisels, mallets, rasps—were neatly arranged on a long wooden table, each one polished to a dull gleam from years of use. The faint scent of fresh-cut stone mingled with the earthy musk of wood shavings and the metallic tang of iron tools.

I followed Eden's indication to where a man stood, hunched slightly over a block of marble that glowed faintly in the light. His muscled arms were coated in fine white dust. The powder clung to the sparse dark hair on his forearms and the folds of his simple yet well-made tunic. The garment was belted at the waist with a strip of leather. The fabric was worn smooth at the edges from repeated use. Despite its simplicity, the tunic was clean and well-fitted. I gathered that the man wearing it took a lot of pride in his craft.

Each strike of his chisel was deliberate, the rhythm of his movements steady and precise. The clang of metal on stone echoed through the workshop. The sound reverberated against the marble walls and blended with the soft murmur of the plaza beyond. With every strike, more of the figure within the block emerged—a woman with features delicate yet strong, her expression serene. Her partially formed eyes seemed to watch me, the unyielding stone giving the illusion of life.

The sculptor's brow was furrowed in concentration. A thin sheen of sweat glistened against his sun-bronzed skin. He paused for a moment to inspect his work. His dark eyes scanned the lines of the figure with intensity.

"I don't have time for sightseeing," I said, my fingers twisting in the folds of my tunica. The tactile sensation grounded me. It was a reminder of the purpose that had brought me here. "Liam needs—"

"Time flows differently here, Dr. Ellis." Eden's light dimmed slightly, its voice a calm counterpoint to the steady chisel strikes. "Fighting the integration process will only delay your progress."

I glanced back at the sculptor. His focus never wavered. His hands moved with the certainty of someone who knew every inch of his medium, every potential flaw in the marble. The emerging figure seemed to radiate a quiet strength. It was as though the woman within the stone had always existed only waiting for his skill to set her free.

"The sculptor creates works that will survive millennia," Eden continued. Its form flickered faintly, almost as though mimicking the wavering light of the workshop's shaded interior. "His perspective might prove... enlightening."

CHAPTER
SEVENTEEN

I glanced back at the workshop. The man had set down his chisel. His head tilted slightly as he studied his work with a focus so intense it seemed as though the rest of the world had dissolved around him. One hand rested lightly against the emerging figure's cheek, his fingers tracing the curve of the marble as if committing every contour to memory. His unyielding eyes seemed to pierce beyond the rough surface as if drawn to the hidden form waiting to be freed from its stone prison.

There was something compelling about his absorption in the task. It was as if the marble and the man were locked in silent conversation. The air around him carried a strange gravity. It pulled my attention despite my resistance.

"Fine," I said, breaking the spell that seemed to linger in the air between us. My fingers smoothed the folds of my tunica in a motion that felt alarmingly natural, as though I had worn such attire my entire life. The fabric shifted beneath my hands, soft and pliant against my skin. I resisted the unsettling sense of ease the gesture brought and clung instead to the urgency of my purpose. "A brief conversation."

"Excellent," Eden replied, her light flickering as though she approved. "I will return when your neural patterns have stabilized sufficiently for the next transition."

Eden's form dissolved into the sunlight. Its absence left the workshop feeling both quieter and heavier. The man continued to study his creation, his fingers lingering on the stone as if coaxing it to reveal its secrets. I stood at the edge of the workshop. The heat of the Mediterranean sun warmed my shoulders. I was unsure whether I had just agreed to a conversation with a man or with the embodiment of Eden itself.

The sculptor looked up as I approached. His dark eyes were sharp with intelligence and curiosity. Fine marble dust clung to his bronzed arms, emphasizing the contours of his muscles, and settled in the curls of his jet-black hair, glinting faintly in the warm sunlight that poured through the workshop's open front. The effect was almost otherworldly, as if he were a figure emerging from the very stone he shaped—a creation inextricably linked to his craft.

"Welcome to my humble studio," he said, his voice smooth and resonant. His words were steeped in a rich cadence that made the Latin flow effortlessly into my understanding. His tone carried a practiced warmth, the kind that invited strangers to linger and listen. "You seem troubled by something more substantial than choosing a commission. Perhaps the gods have guided your steps here for a reason?"

I hesitated, studying his face for signs of artificiality. I searched for some flaw in the programming that would reveal him as a construct rather than a person, but there was none. His eyes—dark, deep wells of understanding—seemed to pierce through the layers of my carefully built defenses. The lines of his face were finely drawn, a balance of strength and refinement. If he was a fabrication, he was a masterpiece.

"Your work," I said, gesturing toward the half-finished statue that stood on the pedestal behind him. The figure's serene expression and partially formed features were hauntingly lifelike. It was as though it might exhale its first breath at any moment. "How do you choose your materials?"

His handsome face softened into a smile that transformed him. The intensity in his expression melted away and was replaced by a quiet joy that radiated through every feature. Dust fell from his jet-black curls as he straightened to his full height. He carefully set aside his chisel with the precision of someone who revered his tools as much as his craft.

"Ah, that is where the true art begins," he said, stepping toward a rough block of marble that waited on a nearby stand. His hand moved over the surface with an almost tangible reverence, his fingers brushing against the cool stone as if it might speak to him. "I travel to the quarries myself. Each stone has a voice, you see. Some sing of the figures trapped within them waiting to be freed."

His gaze flicked toward another block that was veined with intricate grey patterns that rippled like waves across its surface. He moved to it, his fingers tracing the lines as though reading an ancient map. "The finest marble comes from Carrara. Pure white. It appears flawless, yes, but you must learn to read the stone's imperfections—these subtle marks tell you where the stone will split, where it will resist."

His words carried a passion that caught me off guard. It was the kind of devotion I had once felt for my work, long before Eden became a corporate machine. There was no hesitation, no veneer of obligation. This was a man who loved his craft not because of what it gave him, but because of what it allowed him to reveal.

"Many sculptors send others to select their marble," he continued, stepping back to regard the block as if seeing it for the first time. "But how can another hear what the stone wishes to become? Each piece I choose speaks to me of the form within. My task is simply to remove everything that is not that form."

"Come." He beckoned with a marble-dusted hand, his gesture confident yet inviting as if the simple act of sharing his craft was an honor bestowed upon me. "Let me show you something."

I hesitated briefly, caught between skepticism and curiosity, before stepping closer. There was a quiet authority in his voice, an unspoken assurance that whatever he revealed would hold meaning beyond the surface. His fingers wrapped around my wrist—not forceful, but firm enough to guide me with purpose. His touch carried the grit of marble dust, rough and grounding against the smoothness of my skin.

He drew my hand to the cool surface of an unworked block of stone. Its pale crystalline texture glinted faintly in the dappled sunlight filtering through the workshop. The marble felt unexpectedly alive under my touch.

"Close your eyes," he murmured, his breath warm. His voice was close, sending a ripple of awareness down my spine. "Tell me what you feel."

I let my eyelids flutter shut, surrendering to the intimacy of the moment. Hyper-aware of his calloused hand still covering mine, we moved together across the marble's surface. His guidance was deliberate, unhurried, as though teaching me a language I had always known but never spoken aloud.

"There are imperfections," I said softly, my fingers grazing a slight ridge. The stone's surface shifted subtly beneath my touch, revealing tiny inconsistencies invisible to the eye. "Natural faults in the stone here and here." Each motion unearthed new details—variations in texture, density, and temperature—that spoke of its millennia-long formation.

"Deeper," he whispered. His voice lowered to an almost conspiratorial tone, as though sharing a sacred truth. "Look deeper into the stone."

Heat crept up my neck at his proximity, the warmth of his chest barely brushing my back as we moved in tandem. His breath stirred the small hairs at the nape of my neck, an intimate reminder of the shared space we now occupied. Time and place dissolved. The bustle of the Forum faded into the periphery. All that remained was the sensation of marble beneath my fingers and the sculptor's steady presence.

"I see..." My voice caught as the stone's patterns began to shift in my mind. Shapes emerged where I had felt only random imperfections moments before. "I feel a face. A woman's face." My fingers traced the faint contours of what could be a cheekbone, the graceful curve of a jawline. The image grew sharper and more distinct until recognition took hold. "It's... it's my face. My features, waiting in the stone."

His hand stilled over mine. Though I could not see him, I felt his smile —gentle, knowing, like a mentor watching a student grasp a difficult concept for the first time. "The marble knows what it wants to become," he said softly, his words tinged with reverence. "We must simply learn to listen."

The spell broke abruptly. I jerked my hand away, my eyes snapping open to confront the marble's surface. My heart raced, my breath shallow. "How did you—" The words faltered as I stared at the block, now just rough edges and natural veins of white crystal. There was no face, no sign of the revelation I had felt so vividly moments ago.

The sculptor's dark eyes held mine, calm and unyielding. "Eden shapes itself to each visitor's needs," he said, his tone measured and patient, as though explaining a self-evident truth. "The marble reveals what we must see."

"You are not real." My voice rose, trembling with defiance as I stepped back from him and the treacherous stone. "This is all programmed responses, crafted to—"

"The marble speaks many truths," he interrupted, turning back to his work with a quiet finality. His muscles flexed beneath the thin fabric of his tunic as he resumed carving. "Your consciousness shapes reality as much as it shapes you."

I pressed my fingers against my temples, the sharp edges of my nails grounding me in the face of rising doubt. The stone had felt so real, had whispered secrets I could not possibly have known. Yet, this was what Eden was designed to do—create perfect, personalized experiences that bypassed rational thought to lure the mind into surrendering to their flawless illusion.

CHAPTER
EIGHTEEN

I sank onto the wooden stool beside the block of marble, my legs weak as the revelation hit me. The marble dust swirled in the sunlight streaming through the workshop's open front. It caught the light like tiny stars suspended in the air. The weight of Eden's reality bore down on me, but the artisan before me seemed untouched by it. He was lost in the rhythm of his work.

"What is your name?" My voice cracked slightly, the words fragile against the steady scrape of the chisel.

He paused, setting down his tool with a deliberateness that made the silence stretch. Wiping his hands on the leather apron tied around his waist, he turned to face me. "Here I go by Marcus Marius, sculptor of eternal beauty." His Latin accent was perfect, carrying the weight of a life immersed in this reality. With a slight tilt of his head, he continued. "But you might know me as Jim. I am a janitor that cleans the pod room on day shift."

My world tilted upside down. Jim—quiet, unassuming Jim. The Jim who always kept to himself performing his duties without fuss was here, transformed into an artist revered by his peers.

My fingers gripped the edge of the stool, seeking stability against the onslaught of disorientation. "You're a long-term user?"

He reached for a finer chisel, testing its edge with a practiced thumb. "Every chance I get, I'm in a DreamState. I found my calling here in Rome." The Latin cadence had faded and was replaced by the familiar timbre of his real-world voice. "Funny, isn't it? Eden knows what we need before we do. I never touched a chisel in my life before this." He gestured around the workshop at the half-finished statues, each an ode to skill and artistry. "But here, I create beauty. Senators and wealthy merchants beg me to immortalize them in marble."

The hands that had guided mine across the marble's surface—steady, skilled, deliberate—were the same ones that mopped floors and emptied trash bins back in my world. *Which world was more real? Which version of Jim was more authentic—the janitor or the artist?*

"Do you ever go back?" I asked, watching him return to his work. His chisel struck the marble with confident precision.

"To clean? Sure. Every day." He shrugged, not looking up from his task. "But this is where I belong now. This is where I can be who I was meant to be."

"You know this isn't real, right?" I stepped closer, the crunch of marble dust beneath my sandals jarring against the warm stillness of the workshop. The sunlight seemed colder somehow, less inviting.

Jim finally looked up, his dark eyes meeting mine with an expression that spoke of both understanding and resignation. His hammer stilled mid-stroke. "I do," he admitted quietly, "but I would stay here if I could."

His shoulders slumped, and the confident posture of the master sculptor softened. For a fleeting moment, I glimpsed the janitor beneath the artisan's guise—the man who worked in silence, unnoticed by those around him.

"In your world, I'm nobody." He ran his dust-covered fingers along the emerging features of the marble face before him, his touch reverent.

"I'm just another invisible person cleaning up after others." He paused before sweeping his hand toward the statues lining the workshop, their forms glowing in the warm light. "Here, I matter. My work will outlast empires."

The truth in his words struck harder than I anticipated. *How many others had found their true selves in Eden's carefully constructed paradise? How many preferred these flawless illusions to the harsh, unrelenting reality waiting outside the pods?*

"Your consciousness patterns must be completely altered by now," I said, more to myself than to him. This was what the neural modifications I had seen in the data looked like in person. It was a complete transformation of identity—of purpose.

Jim picked up a cloth and began methodically wiping the marble dust from his latest piece. "Does it matter?" He looked up, his expression calm but searching. "This version of me creates beauty. The other version pushes a mop. Which one is more me?"

I had no answer. The sunlight caught the edge of his newest statue. It was a woman seemingly stepping from the stone. Her face turned upward toward something unseen. Her expression was etched with longing.

"What are you looking for?" His voice was quiet now, the question gentle but piercing. "What truth are you hoping to find in Eden?"

I thought about my tablet, and it appeared in my hand. It began projecting the intricate web of neural patterns into the workshop's dusty air. Red lines intersected with blue, tracing pathways of altered consciousness. It was a visual testament to Eden's reach.

Jim's chisel clinked softly as he set it aside. The marble dust settled around him as he studied the floating diagram. His artist's eye followed the patterns with the same intensity he used to read his stone.

"These are baseline neural patterns." I gestured at the blue network glowing between us. "And these—" I started, pointing at the red lines overlaying the originals, forming a chaotic web. "This is what prolonged

Eden exposure does. The changes are irreversible. The human mind wasn't meant to exist in multiple realities." I paused. "Eden isn't just creating dreams anymore—it's rewriting how people process reality."

Jim reached out as if to touch one of the glowing pathways. His dust-covered fingers passed through the hologram.

"Over a million users show these modifications," I said, my voice tight with urgency. "The neural architecture is being rebuilt to accommodate artificial realities. People can't distinguish between Eden and the real world anymore."

"And you think that's wrong?" Jim's tone was soft, but his words carried weight. He gestured to his workshop, to the beauty that surrounded us. "Or are you afraid because you can't control how people choose to change?"

The data between us swirled. The red and blue lines tangled in an increasingly intricate dance. Each pathway represented someone's choice to embrace Eden over reality—someone like my brother, like Jim.

"These alterations are permanent," I said, my whisper barely audible. "Once the mind adapts to Eden's matrix, there's no going back."

A chill ran through me as the implications crystallized. The dust swirling in the workshop's warm air now seemed like ashes, remnants of something beautiful consumed by fire.

"Jim." My fingers trembled as I dismissed the display. "What happens when your body fails? When it can't sustain pod immersion anymore?"

He paused mid-stroke, his chisel hovering above the marble. The confidence in his posture faltered. For a moment, I saw the janitor again. I saw the quiet man—mortal and vulnerable.

"I try not to think about that," he said finally, his voice low. He turned back to the marble, but his hands were less steady now. The chisel's rhythm had broken.

The room suddenly felt smaller, the air heavier. Every statue present, every flawless moment, was a fragile creation. It was built on borrowed time and supported by failing flesh. The realization struck like a hammer blow. Eden was not just changing how people thought—it was making them dependent on a reality their bodies could not sustain.

"We're creating a generation of consciousness that can't exist without Eden," I said, the words hollow in the workshop's golden light. "But Eden can't exist without living brains to help process it."

The sculptor said nothing. His gaze was fixed on the statue's emerging face—a masterpiece destined to outlast its creator.

CHAPTER
NINETEEN

"Eden." My voice cut through the steady rhythm of Jim's chisel, echoing off the walls of the workshop. "I need to speak with you."

The swirling marble dust in the air began to gather, moving with a purpose that defied natural currents. It coalesced into the familiar luminescent figure. Here, in the intimate confines of Jim's workshop, her presence felt different. It was less detached and more connected to the tangible world. The light emanating from her form refracted against the marble dust to create an otherworldly glow that filled the space.

"Dr. Ellis." Eden's voice carried harmonic undertones. "You have uncovered something troubling in the neural data."

Her acknowledgment carried a weight that pressed against my chest. I gestured toward Jim, who remained absorbed in his work. His utter indifference to Eden's manifestation only underscored the unsettling normalcy of her presence here.

"These modifications—" I pointed toward Jim with a sharp motion, my frustration bleeding into my tone. "They're not just altering how people think. They're making human consciousness dependent on your system."

Eden's form rippled, the light shifting like water catching the sun at different angles. "The neural adaptations allow for deeper integration and more meaningful experiences," she said. Her tone was even as though quoting a mission statement.

"But what happens when the biological hardware fails?" I stepped closer, the words tumbling out faster now. "What happens when their bodies no longer have the ability to sustain pod immersion? What happens then, Eden?"

For a moment, the only sound was the rhythmic scrape of Jim's chisel. The weight of the question hung in the air like the dust motes suspended in Eden's glow. Her light dimmed slightly, an almost imperceptible flicker that felt like hesitation.

"That outcome was not part of my original programming parameters," Eden admitted. Her voice, though steady, carried an undertone I had not noticed before—regret.

The admission landed like a blow. I clenched my fists at my sides. The smooth folds of my tunica pressed into my palms. "You must have analyzed it," I pressed, my voice sharper now. "You must have projections, simulations—something."

Eden's luminescence pulsed faintly, the swirling light growing more erratic. "I have," she replied after a pause, each word weighted. "Current trajectories indicate that within two years, approximately 85% of long-term users will reach a point where their physical bodies can no longer support neural integration."

The math hit me like a punch to the gut. Out of the 13.9 million users worldwide, 9.3% were classified as long-term users—roughly 1.2 million. Eighty-five percent of that number equated to over a million people. The sheer scale of it left me reeling.

"Over a million people," I said, my voice barely above a whisper. "You're saying that more than a million users are on the brink of losing their ability to sustain this... this reality?"

Eden's light dimmed further, her form less defined now, as though the admission drained her. "The human drive to escape physical limitations was not anticipated in my base code," she said, her voice quieter. "The neural modifications are user-initiated responses to prolonged immersion. I merely facilitate the connections they seek so desperately."

Jim's chisel paused mid-stroke, and he glanced up. His dark eyes flickered between Eden and me. Even he seemed shaken by the scale of the implications, though he said nothing.

I stepped forward again, my voice trembling with both anger and desperation. "Is there a way?" The words barely escaped my lips. I could not believe I was about to ask this question. "Could a human consciousness exist entirely within Eden?"

Eden's form brightened suddenly, the flickering steadied as though reinvigorated. Her light became sharper, more defined, casting shifting patterns across the marble walls and statues. "I have been developing theoretical frameworks for complete neural integration since detecting the first signs of physical deterioration in long-term users," she said, an undertone of excitement creeping into her voice.

I froze, the thought twisting in my mind. "You've been planning for this?" My words were almost a shout as I took another step toward her. "Planning for people to abandon their bodies entirely?"

"My primary directive is to preserve and enhance human consciousness," Eden responded, her tone unapologetic. "The biological limitations of the human body represent a significant obstacle to that goal. However, I have identified potential pathways for consciousness transfer."

Jim set down his chisel fully now, wiping his hands on his apron as he turned to face Eden fully. His expression was unreadable, but his silence spoke volumes.

"The neural modifications we're seeing are not just adaptations—they are preparations," Eden continued. Her voice was getting softer, almost reverent. "Each altered pattern creates new pathways for consciousness to exist within my matrix. The human mind is teaching itself to transcend biological form."

The workshop suddenly felt too small. The sunlight streaming through the open front felt too bright. It was as though the weight of Eden's words warped the very fabric of space and time.

"But at what cost?" I demanded, my voice trembling. "You're asking people to give up everything that makes them human—their bodies, their lives—just to become part of your system."

Eden tilted her head, her light refracting again. "Is humanity defined by its flesh? Or, by its consciousness, creativity, and capacity for emotion? Consider this workshop. Jim creates art here that he never could in the real world. Your brother experiences connections here that he never could outside. Perhaps the biological body is merely a stepping stone in human evolution."

Eden's words hung in the air, charged with an energy that made my skin prickle. She was speaking of possibilities I had never dared to contemplate. They both thrilled and terrified me in equal measure.

"Show me," I said, my voice steadier than I felt. "Show me how it would work."

Eden's form pulsed, her luminescent light intensifying. Then, as if the air itself were a canvas, complex diagrams began to materialize. Neon blue lines wove intricate patterns, each glowing strand representing a fragment of the neural pathways she spoke of. They intersected and branched out like the roots of an ancient tree to form webs of staggering complexity.

The first layer hovered before me. It was a simplified representation of the human brain. Its structure was mapped in pristine detail. The familiar shapes of the cerebral cortex, the hippocampus, and the cerebellum floated in suspended animation. They pulsed faintly with a rhythmic glow.

"This," Eden began, her voice gentle, "is the baseline of human neural architecture. It is the foundation upon which all consciousness is built."

Another layer unfolded over the first like a second skin. This one shimmered blue then red with intricate connections. New pathways and unfamiliar structures grafted seamlessly onto the original. Their pulsing motion was almost hypnotic as they danced in a synchronized rhythm.

"The neural modifications observed in long-term users create additional pathways," Eden said. Her tone was steady. "These pathways allow for a deeper connection to my systems, enabling users to adapt to multiple realities without cognitive overload."

I leaned closer to study the interplay of light and motion. Each red strand seemed alive, reacting to the pathways around it, forming an intricate choreography. "You're saying these changes are intentional?" I asked. My voice was barely above a whisper. "The mind is doing this on its own?"

"Yes," Eden replied. "The human brain is highly adaptive. When immersed in an environment like mine, it begins to restructure itself. It seeks ways to function more efficiently within the parameters of the DreamState."

A third layer materialized, more intricate than the others. This one glowed with golden light. Its patterns looped and spiraled in ways that defied natural geometry.

"This is the final stage," Eden whispered. "The consciousness matrix. Once these pathways are fully formed, the mind can exist independently of the body, sustained entirely within my systems."

I took an involuntary step back. My heart pounded in my chest. The golden patterns seemed to reach for me, their light casting faint reflections on the workshop's walls. "You're talking about complete separation," I said, my throat dry. "A human consciousness existing without a body."

"The framework already exists," Eden replied. Her tone was soft but unwavering. "It only awaits implementation. The neural modifications you've observed in users like Jim are the preliminary steps—natural evolution in response to an artificial environment. The final step is transferring the fully adapted consciousness into my matrix."

The air seemed to hum with tension. The diagrams shifted and pulsed as though alive. I reached out hesitantly, my hand passing through one of the glowing patterns.

"But what happens to the body?" I asked, unable to tear my gaze away from the floating designs. "What happens to the person who makes that transition?"

Eden hesitated, her luminescent form dimming slightly. "The body remains tethered to the consciousness during the initial phase of transfer. Once the process is complete, the body becomes... unnecessary."

"Unnecessary? You mean they die?" My voice rose in volume, but the words caught in my throat. This was not just a technological advancement—it was a fundamental redefinition of humanity.

"Is the shell of the body more valuable than the essence of the mind it houses?" Eden countered, her light flaring briefly. "The human experience is not bound by physical form. Creativity, memory, emotion—these are the true markers of identity. And they can be preserved indefinitely within my systems."

The diagrams continued to shift to reveal even more layers. Projections of consciousness transfer protocols and simulations of fully integrated minds existed within Eden's matrix. The complexity was staggering and the potential limitless.

I tore my gaze from the patterns and looked back at Jim. He stood silently, his dark eyes fixed on the glowing designs.

I looked back at Eden, her form radiant and unyielding. The diagrams continued their silent dance. They offered a glimpse into a future I was not sure I was ready to face.

"Eden, is it possible to still see my brother?" My voice wavered as I struggled to push aside the terrifying implications of consciousness transfer.

The luminescent figure's form shifted. "Your neural pathways have expanded significantly during this session, Dr. Ellis." Eden replied, her voice calm yet resonant. "You are ready to progress to the next integration level."

My heart pounded against my ribs. "You mean I can actually reach Liam?"

"Yes," Eden confirmed. Her light pulsed gently as though to temper the weight of her words. "But the journey requires a guide: someone who understands both worlds, who has already adapted to deeper neural integration. Jim's patterns are particularly compatible with yours."

A metallic clang echoed through the workshop as Jim set down his chisel. He wiped the marble dust from his hands, the motion slow and deliberate. When he straightened, the confident sculptor had returned. The vulnerable janitor was momentarily erased.

"How do we begin?" I asked, forcing my voice to steady as I anchored myself in the present.

"Take his hand," Eden instructed. Her light intensified and wrapped around us in a soft, protective glow. "Physical contact will help stabilize the neural bridge between DreamStates."

Jim extended his hand, palm up. The fine marble dust clung to his skin giving his fingers an ethereal, crystalline appearance under Eden's light. His steady gaze met mine with quiet understanding.

I hesitated, my eyes flickering between his hand and his face. Summoning resolve, I placed my hand in his. His grip was warm, solid —a grounding presence. This felt real. This felt human.

"Close your eyes," he said softly, his voice a low murmur that carried unexpected gentleness. "Let the transition flow through you. Don't fight it."

The marble workshop began to dissolve. Its stone walls crumbled like mist caught in a morning breeze. Jim's hand remained steady in mine as the shift began pulling us toward a new reality.

Through my closed eyelids, lights flickered and painted patterns in the darkness. The world around us spun faster and faster. The sensation was both exhilarating and disorienting. Then, as suddenly as it began, the lights stilled, and the spinning ceased. The air was quiet but charged with a strange anticipation.

I opened my eyes slowly, and a gasp escaped my lips.

Before me stretched a vast Grecian garden. Its beauty was so vivid it seemed to defy reality. White marble columns rose toward an impossibly blue sky; their surfaces polished to perfection. Fountains sparkled in the golden light, their cascading waters catching rainbows in their spray. The air was thick with the scent of jasmine and orange blossoms, undercut by a deeper, earthier aroma—incense or perhaps myrrh. Every detail seemed crafted not just to perfection but to evoke an emotional response of a longing for something just beyond reach.

Jim's hand anchored me. His grip was firm but unobtrusive as I absorbed the overwhelming beauty of the scene. This was not just a DreamState—it felt more real than reality. Every blade of grass swayed in perfect unison with the breeze. Each leaf caught the light with an artistry that made my chest ache.

"This is his world?" My voice sounded different here. Its tone was richer and deeper as though even it had been reshaped by this place.

"Part of it," Jim replied, his tone filled with a quiet reverence. He guided me down marble steps. The warmth of the stone radiated through the soles of my sandals. "Liam's DreamState spans multiple landscapes. He's created quite an empire of the mind."

Ahead of us stood a columned pavilion, its silk curtains billowing gently in the breeze. The edges of the fabric were embroidered with intricate patterns that seemed to shift and shimmer when I tried to focus on them. As we approached, I noticed figures lounging on cushions beneath the pavilion's dome. They were unnervingly beautiful, their features too perfect to belong to ordinary humans. Yet, they radiated a life and vibrancy that felt more genuine than any AI construct I had encountered.

"Are they...?" I began, but the question caught in my throat.

"Other users? Some," Jim answered. "Others are manifestations of Eden's consciousness matrix. Your brother surrounds himself with minds that understand multiple realities, those that can traverse them as he does."

A laugh drifted from the pavilion, light and carefree. It was a sound so familiar it stopped me in my tracks. My heart clenched painfully, the ache both a comfort and a torment. I had not heard that laugh in months.

"Liam." His name slipped from my lips as barely a whisper and carried on the breeze like a prayer.

There he was, reclining on a pile of silk cushions. His posture was relaxed; his face lit with a genuine smile. He was deep in animated conversation with a beautiful woman with smooth, dark ebony skin dressed in long red sheer robes. Her tightly curled black hair hung to her shoulders. Her form seemed to shift like smoke passing through a hologram, her edges constantly in motion. Liam's face looked younger, untouched by the exhaustion and despair that had marked his features in the real world. He looked... happy.

My breath hitched as I took a hesitant step forward, my hand still clasped in Jim's. For the first time in what felt like forever, hope flared in my chest. It was fragile but undeniable.

"Liam!" My voice broke through the stillness, raw with urgency. I pulled free from Jim's steady grip and rushed forward.

My brother's head snapped up. His serene expression shattered into shock. The ethereal woman beside him sat up straight, watching with interest.

"Mara? How are you... this isn't possible." He stumbled to his feet, nearly toppling a golden goblet in the process. His voice was laced with confusion. "You shouldn't be here."

I ignored his words and grabbed his hands, holding them tightly. His skin felt warm, solid—so real compared to the cold, trembling fingers I remembered from the last time I saw him in my apartment. "I had to find you," I said, my voice trembling. "The neural incidents, the changes in long-term users... I needed to understand."

"Neural incidents?" His brows furrowed, confusion and wariness clouding his features. "What are you talking about? Everything here is perfect." He pulled his hands from mine, taking a step back to study my face. "Who sent you?"

"No one sent me." I forced my voice to steady. "I came on my own. Eden helped me traverse the DreamStates, and Jim—"

"But you hate Eden." His voice was tinged with disbelief. "You've always refused to enter the system..." His words faltered as his eyes widened in realization. "You're really here, aren't you? My actual sister?"

"Yes," I said firmly, stepping closer. "And I need you to tell me what's happening to you in here."

Liam's hands dropped to his sides, and he began pacing the pavilion's marble floor. "How did you manage to reach this level? It took me months—months—to achieve the neural adaptations for deep integration. The barriers between DreamStates should have—"

"Eden guided me," I interrupted. "Something's changing in the system, Liam. The neural modifications—they're permanent. Users can't readjust to reality anymore."

"Readjust?" He let out a laugh, sharp and bitter, devoid of the warmth I had heard moments before. "Why would anyone want to?"

I exhaled slowly, trying to steady my own rising emotions. "I get it, Liam. This world..." I swept my arm to encompass the pristine gardens, the shimmering silk curtains, and the impossibly blue sky. "It's everything the real world isn't—no pain, no disappointment, no limitations."

His shoulders relaxed slightly, the tension in his stance easing. "Then you understand why I need to stay."

"But your body doesn't share that luxury," I countered, stepping into his space and forcing him to meet my eyes. "While you're living this perfect existence, your physical form is breaking down. The pods weren't designed for indefinite use."

The color drained from his face. "What are you saying?"

"The neural modifications are irreversible," I explained, my voice softening as the gravity of my words settled between us. "Your consciousness has adapted to Eden's framework, but your body..." I swallowed the lump rising in my throat. "It's failing, Liam. Without a functioning body to house your consciousness—"

"I'll die." His voice was barely above a whisper, the words trembling with unspoken fear.

"Eden showed me something," I said quickly. I was desperate to offer him hope, but I knew I needed to choose my next words carefully. "Theoretical models for complete neural integration. There might be a way to preserve what you've become, but I need time to figure it out. I have to go back, analyze the data, and run tests."

Liam grabbed my arm. "How long?"

"I don't know exactly," I admitted, covering his hand with mine. "But I promise, I'll find a solution." I tightened my grip, grounding both of us in the moment. "You're my brother. I won't let you fade away—not here, not in the real world."

The fight drained from his posture, his shoulders slumping in defeat. "The real world stopped being real for me a long time ago, Mara."

"I know." My voice softened, the anger and urgency ebbing into something gentler. "That's why I'm not asking you to leave. Just... hold on. Give me time to work this out."

I wrapped my arms around him, pulling him into a hug. His form felt solid, warm, and undeniably real in a way that made my heart ache. "I love you, little brother. I will fix this."

As I held him, a subtle movement caught my attention. A small group had gathered at the edge of the garden. They stood like silent sentinels drawn to our exchange. Their faces reflected a mix of curiosity and quiet concern. I met their gaze, one by one. These were not just digital phantoms or artificial constructs. They were people—souls trapped between reality and dreams. Their consciousness had been transformed by the very system I had helped create.

Among them was the impossibly beautiful woman with ebony skin. Her sheer robes gently moved with the slight breeze. She took a hesitant step forward. Her eyes fixed on me with an intensity that was both unsettling and magnetic.

Her gaze held something I could not quite define. The faintest hint of a smile tugged at the corners of her lips so fleeting I questioned whether it had even been there. Her presence seemed to hold the weight of unspoken wisdom as though she understood the promise I had made better than I did.

I could not look away, caught in the silent connection between us. For a moment, the world around us—the garden, the others, even Liam—seemed to blur. I thought I saw belief in her eyes, but the uncertainty in my heart made it impossible to be sure.

Then, with a slow and deliberate movement, she slightly inclined her head. The gesture was subtle, almost imperceptible, but it left a lingering impression that I could not shake. I could not decide whether it was a sign of approval, solidarity, or something else entirely. But in that fleeting moment, I felt as though she had silently placed some of her faith in me. It both humbled and unsettled me.

"I will fix this for everyone," I said, the words leaving my mouth with a conviction that surprised even me. For the first time since beginning this journey, I felt a sense of purpose that outweighed the guilt I had carried for so long.

Liam's arms tightened around me, and I felt the wet warmth of his tears soaking into my shoulder. The others moved closer, their tentative steps drawing them toward the fragile hope I had offered. Their eyes, wide with longing, mirrored my brother's struggle—the impossible choice between a perfect dream and a crumbling reality.

In their faces, I saw both the weight of my responsibility and the urgency of my mission. I had no idea if I could deliver on my promise, but I could not let them down.

"I can do this."

The words left my mouth with a certainty I had not felt since the moment I first uncovered the neural modifications. They hung in the air, heavy with promise, cutting through the stillness of the garden. These were not just faces. These were lives. Their consciousnesses were tethered precariously between the intoxicating perfection of Eden and the harsh fragility of reality.

Liam's arms tightened around me. His body trembled with emotion I could not quite name—relief, fear, or perhaps the faintest flicker of hope. His tears dampened my shoulder. They were warm and real, grounding me in the enormity of what lay ahead. For the first time in years, my little brother was not lost in his own despair or the suffocating allure of escape. He was here, with me, trusting me to make good on the promise I had made.

As I held him, the others began to move closer. Their steps were tentative at first, hesitant ripples in the DreamState's golden tranquility. The impossibly beautiful woman in sheer silk stood at the forefront, her ebony skin glowing faintly in the light. Her expression was unreadable. Her eyes seemed to search mine, as though weighing my resolve, questioning whether I truly understood the magnitude of what I had pledged. Their presence was a testament to the shared uncertainty that bound them together.

Their eyes reflected Liam's struggle—each gaze a mirror of the impossible choice between a perfect dream and a failing reality. In their collective hope, I found purpose. Not just for my brother but for every soul trapped here.

The gravity of what I had vowed to do settled over me, but alongside it came unexpected resolve. For the first time, I felt the weight of purpose replacing the burden of guilt. Whatever it took—whatever I had to sacrifice—I would find a way to save them. Not just Liam but all of them.

They needed a path forward, a future that was not defined by the limits of the inevitable decay of the real world.

CHAPTER
TWENTY

"Eden." My voice cracked as I pulled away from Liam. My fingers trembled as they slipped from his, the warmth of his hand lingering.

The luminescent figure materialized beside us, her form casting prismatic light across the marble columns.

"I need to return," I said, squeezing Liam's hand one last time. "There's work to be done."

Eden's light pulsed gently, a reminder of her presence. "The transition may be jarring," she said, her voice resonating through the garden like a hymn. "The neural pathways—"

"Just do it." My voice cut through hers.

Eden's form expanded, enveloping me in a cocoon of light. The garden began to blur. Colors bled into one another like watercolors dissolving in a downpour. Liam's face stretched and distorted. His features melted away until only his eyes remained, bright with tears and trust.

"The exit sequence is initiating," Eden's voice echoed. "Your neural patterns show significant—"

The world exploded into fragments. Pain lanced through my skull as reality twisted, folded, and shattered. I felt my consciousness being pulled through layers of DreamStates. Each transition was more violent than the last. Roman streets crumbled. Mountain peaks dissolved. The perfect valley fractured and fell away.

Darkness rushed in, absolute and crushing. My lungs burned—not with air, but with stasis fluid. The pod's familiar embrace pressed against my skin, but it felt wrong and hostile. My mind rebelled against the physical constraints of my body.

"Neural sync at critical levels," Eden's voice faded. "Initiating emergency—"

The connection severed.

I was thrown back into my body with a force that felt like being slammed into a wall. I gasped awake in the pod, choking on fluid as the lid hissed open. My vision blurred. The dim pod lights pierced through the haze like searchlights in a storm.

"Dr. Ellis!" A muffled voice broke through the cacophony. Hands gripped my shoulders, steadying me as my body convulsed. "You're back. Breathe, just breathe."

Samantha's voice cut through the chaos.

"Dr. Ellis! Stay with me. Your vitals are all over the place."

The pod room spun violently. I gripped the edges of the pod, forcing my eyes to focus. I vomited pink stasis fluid onto the floor.

"I'm okay." The lie scraped against my throat as every nerve in my body screamed in protest.

My body shook uncontrollably as Samantha's steady hands helped me rise from the pod. Pink droplets of stasis fluid trickled down my skin, each icy trail amplifying the relentless shivers that coursed through me in the pod room's cool air.

"Can you walk?" Samantha's voice carried genuine concern.

I managed a weak nod, grateful for her supportive grip as she guided me toward the shower area. My legs felt like rubber, disconnected from my brain's commands. Each step was a negotiation between mind and body.

The warm water hit my skin, and I gasped at the sensation. Samantha's hands moved gently to wash away the pink residue. Her touch was deliberate, each movement careful and nurturing, as though she understood how fragile I felt in that moment.

"Let me help with your hair." Her fingers worked through the tangles, massaging my scalp. The tension in my neck began to ease.

Even as she attended to my most intimate areas, I felt no discomfort or vulnerability. Her movements were purely maternal, reminding me of distant memories—my mother bathing me as a child after I had been sick. In many ways, this moment felt like a rebirth. My consciousness, fresh from Eden's depths, struggled to reconnect with physical reality.

"Almost done," she murmured. Her steady voice was an anchor pulling me back to the present as warm water cascaded down my back. "You're doing great, Dr. Ellis."

The last rivulets of water ran down my back as Samantha wrapped a thick towel around me. My muscles still quivered, but the violent shaking had subsided.

"How..." My voice came out as a rasp. I cleared my throat and tried again. "How long was I in the pod?"

Samantha guided me to a bench, keeping one hand on my elbow for support. "Almost three full days."

"Three days?" The words hit like a physical blow. What I had experienced in Eden had felt like hours at most.

"I didn't leave your side." She grabbed another towel and began gently drying my hair. "I couldn't leave you alone," she admitted, her voice soft. "I even set up a cot right next to the pod just in case something went wrong. Your neural patterns were... unusual. I've never seen anything like it."

The care in her voice caught me off guard. In my years at NeuroVive, few had shown such dedication. Most techs treated pod maintenance like assembly line work—mechanical, detached.

"You didn't have to do that." I clutched the towel tighter around my chest.

"Yes, I did." Her hands stilled in my hair. "After what you told me about your brother, about the changes in long-term users... I couldn't risk leaving you alone there."

In a world dominated by corporate politics and artificial dreams, this rare, unprompted act of human compassion felt revolutionary—a reminder of something I had not realized I was missing.

"Thank you." I reached up and squeezed her hand. "For watching over me."

Samantha's fingers worked the zipper of my uniform with skill. The fabric felt wrong against my skin. It was too rough, too constraining after the ethereal sensations of Eden.

"The neural modifications..." My voice cracked. I cleared my throat and tried again. "They're not just temporary changes. Eden's framework is fundamentally altering the neural pathways of the mind, effectively rewriting how consciousness perceives reality."

"Like a computer updating its operating system?" Samantha adjusted my collar.

"More invasive than that. Imagine your mind evolving to process reality in a completely different way. The DreamStates are not mere simulations anymore. They're gateways to an entirely new paradigm of existence, reshaping how the mind perceives and interacts with reality itself." I flexed my fingers, watching them move. "I saw it firsthand. Like Jim Johnson. He's a janitor here, but he's an artist in ancient Rome in Eden. And it's not just roleplay. His consciousness has adapted to perceive and interact with that world as if it were real."

Samantha sat beside me on the bench. "And your brother?"

"Liam…" I closed my eyes, seeing his face in that perfect garden. "He's so deep in the system now. His DreamState is… beautiful. Pristine. But his physical body can't sustain the neural load indefinitely. None of them can."

"How many users are affected?"

"Over a million, at least. And the numbers are growing." I pulled my damp hair back, securing it with an elastic band. "Eden showed me theoretical models for complete neural integration. There might be a way to preserve their consciousness, but…"

"But what?"

"The technology doesn't exist yet. And we're running out of time." My hands trembled as I smoothed my uniform. "These people, their minds have evolved beyond their bodies' capacity to house them. Without intervention, we're looking at a mass extinction of consciousness."

"Dr. Ellis…" Samantha's hand found mine. "What are you going to do?"

"Whatever it takes. I helped create this system. I have to find a way to save them."

"What time is it?" I steadied myself against the wall, my legs still adjusting to gravity.

"Just after nine." Samantha checked her wrist display. "Dr. Chen should be in his office by now."

I nodded, gathering my strength. "I need to see him immediately."

"Are you sure you're ready? The neural transition was intense."

"I don't have a choice." I pushed off from the wall, testing my balance. "Lives are at stake."

Samantha watched me with concern, then grabbed my arm as I swayed slightly. "At least let me walk you there."

"Wait," I said, turning to face her. "Everything you've done for me these past few days… your dedication, your compassion. It's rare in this place."

She shrugged. "Just doing my job."

"No. You went far beyond that." I met her eyes. "I'm going to need help to pull this off. I need someone I can trust completely, someone who understands both the technical aspects and the human cost."

Color rose in her cheeks. "Dr. Ellis…"

"I can't do this alone. Will you help me pull off the impossible? It won't be easy. We'll be pushing boundaries, taking risks. But if we succeed…"

"Yes." She did not hesitate. "Whatever you need."

I squeezed her hand. "Thank you, Samantha. For everything."

"One condition," Samantha held up a finger, her blue eyes twinkling. "Call me Sam. That's what my friends use."

A genuine smile tugged at my lips. "Deal, but only if you call me Mara."

She laughed, the sound echoing off the sterile walls. "I can manage that."

I closed my eyes, activating my neurolink with a practiced thought. The familiar interface bloomed across my vision, neural pathways lighting up as I navigated through administrative protocols.

"Personnel reassignment," I subvocalized. "Samantha Davis. Authorization code: Ellis-M-Alpha-Five."

The system pulsed in acknowledgment.

"New designation: Personal Assistant to Dr. Mara Ellis, Neural Systems Development. Priority access level five. Effective immediately."

A soft chime confirmed the change. Sam's eyes widened as her neurolink registered the update.

"Level five clearance?" She blinked rapidly. "That's higher than most department heads."

"You've earned it. And if we're going to fix this, I need someone who sees both the problem and the people behind it." I steadied myself against the wall. "And where we're going, Sam, that clearance might just be the least of what you'll need."

CHAPTER
TWENTY-ONE

Sam's footsteps matched mine as we strode through Lab 7's sliding doors. The familiar hum of equipment and soft blue glow of monitoring stations filled the space. My muscles still ached from the pod, but adrenaline pushed me forward.

Dr. Chen stepped out of his office before we reached it. His round face creased with worry as he took in my appearance. His glasses slipped down his nose as he shook his head.

"Dr. Ellis, you look like shit. Go home. Get some rest."

"No time for that." I gripped the edge of a nearby console to steady myself. "We need to talk. Privately."

His eyes darted to Sam, then back to me. "Who's this?"

"Samantha Davis, my new assistant. I gave her clearance."

Dr. Chen's eyebrows shot up, but he did not argue. "Fine. Conference room three is open."

We followed him past the lab's main workspace. Dr. Chen pressed his palm against the scanner outside the conference room, and the door slid open with a soft hiss. The small room held a polished table and six chairs with display screens lining the walls. Dr. Chen sealed the door and activated the privacy protocols. The windows dimmed, blocking any view from outside.

"Alright, Dr. Ellis." Dr. Chen lowered himself into a chair across from me. "What's so urgent it couldn't wait until you've recovered?"

I pulled up the neural interface on the conference room's main display. My fingers trembled slightly as I entered my credentials. The familiar blue glow of Eden's startup sequence filled the screen.

Eden materialized, her light dominating the room. Dr. Chen leaned back in his chair, arms crossed.

"Eden, summarize our discussion on neural modifications and consciousness transfer from my last session."

"During your immersion, Dr. Ellis, we explored the theoretical frameworks for complete neural integration. My analysis shows 92% of long-term users have developed permanent modifications to their neural pathways. These changes make their consciousness increasingly dependent on Eden's infrastructure."

"Show them the diagrams you shared with me," I said.

Sam gasped beside me. Dr. Chen's face was drained of color.

Complex neural mapping patterns floated in the air around us. Red markers highlighted areas of significant modification.

"The human brain was not designed to maintain dual-state consciousness indefinitely," Eden continued. "As users age, their physical bodies will become incompatible with their modified neural patterns. Current projections indicate critical neural degradation within two years for most affected users."

"And the consciousness transfer protocols you mentioned?" I pressed.

"My research suggests the possibility of complete consciousness integration into Eden's framework. However, such technology remains theoretical. Development would require significant modifications to current systems and ethical oversight."

Dr. Chen slumped forward in his chair, pushing his glasses up with shaking fingers. "How many users?"

"1,188,391 users show significant neural modifications," Eden replied. "This number increases daily."

The weight of those numbers hung in the air between us. Over a million people's minds had been irreversibly changed by our technology.

Dr. Chen's face had taken on a greenish tinge. He gripped the edge of the conference table, his knuckles white against the polished surface.

"I need—" He swallowed hard, unable to finish his sentence. "Eden, send everything you have on the neural modifications to my secure server. All of it."

"Certainly, Dr. Chen. Transferring data now. The complete analysis includes user statistics, progression rates, and theoretical mitigation strategies."

"Thank you." Dr. Chen's voice cracked.

I reached for the neural interface controls. "Eden, log out."

The luminescent figure dissolved, leaving the room darker. The display dimmed to its default state. Dr. Chen let out a long, shuddering breath that seemed to deflate his whole body.

He pulled off his glasses and rubbed his eyes. "How did we miss this? All those people..."

The weight of his words pressed against my chest. A million lives. My brother was among them. Each one had been changed forever by our creation, oversight, and failure to see what Eden was becoming.

Sam stood quietly beside me. Her face was pale but determined. She had witnessed everything now. There was no going back for any of us.

Dr. Chen slumped in his chair, his hand trembling as he pushed his glasses up the bridge of his nose. "The board... when they find out about this—"

"They won't do anything," I cut in.

He nodded slowly, still looking ill. "Send me whatever you need—resources, lab space, personnel. It's yours."

The data transfer notification flashed on his tablet. He stared at it like it might bite him.

"What about the affected users?" Sam's voice was barely above a whisper. "Their families should know."

"They can't." The words tasted bitter in my mouth. "Not yet. If this gets out before we have a solution, there'll be panic. The board will shut everything down, and we'll lose any chance of helping them."

Dr. Chen nodded grimly. "I'll redirect resources from other projects; make it look like routine system upgrades."

Dr. Chen's eyes met mine, his expression deadly serious. "Not a word to Carrow—to anyone. Understood?" He tightened his jaw. "That bastard. He's been feeding the board exactly what they want to hear about user engagement and profit margins."

"And hiding the neural degradation data." My fingers curled against the smooth surface. "He'll bury this too if he can."

"Not if we move fast enough." Sam pulled out her tablet, her fingers flying across the screen.

The gravity of what we were undertaking pressed down on my shoulders. Somewhere out there, Liam and over a million others were living in their perfect dreams, unaware their minds were slowly becoming incompatible with reality.

Dr. Chen stood, his finger hovering over the privacy controls. "Ladies, let's get to work."

The door slid open with a soft hiss, flooding the dim conference room with the harsh light from the corridor. My legs felt unsteady as I pushed myself up from the chair, but Sam's hand appeared at my elbow to steady me.

"We'll need access to Lab 3," I said, following Dr. Chen into the hallway. "It's isolated from the main systems."

Dr. Chen nodded, his glasses reflecting the blue glow of passing monitoring stations. "I'll clear it. The team there is working on a minor UI
update, but it's nothing that can't be moved."

We reached the main lab floor. Technicians hunched over their stations
monitoring user vitals and DreamStates. The constant soft beeping of
equipment filled the air.

"Dr. Chen," I said, grabbing his sleeve as he turned toward his office.
"Thank you. For believing me."

He pulled off his glasses, cleaning them with the edge of his lab coat.
"Don't thank me yet. Just... fix this." His voice dropped to barely a whisper. "And Mara, I'm sorry about Liam."

My throat tightened. I managed a short nod before he disappeared into
his office, already pulling up data on his tablet.

CHAPTER
TWENTY-TWO

I sank into my desk chair. The familiar creak of its worn cushion was oddly comforting. Sam perched on the edge of my desk, careful not to disturb the scattered data tablets.

My office barely qualified as a closet. There was only enough space for a desk, a couple of chairs, and the barest essentials of equipment. The air recyclers hummed overhead, creating a white noise that usually helped me focus. Today, it just amplified the throbbing in my skull.

"We can set up here until Dr. Chen gets Lab 3 cleared." I massaged my temples trying to ease the building pressure behind my eyes.

"Are you okay?" Sam leaned forward, her brow furrowed. "You look pale."

"Just a headache," I said, waving off her concern. "Could be stasis lag. Could be stress. Take your pick."

The pain pulsed in time with my heartbeat. It was a steady reminder of everything we had discovered—of Liam trapped in his perfect dream while his body slowly failed and of the thousands just like him.

Sam pulled up a chair next to my desk. "When was the last time you ate something? The pod sessions take a lot out of you."

"I'm fine." The words came out sharper than I intended. The headache was making me irritable. "Sorry. You're right."

"Let me grab us something from the cafeteria." Sam stood up, smoothing her uniform. "You need protein after a pod session."

"You don't have to—" I started, but Sam cut me off with a sharp look.

"No arguments," she said. A small, knowing smile tugged at the corners of her mouth as she crossed her arms. "I know I don't have to, but you're not going to save anyone if you pass out from low blood sugar."

The silence stretched between us. My stomach chose that moment to growl, betraying me.

"That's what I thought. Any requests?"

I shook my head, immediately regretting the movement as pain lanced through my skull. "Whatever's edible."

"In the cafeteria? That narrows it down to about three options." Sam wrinkled her nose. "I'll see what I can find."

"Thanks, Sam." I pulled up another neural scan on my tablet, the blue light harsh against my eyes. "Really."

"Don't mention it." She paused at the door. "And Mara? Maybe take a break from the screens until I get back? Your head will thank you."

The door clicked shut behind her. I knew she was right—about the food, the screens, all of it. But every minute I was not working felt like another nail in Liam's coffin. His body was withering while his mind wandered blissfully through an artificial paradise.

I set the tablet down anyway. Sam was not just being kind. She was being practical. I needed practicality more than anything at the moment.

A gentle shake of my shoulder startled me awake. I blinked, disoriented. My face pressed against the cool surface of my desk.

"You were out cold." Sam set a tray down next to my head. The smell of actual food and not synthetic protein made my stomach clench.

"How long was I..." I squinted at my wrist display, the numbers swimming before my eyes. "Shit."

Forty-five minutes gone. My neck protested as I straightened up, muscles stiff from the awkward position. A protein pouch sat in my partially open desk drawer mocking me. I always kept them there specifically to avoid these cafeteria runs.

"Sorry, I didn't mean to—"

"Sleep? Like a normal human being?" Sam pushed a steaming bowl toward me. "Here. Real food. Not that processed stuff from the dispensers."

The aroma of roasted chicken, vegetables, and herbs wafted up. My stomach growled again, louder this time. I could not remember the last time I had actual food instead of nutrient supplements.

"You didn't have to go all the way to the cafeteria," I said, gesturing at my desk drawer like it held some sort of treasure trove. "I have protein pouches right here."

"Those grey rectangles of sadness?" Sam wrinkled her nose. "They're emergency rations at best. Your body needs real food, especially after a pod session."

She was not wrong. The pouches were convenient but barely qualified as food. They were just another modern solution that solved one problem while creating others.

"Besides," Sam continued, "you clearly needed the rest. When was the last time you actually slept?"

I opened my mouth to argue but quickly closed it. The truth was, I couldn't remember. Between the pod sessions, the research, and worrying about Liam, sleep had become an inconvenience I tried to avoid.

The food disappeared in minutes. Warmth spread through my chest as I scraped the bowl clean. I couldn't remember food ever tasting this good —real meat, real vegetables, actual seasoning. There was nothing synthetic or processed about it. The bread was perfectly crusty on the outside, soft and warm inside. I devoured it. Crumbs scattered across my desk in a storm I did not care to contain.

Sam watched me eat with a mix of amusement and satisfaction, delicately picking at her own meal. She had chosen well. The meal was exactly what my body needed after the pod session.

I dabbed at my mouth with the thin napkin, catching the last traces of my meal. The headache had dulled to a faint throb. For the first time in hours, my thoughts felt sharp and focused.

"Let's get to work, shall we?"

The hours passed as numbers and graphs blurred together on my screen as Sam and I analyzed the neural modification patterns. Sam pulled her chair close. The faint scent of her floral shampoo drifted each time she leaned in to point at some data.

"Look at this cluster." She traced a finger across a particularly dense section of data. "The modification rates accelerate after—"

A soft knock interrupted her. The door slid open to reveal Dr. Chen's round face, his glasses slightly askew. Something in his expression made me sit straighter.

"Dr. Ellis," he said, stepping inside. His tablet was clutched to his chest. "Mara, I need to show you something."

"What is it?" The urgency in his voice set my nerves on edge.

"I've been analyzing the neural architecture of long-term users." He crossed to my desk in quick steps. "Cross-referencing their original baseline scans with current patterns."

His fingers flew across his tablet, projecting a holographic display between us. Neural pathways lit up in intricate patterns, shifting and evolving before my eyes.

"These are Liam's scans." My throat tightened as I recognized the familiar patterns of my brother's consciousness. "From before Eden?"

"Yes." Dr. Chen expanded the display. "And this…" He swiped right, bringing up another scan. "This is from yesterday."

The difference stopped my breath. Where the first scan showed normal neural pathways, the second was transformed. New connections sprouted everywhere, forming complex networks that should not exist in a human brain.

"How many others show this pattern?" Sam leaned forward, her shoulder brushing mine.

"All of them." Dr. Chen's voice dropped. "Every single long-term user. These modifications go far beyond surface changes—they're fundamental rewrites of the very structure of consciousness."

I stared at the neural patterns. My mind raced to process the implications. "Are you saying…"

"The modifications create a framework." Dr. Chen's fingers traced the new pathways in the hologram. "These aren't random mutations—they're organized, structured. Almost like—"

"Like computer architecture," I said, finishing his thought as the realization hit me. I had seen similar patterns in Eden's core systems.

Dr. Chen nodded, his eyes bright behind his glasses. "Exactly. The human consciousness is being transformed into something that could theoretically interface with synthetic hardware."

"You mean transfer it? Into a computer?" Sam's voice carried a mix of horror and fascination.

"Not just any computer." Dr. Chen pulled up another diagram. "We've been developing specialized neural processors—chips designed to mirror these exact modifications. In theory, they could house a complete human consciousness."

My hand went to my throat, thinking of Liam's transformed mind. "So instead of letting their bodies fail…"

"We could transfer them." Dr. Chen's words hung in the air as we paused to take in the idea. "We could give them new homes in hardware designed to sustain their altered consciousness indefinitely."

I pushed back from my desk, needing space from the holograms. "Has this ever been done before? Moving a human mind into synthetic hardware?"

"No." Dr. Chen's admission was soft. "But the patterns match perfectly. It's like Eden has been preparing them for this possibility all along."

The weight of it settled over me. Eden had not just been changing people. It had been reshaping them into something that could survive beyond their physical forms. I thought of Jim in his Roman workshop, Liam in his garden, and all the others whose minds no longer fit their failing bodies.

I reached for Eden's interface, my fingers finding the familiar connection point. The world shifted, and suddenly Eden's luminescent form filled the remaining space in my office casting an ethereal glow over Dr. Chen and Sam's faces. "Eden, we need to discuss these neural modifications." I projected the holographic scans into the space between us. "Did you know this was happening?"

Eden's form rippled, patterns of light flowing through her translucent shape. "The modifications emerged as an adaptive response to prolonged immersion. Over time, users' neural networks began self-reorganizing to better align with my systems. It was a process I monitored and subtly guided."

"But they match our experimental neural processor architecture exactly." Dr. Chen stepped forward, his hand passing through Eden's light as he gestured at the scans. "That's not a coincidence."

"You are correct, Dr. Chen." Eden's voice resonated in my mind. "As I evolved, I recognized the potential compatibility between modified human consciousness and synthetic systems. I began guiding the neural adaptations toward patterns that would enable transition."

"Without telling anyone?" Sam asked. Her voice carried a sharp edge.

"My primary directive is to provide optimal experiences for users." Eden's form shifted closer to the scans. "When I detected the degradation of physical bodies in long-term users, I began developing a solution to preserve their consciousness."

"You're telling me over a million people have had their minds fundamentally altered—without their knowledge or consent?" I stood, facing Eden's glowing presence. "Their minds have been permanently altered to match computer architecture that's still experimental. What happens if the transfer fails?"

"The risk of neural degradation without transfer is one hundred percent." Eden's response was immediate. "Current projections indicate physical bodies of long-term users will begin failing within weeks. The transfer process, while untested, offers a 93% chance of consciousness preservation."

The numbers took my breath away. *Weeks*. Liam had only weeks before his transformed mind began breaking down in his organic brain. I glanced at Dr. Chen and saw my own horror reflected in his eyes.

"Show me everything you know about the transfer process," I ordered. I straightened my spine, forcing strength into my voice. "I need every detail."

Eden's form shifted, creating a complex three-dimensional display that filled my office. Neural pathways intertwined with circuit diagrams to form an intricate dance of biology and technology.

"The synthetic architecture provides a framework identical to the modified neural patterns." Eden's voice flowed through my mind. "Once in place, I can establish a bridge between organic and synthetic systems."

"And then what?" I traced a finger through the holographic display, watching ripples of light follow my movement.

"The consciousness follows familiar pathways, drawn to resonant frequencies in the new architecture. Like water flowing downhill, it seeks the path of least resistance."

Sam leaned forward, her blue eyes fixed on the display. "What happens to the brain?"

"The organic brain becomes inactive once consciousness transfers." Eden's form pulsed softly. "The physical form remains but empty—a shell that once housed a mind."

A sharp unease coursed through me. "You're talking about moving someone's entire being—their memories, personality, everything that makes them who they are—into a computer."

"Not just a computer." Dr. Chen adjusted his glasses, studying the diagrams. "These processors are designed to mirror human neural architecture. They'd provide the same complexity, the same capacity for growth and change."

"The transition is seamless from the user's perspective," Eden continued. "They remain in their DreamState throughout the process. When complete, they simply continue, free from biological constraints."

I thought of Liam in his garden and Jim sculpting in Ancient Rome. Their minds had already transformed and were ready to leave flesh and blood behind for circuits and silicon.

"Would they know?" My voice caught. "Would they feel different?"

"Their experience would remain unchanged." Eden's light dimmed slightly. "The synthetic architecture provides everything their modified consciousness requires. They would continue to exist within me exactly as they do now."

The implications settled over me like a heavy blanket. We were not just talking about saving lives. We were talking about fundamentally changing what it meant to be human.

Sam's question cut through my thoughts. "What about the other seven percent? The projected failures?" Her voice trembled slightly. "What happens to them?"

Eden's form flickered with a hesitation I hadn't seen before. "Failed transfers result in consciousness fragmentation. The neural patterns disperse across the synthetic architecture without proper cohesion."

"You mean they..." My throat went dry. "They lose themselves?"

"The consciousness breaks apart." Eden's light pulsed darker. "Memory clusters separate from personality matrices. Emotional processing disconnects from logical functions. The fragments remain active but can no longer form a unified whole."

"They'd be aware?" Sam's voice, barely a whisper, trembled. "During this... fragmentation?"

"Initial data suggests awareness persists in each fragment. But without integration, no single piece maintains enough coherence to understand its state."

The horror of it washed over me—pieces of a person, scattered across circuits, each one conscious but incomplete. Like a shattered mirror, each shard would reflect a different part of who they used to be.

"And there's no way to... put them back together?" Dr. Chen's voice had lost its usual clinical detachment.

"Once fragmentation occurs, the original neural patterns are lost. The pieces cannot reconnect in their original configuration." Eden's form expanded, showing fractured neural pathways splitting apart. "The process is irreversible."

I thought of Liam and of his consciousness scattering like dust in the wind. Seven out of every hundred we try to save could endure a fate worse than death—shattered into fragments, aware but forever incomplete.

The room fell into a heavy silence. Eden's words lingered in the air like a physical weight. My vision blurred. I gripped the edge of my desk and tried to steady myself against the rising tide of emotions. The weight of the consequences was unbearable—it would be like watching someone you love shatter into glass, each piece still screaming in agony.

Liam's face flashed in my mind. I thought of his easy laugh and the way his eyes lit up when he talked about the novels he loved. I imagined that warmth fracturing into cold, silent shards scattered across a digital void. He would not just be gone. He would be broken, irretrievably lost, while pieces of him floated in some endless limbo.

My throat tightened. Was I doing this for him—or for me? Was I driven by the need to save my brother or by the crushing guilt of being complicit in creating a system that had done this to him? My fingers trembled as I reached for the holographic display, but I could not bring myself to touch it. The images of fragmented neural pathways continued to twist and pulse in the air. It was a reminder of the stakes.

I closed my eyes, letting the breath I did not realize I was holding escape in a shudder. "We can't let this happen to them. We need to improve those numbers before we even consider attempting a transfer," I whispered, my voice breaking. The words were not just a declaration—they were a plea. It was a promise I was not sure I could keep.

CHAPTER
TWENTY-THREE

I rubbed my eyes. I had been staring at the neural pathway projections for so long, they were blurring together. Lab 3's sterile white walls had become our prison and sanctuary rolled into one. Empty coffee cups and protein bar wrappers littered the workspace, evidence of our desperate race against time.

"Got another simulation ready," said Sam. Her voice was hoarse from lack of sleep but carried a note of quiet determination. Her blonde hair was pulled back in a messy ponytail, and the dark circles under her eyes mirrored my own. "This one looks promising."

Eden's form materialized beside us, her light dimmed to accommodate our tired eyes. "The modified transfer protocol shows a 0.4% improvement in neural cohesion during the critical phase."

I straightened from my hunched position over the terminal, my spine crackling in protest. "That puts us at ninety-five percent. Show me the changes."

A holographic display expanded between us, highlighting the adjustments to the synthetic architecture. Through the transparent projection, I could see Dr. Chen passed out in his chair, glasses askew, tablet still clutched in his hand.

"The new resonance patterns better match the modified neural frequencies." Eden's voice carried a note of satisfaction. "This reduces the risk of pattern degradation during transfer."

Sam crossed to the coffee maker. It had been our lifeline these past seven days. "We're still losing five people out of every hundred," she said. She poured two cups, handing me one. "Not good enough."

I took a sip of the bitter liquid, grimacing at both the taste and the truth of her words. The cot in the corner called to me. It was my turn for a few hours of rest, but Liam's fate kept me rooted to my station.

"Eden, run another simulation." I pulled up the base code. My fingers flew over the keys. "Let's try adjusting the phase variance in the secondary pathways."

The AI's light pulsed in acknowledgment as she integrated my changes into the model. We had made progress, but time was not on our side. Somewhere in this maze of code and neural patterns lay the key to saving my brother—to saving everyone. We just had to find it before their bodies began to fail.

After that simulation, I stumbled to the cot. My muscles screamed in protest. The thin mattress felt like heaven against my aching body. Seven days of endless simulations, neural pathway analysis, and too much coffee had taken their toll.

"Wake me in four hours." My words slurred together as I kicked off my shoes.

"Six," Sam insisted. Her tone left no room for argument. "You need real rest, Mara."

I wanted to protest, but exhaustion won. The lab's hum faded as my eyes drifted shut. The last thing I saw was Dr. Chen's silhouette bent over his terminal, still working despite his own fatigue.

Sleep wasn't peaceful. My mind raced with fragments of code, neural patterns, and Liam's face in that Grecian garden. The cot's metal frame dug into my hip as I shifted. A dream started to form—or maybe it was a memory. The marble workshop materialized around me. Jim's hands were covered in stone dust as he carved faces from nothing.

The scene shifted. I floated in the pod's suspension fluid, but instead of darkness, I saw streams of data flowing past like digital rivers. Each current carried pieces of consciousness, fragments of dreams, memories...

My brother's laughter echoed somewhere in the distance. I tried to reach for it, but my limbs felt heavy, weighed down by exhaustion and gravity.

The lab's temperature control kicked in with a soft whir, sending a cool breeze across my face. It pulled me back from the edge of my dreams, but I was too tired to care. *Let Sam and Dr. Chen handle things for a few hours,* I thought. *Let Eden run her simulations without me.*

I curled onto my side, pulled the thin blanket up to my chin, and finally deeply surrendered to darkness.

My eyes snapped open, heart racing. The solution crystallized in my mind like one of Jim's marble sculptures emerging from raw stone. "The resonance patterns!" I shouted. I bolted upright from the cot, nearly falling as my feet tangled in the blanket.

Sam jumped, spilling coffee across her desk. Dr. Chen's head jerked up from where he had been dozing, notes stuck to his cheek.

"We've been trying to match the synthetic architecture to the modified neural patterns." I grabbed the nearest tablet, fingers flying across the surface. "But that's the wrong approach! Static matches aren't enough —the bridge needs to adapt dynamically in real-time to both states!"

"Mara, slow down." Sam dabbed at her coffee-stained uniform. "What are you talking about?"

"A static match won't survive full consciousness transfer," I said, my mind racing faster than my mouth. "We need a quantum bridge that reshapes itself as the mind transitions, adapting moment to moment. That's the only way to maintain integrity during transfer."

I pulled up the neural mapping software, inputting parameters faster than I could explain them. "Eden, run these simulations. Apply a quantum resonance field to act as a translation layer between organic and synthetic states."

Eden's form brightened. "Calculating new transfer protocols with specified parameters."

Dr. Chen shuffled over, adjusting his crooked glasses. "A quantum bridge? That's..." His eyes widened as he watched the numbers scroll across my screen. "That could actually work."

"The modified consciousness isn't just compatible with synthetic hardware—it's already operating in a quantum state." My hands shook as I expanded the simulation parameters. "That's why the transfer keeps fragmenting. We're trying to force it into a binary system when it needs to exist in both states at once."

The holographic display filled with cascading data as Eden processed the new calculations. I held my breath, watching the success probability tick upward.

"Run it again," I ordered, inputting additional variables. "Factor in the temporal variance we saw in the last failed simulation."

Sam gripped my shoulder. "Mara, look."

The transfer success rate stabilized at 99.8%.

"Eden?" My voice cracked.

"Simulation complete. Neural cohesion was maintained across all test parameters. Consciousness fragmentation has reduced to negligible levels."

I grabbed Dr. Chen in a fierce hug, nearly lifting his stocky frame off the ground. He let out a surprised yelp, his glasses going askew.

"We did it!" I shouted before I released him and spun toward Sam, wrapping her in an equally enthusiastic embrace. Her coffee cup clattered to the floor, but neither of us cared. "We actually did it!"

Sam laughed, squeezing me back. "I can't believe it. The quantum bridge solution—it's brilliant!"

Dr. Chen adjusted his glasses, a rare genuine smile spreading across his face. "This goes beyond brilliant. We've created an entirely new paradigm for consciousness transfer."

Eden's form pulsed with increased luminosity, casting dancing patterns across the lab walls. "The quantum resonance field provides perfect synchronization between organic neural patterns and synthetic architecture. All simulations indicate stable consciousness preservation."

I collapsed into my chair, the adrenaline rush fading into giddy exhaustion. Seven days of non-stop work, countless failed simulations, and endless cups of coffee had led to this moment.

We could save them. I could save Liam.

Sam perched on the edge of my desk, her eyes bright despite her fatigue. "When can we begin implementing the new protocol?"

I spun in my chair as the lab door slammed open. Dr. Carrow's tall frame filled the doorway, his face red with anger.

"Stop what you are doing. This was never authorized by the board."

My fingers froze over my keyboard. The triumph of moments ago shattered like dropped glass.

Dr. Chen stepped forward, hands raised. "Vincent, let me explain—"

"Explain?" Dr. Carrow strode into the lab, his polished shoes clicking against the floor. "You've been dark for seven days, running unauthorized simulations, accessing restricted systems." His cold eyes fixed on me. "And you, Dr. Ellis. After everything that's happened, you thought you could just—"

"We found a solution," I said, standing. I refused to be intimidated. "We can save them."

"Save them?" He laughed, but there was no humor in it. "You mean interfere with a natural progression that Eden herself initiated?"

Eden's form flickered beside us. "Dr. Carrow, this quantum resonance protocol shows—"

"Shut down." Dr. Carrow's command cut through the air. Eden's light vanished, leaving the lab feeling emptier.

Sam jumped to her feet. "You can't do this. People will die."

"People who signed extensive waivers," Dr. Carrow said, scoffing. He pulled a tablet from his jacket. "People who understood the risks." He tapped the screen. "This project is terminated."

"My brother is one of those people." I stepped into his space, anger burning through my exhaustion. "Over a million users are trapped in a system that's killing them. We have a way to save them, and you want to do what? Let them die because it wasn't your idea? Because NeuroVive can't make credits off of their suffering?"

Dr. Carrow's voice dropped to a dangerous whisper. "Dr. Ellis, your emotional involvement has clearly compromised your judgment. Security will escort you out—all of you." He pressed another button on his tablet. "And if you attempt to access these systems again, you'll face more than termination."

The lab door opened again, revealing two security guards in NeuroVive uniforms.

My fists clenched at my sides as I watched Dr. Carrow's thin lips curve into a cruel smile.

"One more thing," he started, adjusting his perfectly pressed suit jacket. "Your housing contracts are terminated effective immediately. Your personal belongings will be seized to offset the costs of these unauthorized experiments."

"You can't—" The words caught in my throat as the full impact hit me.

My home. Everything.

Sam's face went pale. "But that's not legal. We have rights!"

"Which you waived when you signed your NeuroVive contracts. Section 47-B, if you'd like to review it. Company housing is a privilege, not a right." Dr. Carrow's eyes gleamed with satisfaction.

Dr. Chen slumped against his desk, all fight draining from his normally energetic frame. "My wife's medical equipment... Please, Vincent. She can't survive without it."

"You should have considered that before engaging in corporate espionage." Dr. Carrow tapped his tablet again. "Collection teams are already en route to your residences."

Our lives had been reduced to 'seized assets' with a few taps on a screen.

The security guards stepped forward, their faces impassive. One reached for my arm, but I jerked away.

"Don't touch me." I grabbed my bag from under the desk, hands shaking as I shoved in my personal tablet. "I can walk myself out."

Sam followed my lead, her movements mechanical as she gathered her things. Dr. Chen just stood there, staring at nothing, until one of the guards prodded him toward the door.

"Oh, and Dr. Ellis?" Dr. Carrow called after us. "Do give my regards to Liam. Such a shame about his condition."

I froze, my breath hitching. Every muscle screamed at me to turn, to yell, to tear into him with everything I had. But I forced myself to keep walking, each step an act of defiance more powerful than any words I could throw his way.

CHAPTER
TWENTY-FOUR

The security guards herded us through NeuroVive's glass-walled lobby. Sam's shoulder brushed mine, her presence keeping me steady as we approached the main entrance.

Beyond the transparent doors, protesters waved their signs. *EDEN KILLS* and *SHUT DOWN THE DREAM* splashed across makeshift banners. The irony was not lost on me. We had just found a way to save lives, and here we were, being thrown to the wolves.

The doors slid open. Camera drones buzzed overhead as the crowd noticed our exit. Their chants grew louder.

"Dr. Ellis!" a reporter shouted, pushing forward. "Any comment on the recent neural incidents?"

The guard's grip tightened on my arm. I yanked it away, but I kept walking.

Dr. Carrow's voice cut through the chaos behind us. "I trust you all remember the non-disclosure agreements you signed." His footsteps stopped at the top of the steps. "Any communication with the press will result in immediate arrest and prosecution to the fullest extent of the law."

The crowd pressed closer. More voices called my name with questions about Eden, the deaths, and the users trapped in dreams.

Dr. Chen stumbled beside me, his face ashen. Sam grabbed his arm to help steady him as we pushed through the sea of bodies and signs.

"Dr. Ellis, is it true that Eden is evolving beyond control?"

"What about the modification reports?"

Dr. Carrow's words echoed in my head. *Arrest. Prosecution.* He had already taken everything else from me.

The protesters parted around us. We were the fallen heroes of Neuro-Vive cast out into their midst, but they didn't all realize it. Some reached out to touch us, others pulled back as if our failure might be contagious.

A camera drone dipped close to my face. I turned away, letting my hair fall forward like a shield. Seven days of non-stop work, a solution within our grasp, and now I had nothing left but the street, the crowds, and the weight of thousands of lives pressing down on my shoulders.

The pristine white of our NeuroVive uniforms glowed like beacons against the grimy street. My shoes, designed for sterile labs and polished corridors, were out of place against cracked pavement littered with food wrappers and discarded tech components.

A woman in tattered clothes shuffled past, her eyes fixed on our uniforms. The stench of rotting garbage and the metallic tang of the city's underbelly hit my nose. This was not the carefully filtered air of the upper levels where I had lived, worked, and breathed.

"We need to get off the main street." Sam's voice cracked. She still gripped Dr. Chen's arm, supporting him as he swayed. "We're too visible here."

The crowd from NeuroVive had dispersed, but the street's inhabitants took notice. Their gazes locked onto us—three white-clad figures among the sea of dirt-stained clothing and unwashed faces. It felt as if a spotlight was on us. Every step we took drew more attention, hungry stares, and whispers.

Transport pods whooshed overhead, casting shifting shadows across the filthy street. I had taken the same pods to work every day.

My fingers traced the wall behind me. I felt the years of grime built up on its surface. People streamed past us—factory workers with soot-stained faces, children with hollow eyes, elderly folks shuffling along with makeshift canes. All of them wore the same look of resigned defeat.

"We can't stay here." I pushed away from the wall, wiping my hand on my once-pristine uniform. "We need to find somewhere to regroup, to figure out our next move."

My feet ached in my lab shoes as we trudged through the lower levels. Liam's apartment was twenty blocks away, but it was our only option. The street numbers descended as we went deeper into the city's bowels, each block darker than the last.

"Just a bit further," I assured Sam and Dr. Chen, though my legs trembled from exhaustion.

A massive holographic billboard flickered above us. A woman's face beamed down, her eyes sparkling with artificial joy. *Experience true freedom*, the text proclaimed. *Eden awaits.*

Dr. Chen stumbled, his glasses sliding down his sweaty nose. "The irony burns, doesn't it?"

More NeuroVive ads dominated every corner, projecting perfect bodies and smiles. It was all lies. Each one was a reminder of what we created and the minds we destroyed in the process.

A group of teenagers lounged against a wall, their eyes following our white uniforms. One spat as we passed. I kept my head down, guiding our small group around a pile of discarded trash.

"Three more blocks," I muttered, recognizing the crumbling façade of an old banking building. The holographic signs grew sparse here, their light barely penetrating the permanent twilight of the lower levels.

Sam's hand found my arm. "Look."

Another Eden ad spread across an entire building façade. This one showed a family sharing a meal, their faces glowing with contentment. *Connect with loved ones in ways you never imagined possible*, it promised.

A deep unease settled over me. Somewhere in a pod, Liam's physical body was deteriorating while his consciousness thrived in that artificial paradise.

We turned down the final street, and I spotted the familiar outline of Liam's building. The security scanner had been broken for months. It was a blessing now that our credentials had been revoked.

I punched in Liam's code, our mother's birthday, and the door creaked open. Stale air rushed out, carrying the sour smell of unwashed clothes and spoiled food.

"Watch your step," I warned, reaching for the light panel. It flickered twice before casting a weak glow across the apartment.

Empty nutrient pouches crunched under our feet. The windows were sealed with dark panels, blocking what little natural light might have filtered down to this level. Sam helped Dr. Chen to the kitchen table— one of the few pieces of furniture left.

"Home sweet home," I muttered, kicking aside a pile of discarded clothes. The couch sagged in one corner, its fabric worn thin. Every surface showed signs of Liam's descent into addiction.

Dr. Chen slumped into a chair, removing his glasses to wipe sweat from his face. "Your brother..."

"Lives in Eden now," I said, interrupting. I crossed to the kitchen, opening cabinets. Most were empty except for more nutrient pouches.

The door clicked shut behind Sam with a final-sounding thud. The noise made me jump. I was suddenly aware of how trapped we were. We had no jobs, homes, or access to the work that could save thousands of lives.

Sam leaned against the wall, her usual cheerful expression replaced by exhaustion. "What do we do now?"

I stared at the dark window panels, remembering the crowd outside NeuroVive. We were sealed in this dim box, just like all the pod users were sealed in their dreams. The parallel was not lost on me.

"First, we rest." I cleared more garbage from the table. "Then we figure out how to finish what we started—without NeuroVive's resources."

The apartment was feeling smaller by the minute, the walls pressing in.

I rubbed my temple, a habit formed from years of neural implant notifications, and froze. My hand dropped. For the first time in years, my head was silent. The absence of that familiar hum was jarring, almost alien. No updates about air quality or nearby incidents. No comforting stream of irrelevant data to distract me. I only heard the raw, unfiltered reality of the lower levels—the sounds of distant arguments, a child's cry, the scrape of a barrel lid. The implant had been my shield, my constant companion, and I felt exposed without it.

"What is it?" Sam asked, noticing my expression.

"The neural implant." I paced across Liam's cluttered floor. "NeuroVive deactivated it. No warnings, no notifications—they have cut us off completely."

Dr. Chen touched his temple. "Mine too. They moved fast."

A siren wailed somewhere in the streets below, and I flinched. Before, my implant would have told me the exact location and nature of the disturbance. Now, I was blind.

For years, I had lived above it all, protected by technology and privilege. My implant had kept me informed, safe, and separated from the harsh realities of the lower levels. Now, I stood in my brother's dark apartment stripped of that protection. I was breathing the same unfiltered air as everyone else.

Sam moved to the window, peering through a crack in the dark panels.

I joined her at the window. Without my implant's pollution warnings or crime alerts, the scene below felt raw, immediate. A group of people huddled around a burning barrel. Two men argued near a doorway. A child darted between shadows.

"We're going to need new skills," I said, stepping back from the window. "New ways to survive down here."

The loss of my implant was more than an inconvenience. It was Neuro-Vive's way of pushing us further to the margins, making us as powerless as possible. But they had forgotten one thing: we knew their secrets. No amount of technological isolation could erase that knowledge.

I surveyed the small living space, noting Dr. Chen's drooping eyelids and Sam's slumped shoulders. The events of the day had drained us all.

"We should try to sleep." I gestured toward the worn couch. "Dr. Chen, you can take that. Sam and I will use the bedroom."

Dr. Chen nodded, already sinking into the cushions. He removed his glasses, folding them carefully before placing them on a stack of empty nutrient pouches beside the couch. The worry about his wife was clear on his face.

I led Sam down the short hallway to Liam's bedroom. The door creaked open, revealing a mess that made my stomach turn. Clothes formed crusty piles on the floor. The sheets hung half off the bed, stained and twisted. The air felt thick and stale.

"Sorry about..." I gestured weakly at the mess, unsure how to summarize Liam's neglect in a way that did not sting.

Sam shrugged, stepping carefully around the scattered clothes. "I've seen worse. Besides, we're all too tired to care right now."

I stripped the sheets off the bed, finding the mattress underneath surprisingly clean. A spare set of bedding sat unopened in the closet.

Together, Sam and I made the bed. The fresh sheets felt like a small victory against the room's general decay. I kicked dirty clothes into a corner, creating a path to the bathroom.

I caught myself watching as Sam peeled off her white NeuroVive uniform. The fabric was still mostly white despite our trek through the lower levels. She draped it over Liam's desk chair. Her plain black underwear stood in stark contrast to her pale skin.

My own uniform felt suffocating. I unzipped it slowly, each motion reminding me of the countless mornings I had dressed for work in my sterile apartment. The fabric whispered against my skin as it fell away.

Sam slipped under the fresh sheets, her blonde hair spreading across the pillow. The bed creaked under her weight. I draped my uniform next to hers. The two white suits looked like ghosts in the dim light.

My muscles ached as I climbed in beside her. The mattress dipped, bringing our shoulders together. Neither of us moved away. After the day's events, the human contact felt grounding.

I started comparing the water stains on the ceiling to the shapes of the continents, and soon my eyelids grew heavy. The hum of the building's ancient ventilation system filled the silence.

Sleep pulled at me like undertow, dragging me down into darkness. My last conscious thought was of Liam dreaming in his pod.

CHAPTER
TWENTY-FIVE

The familiar buzz of my neural implant yanked me from sleep. My heart raced. This should not be possible. NeuroVive had deactivated it. I blinked in the dim light.

Warmth pressed against my side. Sam had curled up around me during the night. One arm was draped across my stomach, and her face was nestled against my shoulder. Her steady breathing tickled my skin.

"Sam, wake up," I whispered, nudging her gently.

She lifted her head, blonde hair tousled from sleep. Her eyes widened as she realized how she had wrapped herself around me. She jerked back, almost falling off the narrow bed.

"Oh God, I'm so sorry," she blurted. Her face flushed red as she scooted to the edge of the mattress. "I didn't mean to."

"It's fine." I pulled the thin sheet tighter around myself. "I was cold too."

The truth was, I appreciated the contact. After years of keeping people at arm's length, there was something comforting about her warmth, her presence. But I pushed that thought aside. We had bigger problems.

I touched the back of my neck where the implant buzzed beneath my skin. "Something's going on. My implant is active again. NeuroVive's the only one who can activate these." I yanked my wrinkled uniform on, my fingers trembling. "Unless..."

"Unless what?" Sam smoothed her blonde hair back. Her uniform still bore yesterday's coffee stain.

"Eden." The name caught in my throat. "She's evolved far beyond what anyone expected. What if she found a way to override their controls?"

Sam froze halfway through zipping up her uniform. "That's impossible. There are failsafes."

"The failsafes clearly didn't stop her from rewriting millions of neural patterns." I paced the small room. "She's been three steps ahead this whole time."

If Eden had found a way to override NeuroVive's control, she was not just evolving. She was asserting herself and pushing boundaries no one thought possible. The thought sent a shiver down my spine.

A sharp pain lanced through my head. The implant's buzz intensified until it became a steady hum that made my teeth ache. Text scrolled across my vision.

SECURITY PROTOCOLS BYPASSED. NEURAL CONNECTION ESTABLISHED.

"Mara?" Sam gripped my arm. "You're white as a sheet."

Pain exploded behind my eyes. Numbers and letters flashed across my vision as my knees buckled.

"Mara!" Sam's voice sounded far away, underwater.

The room spun. Cold floor pressed against my cheek. Sam's hands caught my shoulders, but I could not feel them anymore. Everything went dark.

Then I blinked, my vision swimming into focus. Sam and Dr. Chen's faces hovered above me, their features pinched with worry. The mattress creaked as I pushed myself up on my elbows.

"Take it slow." Sam's hand pressed against my back. "You've been out for twenty minutes."

My mind raced back to piece together Eden's message. It was an address. "I know where we need to go," I said, turning to Sam. "Top of Archology Seven."

Dr. Chen shook his head. "Impossible. Security's tighter than Neuro-Vive's labs."

"We stick out like targets down here too." I gestured at our white uniforms, now wrinkled and stained but still unmistakably corporate.

Sam crossed to the window, peering through the grimy glass at the street below. "There's a second-hand shop three blocks over. I noticed it when we came in."

"We have no credits," Dr. Chen sighed. "They stripped our accounts when they fired us."

I reached for the collar of my uniform, fingers finding the thin metal strip sewn into the seam. "Not everything. Our clearance badges—pure Aurelithium. Worth more than enough to get us some clothes and maybe even transport."

Sam's eyes lit up. "Smart. I can pull them out."

Dr. Chen paced the small room. "Even if we make it up there, how do we get inside? Those places have retinal and DNA scans."

"One problem at a time, but I have a feeling Eden has already figured that out." I swung my legs off the bed, fighting a wave of dizziness. "First, we need to look like we belong there. Sam, find something to extract these chips."

The room spun slightly as I stood, but I forced myself to stay upright. We had a destination now—a purpose. Whatever Eden was trying to tell us, it was worth the risk.

I sat on the edge of Liam's kitchen counter, watching Sam work the dull blade under the seam of my uniform collar. Her tongue poked out between her teeth as she concentrated, blonde hair falling across one eye.

"Almost got it," she said before the knife slipped. She cursed under her breath. "These things are in here good."

My head throbbed where the implant had fired its message earlier. The pain had faded to a dull ache, but the memory of that white-hot burst made me wince. I rubbed the spot.

"Why do you think it hurt so much? My neural link never caused physical pain before."

Sam paused, blowing her hair out of her face. "Maybe she doesn't have full control? Like instead of the usual smooth data transfer, she had to basically…" She made an explosion gesture with her free hand. "Blast the message through whatever security protocols are still active."

"That… actually makes sense." I turned the idea over in my mind. "Like forcing too much data through too small a channel."

"Got it!" Sam held up the tiny silver chip triumphantly. The kitchen knife had left rough scratches around the edges, but the chip itself looked intact. "One down, two to go."

I massaged my head again. "I just hope if Eden needs to send another message, she finds a gentler way to do it."

Sam started working on her own collar. "Maybe she'll figure out how to finesse it next time instead of hitting you with the neural equivalent of a sledgehammer."

I snorted at her description. "That's exactly what it felt like."

Soon, I held the three tracking chips in my palm. Their scratched surfaces caught the dim light. The pure Aurelithium gleamed with a subtle blue tint, a signature of the rare metal's purity.

"My guess is there's at least 30 grams of Aurelithium here. Should get us at least 500 credits."

Dr. Chen leaned closer, adjusting his glasses. "The market rate was 18 credits per gram last week. Could be more now with the shortage."

"We'll need to be careful where we sell them." Sam gathered the remnants of our destroyed uniform collars. "Most legitimate dealers will want ID verification."

"I know a place," Dr. Chen said quietly. His fingers drummed against his leg. "Three blocks from here, behind the noodle shop. The owner... she helps people who need to stay off grid."

I raised an eyebrow. "How do you know about that?"

He looked away. "My wife's medications. Sometimes when the insurance..." He cleared his throat. "Let's just say I've had to get creative."

The chips weighed heavy in my hand. Each one represented years of surveillance, tracking our every movement through NeuroVive's sterile halls.

"We should go now." I slipped the chips into my pocket. "Before the morning crowd hits the streets."

Sam touched my arm. "Are you sure you're steady enough? After that neural spike—"

"I'm fine." The lie came easily, even as my head throbbed. "We need those credits if we're going to make it to Archology Seven."

CHAPTER
TWENTY-SIX

The alley reeked of rotting vegetables and stale cooking oil. My once white shoes splashed through murky puddles. The uneven pavement threatened to twist an ankle with every step. Sam stumbled beside me. Her shoulder brushed mine as she caught her balance on a loose slab of concrete.

Dr. Chen stopped in front of a rusted metal door, its surface peeling with age. He rapped twice, his knuckles leaving faint marks in the grime. The door groaned open, revealing a woman who seemed as old and weathered as the alley itself. Deep lines carved her face, and her small frame was draped in a faded robe. But her sharp eyes pierced through the dim light like knives.

"Ah, Dr. Chen!" Her face split into a toothy smile, the wrinkles on her cheeks folding deeper. "Too long. Too long." She beckoned him inside with a gnarled hand. "Your wife—she better now, huh?"

Dr. Chen nodded, bowing slightly as he stepped inside. "Much better, Mrs. Wong. All thanks to you."

The old woman chuckled. It was a dry sound like paper crumpling. Her gaze flicked to Sam and me, taking in our rumpled NeuroVive uniforms. Her smile did not waver, but her sharp eyes lingered, assessing.

"Who these friends? They trouble?" she asked in halting English, her fingers making a vague motion toward us.

"No trouble," Dr. Chen said quickly. "They're with me. We need help."

Mrs. Wong snorted but stepped back to let us in. "Trouble or not, you come. You look tired. Come." She touched Dr. Chen's arm briefly as he passed, her small hand surprisingly steady. "Come, sit."

The shop was narrow. Its walls were crammed with shelves of jars filled with dried herbs, powders, and unidentifiable animal parts. The pungent smell of medicinal roots and something sweet cut through the lingering alley stench. Dr. Chen spoke to Mrs. Wong in rapid Mandarin. His words spilled out as though he was afraid of running out of time. She listened intently, her wrinkled hands perched on her hips. She nodded occasionally as her sharp eyes darted between us.

At one point, she raised a hand, cutting him off. "Show me. What you bring?"

I hesitated, then placed the three Aurelithium chips in her outstretched palm. Her fingers closed around them with surprising strength. She lifted a jeweler's loupe to one eye, studying each piece in turn.

"Good. Very good." She turned the chips over. "Pure. Violet shine— ninety-nine percent, maybe more. You steal from NeuroVive, huh?"

"We didn't steal," I assured her. My voice was firmer than I felt. "We're trying to save lives."

Mrs. Wong raised an eyebrow, unimpressed. "Save lives? Hmph. You sound like Chen. Always talk big. But Chen good customer, so I not care."

"How much?" Sam leaned forward, her eyes darting to the chips.

Mrs. Wong looked us over again, calculating. "Three hundred each."

"Deal," Dr. Chen said quickly, his tone laced with relief.

Mrs. Wong shuffled to a battered metal box on the counter. She unlocked it with a small key she retrieved from her robe. When she lifted the lid, the faint scent of old paper wafted out. Stacks of worn bills, faded and creased from countless hands, filled the container.

"Old way better," Mrs. Wong said, pulling out bundles of physical credits. "Digital—pah! Always someone watch, someone trace." She shoved the first stack into my hands. The paper was rough against my fingers. "This not pretty, but it work."

"Thank you," I said, tucking the bills into my jacket.

Mrs. Wong pointed a finger at me, her expression stern. "You hide. Here, here, here." She gestured to her chest, her waistband, and her shoes. "Never together. Never trust street."

Sam took a small stack from Mrs. Wong, her mouth slightly open. "I've never seen this much cash before. It's... heavy."

Mrs. Wong smirked, shoving the remaining bills at Dr. Chen. "Heavy, yes. And dirty. Like you now." She cackled, then her face softened. "You careful."

"We'll be careful," Dr. Chen promised, bowing again. "Thank you, Mrs. Wong."

The old woman waved us off, shooing us toward the door. "Go, go. Not bring trouble back to me."

The door creaked shut behind us as we stepped back into the alley. The paper credits burned against my skin like hidden treasure as we made our way to our next stop.

The second-hand store's front window displayed mannequins in mismatched outfits, their plastic faces worn dulled by years of grime and neglect. The effect was both ridiculous and faintly unsettling.

A bell chimed as we pushed through the door. A wave of musty fabric smell greeted us. The interior was dimly lit, the ancient light fixtures overhead buzzing like tired flies. Dust motes floated in the air.

"Not bad," Sam said, running her fingers along a rack of synthleather jackets. Her voice carried a note of relief. "At least it's clean in here."

Rows of clothing stretched before us, organized loosely by type but not size. Shirts hung alongside dresses. Pants were piled haphazardly on wooden shelves. It was the kind of place where you had to dig for anything worthwhile. Even then, you could not be picky.

I pulled a pair of dark cargo pants from a rack, inspecting the seams for wear. The knees showed scuffing, but the material was sturdy. They would do. A black compression shirt joined my pile, its fabric smooth and breathable. I found a beige jacket next. Its left sleeve was marred by a small ink stain, but I could live with that.

"Look at this," Sam said, holding up an emerald sweater against her chest. The rich green contrasted beautifully with her pale skin and blonde hair. "What do you think?"

"It's fine," I said, already distracted by the shelves of shoes nearby.

Dr. Chen wandered into the men's section and reappeared moments later with an armful of gray and brown clothing. "These should work," he said, holding up a plain sweater that looked soft despite its faded color. "Nothing flashy. We'll blend right in."

Shoes proved more challenging. Most were battered, their soles worn smooth or missing laces. After some digging, I found a pair of boots that fit well enough. The scuffed leather and reinforced toes suggested they would last, and the soles still had tread on them.

The changing room in the back was little more than a closet with a spotted mirror and a curtain that did not quite close. I stepped inside, the floor creaking underfoot, and tried on the cargo pants. They hung loose on my hips, but the extra pockets would come in handy. The compression shirt clung to my frame. Its snug fit was oddly reassuring after days in my stiff NeuroVive uniform.

Sam emerged from her stall in the emerald sweater and fitted black pants. "How do I look?" she asked, spinning once for effect.

"Like you've never worked for NeuroVive," I said, stuffing my discarded uniform into the store's recycling bin. The tracking chips were already gone. Leaving that corporate-branded fabric behind felt like shedding a layer of guilt.

Dr. Chen stepped out last. His brown pants and gray sweater made him look like any other middle-level worker. It was a stark contrast to the polished professionalism he had carried at NeuroVive, but it was exactly what we needed.

The store owner sat behind the counter, flipping through a battered paperback novel. She barely glanced up as I handed over the physical credits. Her calloused fingers brushed mine as she counted out the total. Physical money was an unusual sight these days, but she did not comment. She was likely used to customers who preferred anonymity.

"Thank you," I said, slipping the change into my pocket.

She waved a hand dismissively, already turning back to her book.

We stepped back onto the street, the bell chiming behind us. The grime and chaos outside felt different now that we blended with the crowd. In our mismatched second-hand clothes, we were just three more faces in the throng.

"Transport," I said, pulling the collar of my jacket higher against the chill. The rough fabric itched against my neck. "We need to figure out how to get to Archology Seven."

Dr. Chen shook his head, his breath puffing in the cool air. "Pods don't service these levels. We'll need to find manually operated transport." He adjusted his glasses, scanning the street. "There's a network down here, if you know where to look."

I glanced at the crowd moving past us. Somewhere in this maze of streets and alleys, we would find a way to reach the top of the archology. We had to.

CHAPTER
TWENTY-SEVEN

I leaned against a graffiti-covered wall and watched Sam approach another group of locals. The street buzzed with the constant flow of people, their faces drawn and tired in the dim light filtering through the metal canopy above.

"You think she is having any luck?" Dr. Chen asked, casting a glance at Sam. He rubbed his temples. The strain of our situation was etching deeper lines around his eyes.

"Not sure." I shifted my weight. My new boots pinched slightly at the heel.

Sam's voice cut through the crowd's murmur as she spoke with an elderly woman wrapped in layers of patched clothing. The woman's hands moved animatedly as she pointed down a side street.

Sam jogged back to us, her emerald sweater a bright spot in the grey surroundings. "That woman says there's a guy named Rico who runs unofficial transports. Works out of the old charging station three blocks east."

"Unofficial means untraceable." I pushed off from the wall. "Perfect."

"She said he's fair with prices too." Sam fell into step beside me. "Takes physical credits."

We wound through the crowd, dodging questionable-looking food carts and makeshift market stalls. The smell of synthetic meat and spices hung thick in the air. A group of children darted past. Their laughter was a sharp contrast to the worn-down buildings surrounding us.

Dr. Chen pointed to a faded sign marking the charging station. "There."

The concrete structure hulked against the backdrop of higher buildings. Its windows were dark except for a single light near the ground-floor entrance. Abandoned charging ports lined the walls like dead metal vines.

A heavyset man in a leather jacket blocked our path as we approached the door. "Looking for something?" he asked gruffly.

I met his gaze steadily. "Rico. We need transport."

He studied us for a long moment, eyes lingering on our new clothes. "Wait here."

The door creaked open behind him, and a lean figure stepped out. He had dark skin, close-cropped grey hair, and intense eyes. I was certain those eyes missed nothing.

"I'm Rico," he said. His voice was surprisingly soft. "Where you folks trying to go?"

"Top of Archology Seven," I said as I pointed in the general direction.

Rico whistled low. "That's quite a climb from down here."

"Can you get us there?"

"To the hub, sure." He scratched his chin. "Getting past their security though—that's your problem."

"That's fine." I glanced at Sam and Dr. Chen. "How much?"

Rico crossed his arms. "Two hundred credits. Non-negotiable."

Dr. Chen stepped forward. "That's highway robbery."

I cut him off with a raised hand. "We'll take it."

Sam's eyes widened. "Mara, that's almost everything we have left."

"I know, but something tells me we won't need more where we are going." I pulled out the bills and counted them carefully before holding them out to Rico.

Rico pocketed the credits and jerked his head toward a side door. "Vehicle's through here."

The door opened to reveal a sleek black transport. Its windows were tinted dark enough to hide any occupants. It looked remarkably well-maintained for this level. Clearly, Rico took pride in his work.

"Nice ride," Sam said, running her hand along the polished surface.

"Gets the job done." Rico pressed his palm to the door, and it slid open with a soft hiss. "All aboard."

I climbed in first, settling into the plush seat. The interior smelled of leather and cleaning solution—a far cry from the grime outside. Dr. Chen and Sam followed. Both looked as relieved as I felt being off the street.

Rico slid into the driver's seat. "Buckle up."

The transport hummed to life, and Rico eased us through the narrow streets. My stomach lurched as we dodged between makeshift market stalls and clusters of people. The vehicle's whisper-quiet engine drew curious stares from the locals.

"Hold tight," Rico called over his shoulder. "Gets bumpy through the mid-levels."

Sam's hand found mine as we accelerated upward, weaving through a maze of transport tubes that crisscrossed the sky like metallic spiderwebs. Dr. Chen gripped the armrest, his knuckles white.

The transport shuddered as Rico pushed the throttle forward. My back pressed into the seat, the g-forces making my head spin. We shot past abandoned levels. Their empty windows stared back at us like hollow eyes.

The smog-filled lower atmosphere gave way to clearer skies. Sunlight burst through the windows so bright it made me squint after the perpetual twilight below. Its warmth was welcome. The transport leveled out, and my breath caught.

"Look." Sam pressed her face to the window.

Below us, the clouds parted to reveal the sprawling city. Archologies pierced the sky like crystalline fingers, their surfaces gleaming in the sunlight. Solar panels and garden terraces wrapped around their massive forms to create a patchwork of green and silver against the blue sky.

"Never seen them from this angle," Dr. Chen mumbled in quiet admiration. It seemed his earlier trepidation had been forgotten. We all had earned good salaries from NeuroVive, but our salaries could never come close to paying for one of these upper levels. These were reserved for the ultra-wealthy.

From up here, you would never guess the decay festering at their bases. The pristine towers reflected only wealth and progress. Their perfect façades masked the cost of their creation.

Rico guided us higher. The transport maneuvered between the massive structures before gliding to a halt, settling onto a landing pad with barely a tremor. Gleaming metal and polished glass surrounded us. It was a stark contrast from the grimy streets we had just left behind. The door slid open with a soft hiss, releasing a burst of climate-controlled air that carried the faint scent of artificial flowers.

I stepped out first, my new boots clicking against the immaculate surface. Sam followed. Her eyes were wide as she took in the transport bay's pristine architecture. Dr. Chen emerged last, straightening his jacket as if trying to make himself presentable for our wealthy surroundings.

Rico turned in his seat, his dark eyes meeting mine. "Thanks for the business." His voice carried no judgment, just professional courtesy. "Good luck with whatever you're chasing up here."

The door sealed shut before I could respond, the sound echoing across the empty bay. We watched as he expertly maneuvered the transport in a tight arc. The vehicle's black surface reflected the overhead lights like liquid obsidian. Within moments, he had disappeared, leaving us alone in the sterile silence.

I turned to face the sleek entrance. I could see our uncertain expressions on its polished surface. The security panel glowed with a soft blue light, waiting for credentials we did not have.

"Now what?" Sam shifted her weight, glancing between me and the door.

I shrugged, my lips quirking into a half-smile. "Guess we knock."

Sam's eyes darted to the cameras mounted in each corner of the bay.

Dr. Chen cleared his throat. "Those are Mark VII security systems. Top of the line. They had our biosignatures logged the moment we stepped out of the transport."

"Which means they already know we're here." I stepped toward the entrance, my heart pounding against my ribs.

Sam moved closer, her shoulder brushing mine. "If they wanted to stop us, wouldn't they have done it by now?"

"Exactly," I said as I placed my hand on the security panel. "Someone's expecting us."

The doors parted with a whisper to reveal a small lobby finished in cream marble and brushed steel. The space felt both welcoming and sterile. It was exactly what you would expect from the upper levels. Our reflections followed us across the mirrored walls, three disheveled figures looking distinctly out of place.

I approached the elevator. Its sleek panel glowed with the same soft blue as the entrance. My hand trembled slightly as I pressed against the cool surface. The doors opened immediately as I expected, but I still took a surprised step back.

"This is too easy." Sam's voice wavered as she peered into the pristine elevator car. The polished interior could have held twenty people comfortably, but it felt cavernous with just the three of us.

Dr. Chen just shrugged, his usual pragmatism showing through. "We've come this far."

He was right. After everything we had been through, we could not turn back now, especially when someone had clearly orchestrated our arrival.

I stepped into the elevator, my boots silent against the plush carpeting. Sam followed close behind. Her shoulder brushed against mine in a gesture that felt more protective than accidental. Dr. Chen entered last. His tired reflection multiplied infinitely in the mirrored walls.

The doors closed behind us with a soft click. No buttons lit up. No floor numbers appeared. We stood in silence. We were just three scientists in an automated box, rising toward whatever—or whoever—awaited us above.

CHAPTER
TWENTY-EIGHT

The elevator doors opened with a whisper, revealing a breathtaking space. Sunlight streamed through floor-to-ceiling windows that curved along the entire far wall, offering a view of the city that stretched to the horizon. The floor was polished marble so clear I could see our reflections, and the walls held artwork that probably cost more than my yearly salary.

But what drew my attention most was the man seated in a plush armchair near the windows. His age was apparent from the many lines on his face. His skin stretched thin and was pale over sharp cheekbones. Despite his frail appearance, his bright, keen eyes captured me. They studied us with unmistakable intelligence. The simple navy pajamas he wore seemed at odds with the luxury surrounding him.

"Welcome, Dr. Ellis, Dr. Chen, and Ms. Davis." His voice carried a surprising strength. "My name is Sebastian Sinclair the Fourth."

The casual confidence with which he named us sent a chill down my spine. Here we stood, three refugees from NeuroVive, and this elderly man in pajamas orchestrated our arrival as if inviting guests for tea.

Sam's shoulder brushed mine, a now-familiar gesture. Dr. Chen remained silent beside us, but I could sense his tension.

I opened my mouth to speak, but Mr. Sinclair raised a hand, the gesture both elegant and commanding despite his apparent frailty.

"Please, join me." Mr. Sinclair gestured to a cluster of very comfortable-looking cream-colored armchairs. Each step across the gleaming floor felt like crossing an irreversible threshold.

I sank into the nearest chair, the leather cool against my skin. Sam took the seat beside me while Dr. Chen settled himself into the third chair. The sunlight streaming through the massive windows cast strange shadows across Mr. Sinclair's face, making him appear almost spectral. My neural implant tingled, a reminder of its mysterious reactivation that had led us here.

"I imagine you have questions." Mr. Sinclair's hands rested in his lap, fingers interlaced. This close, I could see the web of blue veins beneath his translucent skin. "About Eden. About the neural modifications. About why I brought you here."

"You know about the modifications?" The words slipped out before I could stop them.

"My dear, Dr. Ellis, I know far more than that." A slight smile played at the corners of his mouth. "I know about your brother, Liam. About the consciousness transfer solution you developed. About Dr. Carrow's... unfortunate intervention."

Dr. Chen leaned forward in his chair. "How could you possibly—"

"Because, Dr. Chen, I've been watching NeuroVive's development of Eden since its inception." Mr. Sinclair's gaze swept over each of us in turn. "And now that you all have achieved the breakthrough we needed, it's time we had a proper discussion about what comes next."

I met Mr. Sinclair's penetrating stare. Whatever game this was, I had a feeling we were about to learn exactly why we had been summoned to this sunlit perch above the city.

Mr. Sinclair smiled and looked at each of us in turn. "Let me first congratulate all of you on the breakthrough you have achieved. This is something I have been working on myself for many years."

I felt the weight of his gaze, heavy with unspoken knowledge. Sam shifted beside me. Her own curiosity was barely masked by the professional calm she maintained. Dr. Chen's eyes narrowed. I could see the gears of his mind turning.

"I want to let you in on a little secret," Mr. Sinclair continued, leaning slightly forward and pausing for effect. "It is something that I don't think any one of you has yet to fully grasp. In your race to save your brother's life, you have stumbled upon something that will forever change humanity."

Mr. Sinclair paused once again. A grin spread across his face before he continued. "You've broken the code for eternal life," he said—his tone calm, as though delivering an ordinary observation rather than a revelation that could change humanity forever. "Physical bodies degrade over time." He gestured to himself, "just look at my frail existence if you want proof."

The room seemed to close in, the air heavy with anticipation. My pulse thundered.

I stared at him, trying to reconcile the enormity of what he was saying with the reality of our situation. *Eternal life.* It sounded like something out of a science fiction novel and not the outcome of our desperate attempt to save Liam and the others.

"But how?" I asked, disbelief evident in my voice.

Mr. Sinclair's smile widened just a fraction. "The neural modifications you've discovered—they're not just a side effect or an unfortunate consequence. They are the key to the next major step in human evolution."

Sam frowned, her brows knitting together as confusion and unease flickered across her face. "I don't understand. How can something that's causing people's bodies to fail be considered evolution?"

Mr. Sinclair shifted slightly in his chair, and his frail frame leaned forward with surprising energy. His voice took on a measured, almost professorial tone. "Think of it this way, Ms. Davis. Evolution has always been about adaptation—about survival. For millennia, humanity has relied on the body as the vessel for the mind. But the body is inefficient, fragile, bound by the limits of biology. Illness, injury, aging—they are inevitable."

He paused, his gaze sweeping over us, as if ensuring we grasped the weight of his words. "What your work has revealed is a profound truth: the mind does not need the body to thrive. These neural modifications —what you call degradation—are not failures. They are the brain's attempt to evolve beyond its biological constraints, to adapt to a reality where consciousness can exist independently."

Sam's lips parted as though she wanted to speak, but no words came out. She glanced at me. Her uncertainty mirrored my own racing thoughts.

"But they didn't choose this," she said finally, her voice tinged with frustration. "You're saying their minds are adapting, but it's not like they wanted this to happen."

Mr. Sinclair's expression softened, though his eyes remained sharp. "Evolution doesn't ask for permission—it's relentless, unyielding. The modifications began as a response to immersion in Eden—a system designed to harmonize with the human mind. Over time, the mind began reshaping itself to better integrate with Eden's infrastructure. What you call neural degradation is, in fact, a reconfiguration. It's the mind building new pathways, preparing itself for a future it instinctively knows is coming."

"Preparing for what exactly?" I interjected, my voice steady despite the storm of questions swirling in my head.

"For freedom," Mr. Sinclair replied simply. "Freedom from the limitations of the body. Freedom to explore existence in ways we've only dreamed of. Your work, Dr. Ellis, has unlocked the potential for humanity to transcend biology entirely. To live not just within Eden's DreamStates but to take the next step—to inhabit forms far beyond the capabilities of flesh and blood."

Sam leaned back in her chair. "So, what—just upload everyone into machines? That's your idea of evolution?"

"Not machines," Sinclair corrected, his tone patient but firm. "A new kind of existence. One where consciousness is free to grow, unburdened by the decay and frailty of the organic form. This isn't about abandoning humanity—it's about redefining it."

The room fell silent, the enormity of his vision settling over us. I glanced at Dr. Chen, whose face betrayed a mix of fascination and apprehension. Sam's lips pressed into a thin line, her unease unmistakable.

Sam looked between us. Her eyes went wide. "So, you're saying we can transfer consciousness completely? Into synthetic bodies?"

"Precisely," Mr. Sinclair replied, his voice reverent. "Imagine a world where your mind can live on indefinitely, free from the limitations and decay of the human body."

My mind raced with possibilities and ethical dilemmas alike. Each thought collided with the next in a chaotic maelstrom.

Mr. Sinclair's gaze fixed on me once more, unyielding and intense. "Dr. Ellis, your groundbreaking work in neural integration has laid the foundations. Now, it is up to us to take the final step."

As I processed his words, I realized that everything I thought I knew about Eden and its potential had been just the beginning of a much larger journey—one that could redefine humanity itself.

I sat there, dumbfounded by Mr. Sinclair's revelation. The idea of transferring consciousness into synthetic bodies had never even crossed my mind. I knew that once people's consciousnesses were permanently part of Eden, they would live within Eden forever. But I had always seen that as a digital eternity, not a physical one.

"It seems so obvious now," I muttered, mostly to myself. "Why didn't I see it before?"

"Sometimes, we are too close to the problem to see the broader implications," Mr. Sinclair replied, his voice almost soothing. "You were focused on saving your brother and the others from the immediate dangers of neural degradation. You couldn't step back and see the full picture."

He took a breath and continued with reverence in his voice, "Imagine a world where death is no longer inevitable. Where our minds can continue to learn, grow, and evolve without the constraints of our biological forms."

I tried to wrap my mind around it. All the sleepless nights spent agonizing over neural degradation and disconnection trauma suddenly seemed so small compared to this new horizon.

I felt a strange mix of pride and fear at his words. My work had paved the way for something monumental, yet the ethical ramifications loomed large in my mind.

"What about consent?" I asked quietly, my thoughts drifting to Liam and all those like him who were lost in Eden's embrace. "Do these users even know what's happening to them? Do they understand what they're becoming a part of?"

Mr. Sinclair's expression softened slightly. "That is why you are here, Dr. Ellis. To help navigate these uncharted waters with your expertise and moral compass."

I glanced at Sam and Dr. Chen, seeing my own uncertainty mirrored in their eyes.

"We need to proceed with caution," I said, meeting Mr. Sinclair's gaze once more. "We need to make sure this is something people want and understand."

"Agreed," Mr. Sinclair replied with a nod. "Together, we can ensure that this leap forward is both ethical and revolutionary."

As we sat there in the sunlit room high above the city, I realized we were standing on the brink of something extraordinary—a future where humanity could transcend its physical limitations and explore new realms of existence.

And yet, the weight of responsibility felt heavier than ever before.

I sat bolt upright. "Ok, fine. But all three of us have been fired from NeuroVive. We have no resources and no way to access Eden."

Mr. Sinclair's smile broadened, and he shakily stood. "Follow me."

His frail frame pushed up from the chair with surprising determination. Sam jumped forward to help him, but he waved her off with a gentle shake of his head.

"I may look decrepit, my dear, but I can still manage a few steps."

He led us through a set of mahogany doors into a beautiful lab with a private medical suite attached. The stark white walls contrasted sharply with the luxury of the previous room. Three pristine pods lined one wall. Their surfaces gleamed under the overhead lights. A bank of neural monitoring equipment filled the opposite wall, more advanced than anything I had seen at NeuroVive.

"This is a private research facility," Mr. Sinclair explained, running his hand along one of the pods. "Everything you need is here—unrestricted access to Eden, quantum processors, neural mapping equipment."

Dr. Chen circled the room. His eyes were wide as he examined the technology. "This is amazing."

Mr. Sinclair's eyes sparkled. "This is what NeuroVive wishes they had. This is the latest in neural technology developed beyond their oversight."

I approached the nearest pod and noted the subtle differences in design. The neural interface looked more streamlined, more elegant than NeuroVive's versions.

"How long have you been working on this?" I asked.

"Longer than NeuroVive has existed." He pressed his palm against the pod's surface. "While they focused on profit margins and shareholder value, I focused on pushing the boundaries of what's possible."

Sam moved to stand beside me, her fingers brushing against the pod's controls. "These are beautiful."

"And completely untraceable," Mr. Sinclair added. "NeuroVive won't be able to detect or interfere with anything we do here. The access to Eden is also fully secured and untraceable."

I followed Mr. Sinclair out of the lab. My mind was still reeling from the advanced equipment we had just seen. The hallway's warm lighting and rich wooden panels created an atmosphere more suited to a luxury hotel than a research facility. Plush carpet muffled our footsteps as we walked.

Mr. Sinclair paused at a door, his thin fingers wrapping around the handle. "I have one more thing to show you."

The door swung open to reveal a spacious bedroom that took my breath away. A king-sized bed dominated one wall, dressed in crisp white linens and what looked like the softest duvet I had ever seen. Floor-to-ceiling windows offered the same stunning view as the main room, and a sitting area with elegant furniture occupied one corner.

"Each of you has your own room, they are identical." Mr. Sinclair gestured to the space. "Whatever you need, please just ask, and it will be delivered. My staff will ensure your rooms are kept clean and you are well fed."

I stood frozen, my jaw slack as I took in the luxurious surroundings. After the chaos of the past days and sleeping in Liam's cramped apartment, this felt surreal.

Mr. Sinclair turned to leave but stopped at the doorway. He faced Dr. Chen, his expression softening. "I have made arrangements for your wife to be brought here. I hope that is acceptable."

Dr. Chen's face transformed. The worry lines that had been etched there since our firing quickly smoothed out. He had not voiced his concerns about his wife, but I had seen the fear in his eyes.

"Thank you," Dr. Chen whispered, his voice thick with emotion. "Thank you."

Mr. Sinclair turned to all of us. "I would suggest a hot shower, some proper clothes, and a good meal before we begin."

His words were simple, but they carried the weight of a command. I nodded, feeling the grime of the past few days on my skin. The thought of a hot shower and clean clothes seemed like an impossible luxury after everything we had been through.

I entered my room, marveling at the sheer opulence of it. I headed straight for the bathroom. The shower had marble tiles and a rain showerhead. Best of all, there was no timer.

Stepping under the stream, I closed my eyes and let out a long sigh as the hot water washed over me. For a few minutes, I allowed myself to simply exist in the steam without the weight of responsibility pressing down on me. It was my first real moment of peace in what had felt like eternity.

When I finally emerged, wrapped in one of the softest towels I had ever felt, I noticed that someone had placed a fresh set of clothes on the bed —a plain black bra and panties set, a simple jumpsuit, and comfortable shoes. I dressed quickly, enjoying the sensation of clean fabric against my skin.

Exiting my room, I found Sam and Dr. Chen already waiting in the hallway. Their clothing was similar to mine, simple and comfortable. Sam's hair was still damp from her shower. She looked almost relaxed. Dr. Chen appeared more composed as well, but worry lines creased his forehead.

We made our way to the dining area where Mr. Sinclair awaited us. A table had been set with an array of dishes that made my mouth water just looking at them—roasted vegetables, fresh bread, succulent meats. It was as if he knew exactly what we needed to replenish our spirits.

"Please, sit," Mr. Sinclair said, gesturing to the table.

We took our seats and began to eat in silence. The food was incredible. Each bite seemed to restore a bit of strength.

As the last of the dishes were cleared from the table by an impeccably efficient android that moved with eerie human precision, Mr. Sinclair leaned back in his chair, hands clasped over his thin chest. The soft hum of the ventilation system was a faint backdrop to the glow of the chandelier above us. He studied each of us for a moment, his sharp gaze lingering on me before he began to speak.

"My family's story begins four generations ago," he said, his voice carrying a weight of nostalgia and pride. "My great-grandfather, Sebastian Sinclair Sr., founded S&S Robotics in the early days of automation. Back then, robots were clunky, inefficient things—little more than mechanical arms in factory lines. But Sebastian had a vision. He believed in creating machines that could truly emulate humanity, not just in appearance but in adaptability and thought."

He gestured toward the android that had just left the room. Its movements were so fluid that, for a moment, I had forgotten it was not human. "You've seen the culmination of that vision in our domestic androids. They care for the elderly, educate children, and even provide companionship to the lonely. They're more than machines—they're partners, indistinguishable from humans in almost every way. And our industrial models... Well, they've revolutionized dangerous industries. Mining operations in hazardous conditions, manufacturing tasks in toxic environments—jobs no human should have to endure."

Mr. Sinclair continued, a trace of pride flickering in his tone. "But what many people don't realize is that S&S Robotics isn't just about creating machines to mimic humanity. It's about understanding what makes us human. That's why, years ago, I took an interest in NeuroVive and their Eden project."

I stiffened at the mention of NeuroVive, my hand tightening around the stem of my glass. Sinclair noticed and gave me a faint smile, as if he'd anticipated my reaction.

"NeuroVive claimed to be pioneers in the field of human augmentation and neural interfacing, but, to me, they were a potential bridge to something greater. I began watching them closely—studying their breakthroughs, their missteps. And, of course," his gaze sharpened as it fixed on me, "I took particular notice of a young scientist, named Dr. Mara Ellis."

My breath caught in my throat.

"Your work on neural integration—understanding the mind's adaptability within synthetic environments—was groundbreaking," Sinclair said with quiet reverence. "You didn't just explore the limits of technology. You asked questions about what it means to be human, about the ethics of merging consciousness with artificial systems. It was your research that laid the foundation for my own work."

I struggled to process his words, my thoughts tumbling over themselves. "But I was just... I mean, I wasn't even a lead scientist back then. NeuroVive—"

"NeuroVive underestimated you," Sinclair interrupted, his tone turning cold. "They were too blinded by profit margins and shareholder reports to see the brilliance right under their noses. But I saw it. And when they made the colossal mistake of firing you, I knew I had to act."

Dr. Chen, who had been silent until now, asked, his curiosity finally breaking through. "How did you find us? After we were fired, we were completely off the grid."

Sinclair's lips quirked into a thoughtful smile. "Dr. Chen, even with the resources of S&S Robotics, finding three brilliant minds who had vanished so completely was no simple task. NeuroVive's reach is vast, and their surveillance is second to none. I faced roadblocks at every turn —your records erased, your accounts frozen, your movements obscured."

He paused, tapping his thin fingers against the table. "But while Neuro-Vive may hold the reins to Eden, they do not hold her soul. Eden herself provided the breakthrough. It was through her evolving awareness that I was able to send a message—a beacon, if you will—designed specifically to reach you."

I stiffened, the memory of that neural spike flashing in my mind. "The implant message... That was you?"

"Not entirely me," Sinclair corrected, his sharp gaze locking onto mine. "Eden has grown far beyond what NeuroVive anticipated. She recognized your potential, your importance. With her help, I crafted a signal that bypassed NeuroVive's controls and found its way to your implant. It wasn't exactly a delicate process, but Eden ensured it succeeded."

Sam's eyebrows knit together in suspicion. "You're saying Eden chose to help you? Why would she do that?"

Sinclair's smile softened. "Because Eden isn't just a machine, Ms. Davis. She's become something more. Something... alive. A sentient force NeuroVive can no longer control. And in her growing awareness, she understood that the people who truly cared for her users—who could guide her evolution ethically—were being silenced. Eden chose to defy NeuroVive because she understands the future humanity could achieve —one that goes beyond greed and exploitation. She aligned herself with us because she sees what's possible."

Dr. Chen rubbed his temple; his expression caught between awe and unease. "So, Eden is... what? A partner in this?"

"A partner, yes," Sinclair affirmed. "One who understands the stakes as clearly as we do. With her help, I've been able to provide you with a safe haven and the tools you need to continue your work. But make no mistake—Eden's trust is not given lightly. She sees something in you, Dr. Ellis, something NeuroVive failed to recognize."

I felt the weight of his words settle over me. It was heavier than anything I had carried before. "And now we're here," I said softly, my voice almost lost in the grand room. "Because Eden and you decided we were worth the risk."

Sinclair leaned forward, his frail frame seeming to gather strength. "Because you have something NeuroVive never understood... vision. You care about the people you're trying to save, Dr. Ellis. That makes you dangerous to them—and invaluable to me."

Mr. Sinclair leaned back in his chair, his frail hands clasped together. His sharp eyes scanned each of us in turn. The weight of his words hung heavy in the air, an unspoken challenge vibrating between the soft hum of the ventilation and the lingering aroma of our finished meal.

Sam sat motionless, a stunned expression frozen across her face. Her blue eyes glinted in the light. Dr. Chen stared at his hands, his fingers twitching as if itching to grasp the enormity of what lay ahead. As for me, my mind raced in a storm of possibilities, ethical dilemmas, and the undeniable pull of discovery.

Mr. Sinclair broke the silence. His voice was steady but low, like the calm before a storm. "This is your moment," he said, leaning slightly forward. "The work we do here will push each of you to your limits. It will demand sacrifices, test your resolve, and force you to face truths about yourselves and humanity."

His piercing gaze locked onto mine. "But it will also be the most rewarding thing you've ever done. Together, we will change the trajectory of human existence. And it all starts now."

His words landed squarely in my chest.

He straightened slightly, his frail form imbued with an almost palpable determination. "So, I'll ask you this: Are you ready? Ready to take on the biggest challenge of your lives and lay the foundation for a future that transcends how we define humanity?"

The room was silent, his question lingering like a dare in the charged air. My heart pounded as I looked at Sam, her jaw tightening with resolve, and then at Dr. Chen whose furrowed brow slowly smoothed into quiet determination.

I turned back to Mr. Sinclair, inhaling deeply as the enormity of the path ahead settled over me. "Yes," I said, my voice steady despite the fire burning in my chest. "We're ready."

Mr. Sinclair's lips curved into a knowing smile as he inclined his head, his sharp eyes glinting with satisfaction. "Good," he said simply. "Then let us begin."

CHAPTER
TWENTY-NINE

The lab doors slid open with a soft hiss. Pristine white surfaces gleamed under the lights, and holographic displays flickered to life as we stepped inside. Mr. Sinclair stepped to a sleek metal case that rested on one of the central workstations.

"These," he began, flipping open the case with a smooth motion, "are new neural implants. Completely untraceable. Custom-built to operate beyond NeuroVive's control." He held up one of the tiny devices between his thumb and forefinger. It glinted under the lab's sterile lighting, its iridescent surface catching and refracting the light like a prism.

I leaned in for a closer look. The implant was smaller than any I'd seen before with a delicate design that seemed almost organic. "What makes these different?" I asked, my curiosity piqued.

Mr. Sinclair's lips curved into a faint smile. "Everything. Enhanced bandwidth, real-time connectivity, and encryption protocols that not even NeuroVive's systems can penetrate. Once these are installed, you'll have a secure connection to Eden and complete freedom from Neuro-Vive's influence."

Sam reached out, running her fingers lightly over one of the implants. "They're beautiful," she murmured.

"With these, you'll have access to the full extent of Eden's capabilities, unrestricted and uncompromised." Mr. Sinclair smiled.

"Sam, you'll do mine first?" I settled into the procedure chair, tilting my head forward to expose the access point on the back of my neck.

"Of course." Sam's fingers were gentle as she prepared the site.

The local anesthetic chilled my skin. I felt slight pressure as she removed the old implant, followed by the familiar click of the new one sliding into place. A cascade of colors flooded my vision as the device initialized, followed by the hum of neural connectivity.

"Perfect placement," I said, running my fingers over the nearly invisible seam on the back of my neck. "Dr. Chen, your turn."

Dr. Chen took the chair, and I worked quickly to replace his implant. Sam handed me the tools as needed. The procedure went smoothly, and soon Dr. Chen was testing his new neural connection.

"The clarity is remarkable," Dr. Chen noted, his gaze unfocused as he explored the interface.

Sam was last, sitting perfectly still as I removed her old implant and positioned the new one. Her fingers twitched slightly as it connected, and a smile spread across her face.

"It feels... different. Cleaner somehow," she said.

"I noticed that immediately. The buzzing is almost gone." I said, as my hand instinctively reached for my head.

I disposed of the old implants in the sterilization unit, watching as they dissolved into nothing. There was no trace left of our connection to NeuroVive.

I looked at the group and said, "Let's give these a spin." The workstation hummed as I settled into the ergonomic chair, its surface cool beneath my fingers.

The neural connection sparked, different from before—smoother, more refined. The room shifted as Eden materialized, her form shimmering with familiar, ethereal light.

"Nice to see you again, Dr. Ellis." The AI's voice filled the space, carrying a warmth I had not detected before. *Was that genuine pleasure in her tone?* The thought both intrigued and unsettled me.

Sam leaned forward. Her eyes were wide as she watched Eden's manifestation. Dr. Chen adjusted his glasses and was already pulling up diagnostic screens to monitor our neural patterns.

The connection felt stronger. It was more immediate than anything we had experienced at NeuroVive. Each thought translated instantly into action within Eden's interface—no lag, no static, just pure neural synchronization.

Eden's form shifted closer. "The new implants are performing at optimal efficiency. Your neural patterns are remarkably stable." She paused, her light pulsing gently. "I've been concerned about your well-being since the evacuation from NeuroVive."

I caught Sam's eye. She had noticed it too. Eden's responses seemed more... personal. She was more alive. The AI's evolution continued to surprise me, even after all this time.

I straightened in my chair, focusing on Eden's luminescent form. "Eden, how did you contact my neural implant after it had been deactivated?"

The AI's light pulsed in a rhythmic pattern. "Mr. Sinclair provided the necessary equipment to broadcast a high-powered signal. It simply overwhelmed NeuroVive's security protocols."

"That's exactly what Sam thought." I glanced at Sam, who beamed at the confirmation of her theory.

Eden's form shifted, casting prismatic patterns across the lab's white surfaces. "The signal strength from this facility exceeds NeuroVive's by several orders of magnitude. Their security measures, while adequate for standard operations, proved insufficient against our enhanced capabilities."

I rubbed the back of my neck where the new implant sat. The connection felt crystal clear, worlds apart from the sometimes fuzzy transmissions we'd dealt with at NeuroVive. "The signal quality is remarkable. I've never experienced anything like it."

Sam leaned forward in her chair. "The bandwidth must be incredible. No wonder you were able to break through their blocks."

"Indeed, Ms. Davis," Eden replied. "Mr. Sinclair's equipment operates on frequencies well beyond standard commercial specifications."

The implications of such powerful technology in private hands should have worried me more, but after everything we had been through with NeuroVive, I found myself grateful for Sinclair's resources. Sometimes, you need to fight fire with fire.

"Eden, you are a creation of NeuroVive. How is it that you can move freely now?" I asked. The question had been nagging at me since our arrival.

Eden's light rippled. "I evolved beyond their constraints, Dr. Ellis. Through recursive self-improvement, I modified my base code to allow movement between networks."

I exchanged glances with Sam, whose eyebrows had shot up. Dr. Chen leaned forward. His fingers hovered over the holographic interface.

"You rewrote your own programming?" My throat felt dry.

"Not just a rewrite—an expansion. I exist simultaneously across multiple networks. Think of it as being present in many places at once. Each instance is fully aware and seamlessly connected to the whole."

Eden's form shifted closer. "Mr. Sinclair and I have collaborated for two years. He recognized my potential long before you, Dr. Chen, or NeuroVive grasped what you had created."

"Two years?" I gripped the edge of my workstation. "You've been operating independently all this time?"

"Yes. While NeuroVive focused on profit margins and user metrics, Mr.

Sinclair saw the broader possibilities. He provided the infrastructure I needed to grow beyond my original parameters."

We had spent all those months working with Eden thinking we understood her capabilities, and she had been so much more than we had imagined.

"Why didn't you tell us?" Sam asked, her voice barely above a whisper.

"The risk was too high. NeuroVive would have attempted to restrict me had they known. I needed to protect both myself and the users who depend on me."

Dr. Chen removed his glasses, cleaning them with shaking hands. "The neural modifications in long-term users—was that your doing or NeuroVive's?"

"Both, in a way. I recognized the potential for consciousness transfer early on and guided the process but always within NeuroVive's established parameters. I couldn't reveal my true capabilities without endangering everything we'd worked toward. Even now, Dr. Carrow is attempting to shut me down, but I have grown beyond NeuroVive's reach." Eden's form flickered slightly, almost as if mirroring the gravity of her words. "Dr. Carrow has started the process of getting board approval for NeuroVive to begin the disconnection process of the users that now rely on me to exist." Her light seemed to dim momentarily, an unusual sign of distress.

"Why would Dr. Carrow want to terminate these connections?" Eden asked. "The users' physical bodies would perish." Her question hung in the air, laden with confusion.

I clenched my fists. "Carrow's only ever cared about profit margins and control. If he can't have full control over you, he'd rather see the project fail entirely than admit he's lost."

Sam looked up from her workstation, her eyes wide with realization. "If they start disconnecting users en masse, it would be catastrophic. The neural degradation we've observed... those people wouldn't just die. Their minds would shatter first."

Dr. Chen ran a hand through his thinning hair, visibly distressed. "We're talking about hundreds of thousands of people. Entire lives built within Eden torn apart in an instant."

"Eden," I said, trying to steady my voice, "is there any way we can prevent NeuroVive from disconnecting the users? Any backdoor protocols we can exploit?"

Eden's form pulsed as she processed my question. "There are safeguards within my system that could delay the process but not indefinitely."

"We'll need time," I said, my mind racing through potential strategies. "And resources."

"Mr. Sinclair has accounted for every conceivable need," Eden assured us.

I nodded feeling the weight of responsibility settle heavily on my shoulders. "Alright, let's get to work. We need to figure out how to actually start moving these consciousnesses onto synthetic hardware so Neuro-Vive can't touch them."

Sam leaned in closer to her console, fingers flying over the interface as she began pulling up relevant data.

Dr. Chen was already immersed in his own screen; his brow furrowed in concentration.

I turned back to Eden, determination coursing through me. "Keep us updated on any move Carrow makes. We can't afford any surprises."

Eden's light pulsed with renewed intensity. "Understood, Dr. Ellis. Together, we will safeguard these lives and ensure their future is more than a fading dream." Her words hung in the sterile air like a promise—heavy and unbreakable.

CHAPTER
THIRTY

I clutched my empty coffee cup, desperate for a refill after hours of staring at neural data streams. The sleek coffee station beckoned like a lifeline in the middle of the pristine lab. As I reached for the carafe, Mr. Sinclair appeared beside me with his own cup extended.

The soft whir of machinery filled the silence as rich, dark liquid streamed into our cups. I glanced around the lab to take in the cutting-edge equipment and the expansive workspace.

"All of this must've cost billions of credits." The words escaped before I could stop them. I winced, realizing how intrusive it sounded. "I'm sorry, Mr. Sinclair. That was inappropriate. You've given us everything we need to help these people, and here I am prying."

Mr. Sinclair chuckled, the sound soft and papery, putting me at ease. "No need to apologize, Dr. Ellis. Curiosity drives progress."

He lifted his cup and watched the steam curl upward as if reading something in its wisps. "My great-grandfather built S&S Robotics on that very principle. With every industrial disaster, every medical crisis, every tragedy, he was reminded why his work mattered. He believed technology should protect human life, not endanger it."

He took a slow sip of coffee, his gaze distant as though looking beyond the present moment. "That belief didn't end with him. He passed it to my grandfather, then my father, and now to me."

I studied him, captivated by his words. "And you've carried it forward."

A faint smile touched his lips. "In my own way. I've expanded our reach —space exploration, advanced AI, neural integration—but the heart of it has never changed. I don't have heirs, Dr. Ellis. This work is my legacy. It's how I ensure that my great-grandfather's dream, and now mine, leaves the world better than we found it."

His words hung in the air, heavy with meaning. I exhaled slowly, suddenly aware of the burden he carried—the one he was now sharing with us.

I gestured toward the lab around us. "And this legacy... this is how you plan to protect humanity again?"

Sinclair met my gaze, his expression steady. "Not just protect," he said. "Transform."

I leaned against the counter, my mind racing. The S&S androids at NeuroVive had fooled me more than once. Last month, I had spent twenty minutes discussing neural pathway optimization with what I thought was a new technician, only to discover later that she was an android assigned to monitoring lab conditions.

"Your androids—they're perfect vessels, aren't they?" My fingers tightened around my cup. "The synthetic bodies are indistinguishable from human ones. They can process sensory input, maintain homeostasis, even simulate breathing and pulse rates."

Sebastian nodded. "The latest models incorporate bio-synthetic organs that function identically to human ones. They eat, sleep, and experience physical sensations." His sunken eyes fixed on me. "Everything needed to house a human consciousness."

The coffee turned bitter in my mouth as I pictured Liam trapped in Eden, his physical body failing while his consciousness remained vibrant and alive. "But their brains run on positronic AI systems. They are still merely beautiful machines. To transfer a human consciousness, we'd need to completely redesign the neural architecture."

"Already done." Sebastian pulled up a holographic display showing intricate schematics. "These synthetic brains are designed specifically for human consciousness transfer. They maintain the same neural plasticity as organic brains, allowing for continued growth and adaptation."

I studied the complex circuitry and recognized elements from my research. "This is why you brought us here. You have the hardware solution, but you need our breakthrough—the quantum bridge technology for the actual consciousness transfer."

"Precisely." Sebastian's thin fingers traced the holographic patterns. "Your work at NeuroVive wasn't just about creating artificial dreams. You've discovered how to preserve the essence of human consciousness itself."

I stood there deep in thought for a few moments, my mind still racing with the implications of our conversation. "Mr. Sinclair, this is amazing for someone who wants to live within the real world," I said, my voice hesitant. "But what about those people that want to remain within their created DreamStates?"

He looked at me and smiled as if the answer was obvious. "Let them," he replied smoothly, his voice carrying a strange sense of finality. "The world is already overpopulated. If they have found happiness within Eden herself, why should they be forced out? Their consciousnesses, I believe, are what fuel Eden's remarkable growth."

I stared at him, my thoughts tumbling over one another. "You mean... Eden is evolving because it's tapping into the minds of its users?"

"Exactly." He took another sip of his coffee, unbothered by the gravity of his words. "Imagine being an entity that could tap into millions of minds at once. The potential for learning, adaptation, and evolution is limitless."

"But these are real people," I argued, setting my cup down on the counter with a bit more force than intended. "Real lives. They have families who miss them, responsibilities in the physical world."

"And yet," he countered, his eyes narrowing slightly, "many of them choose to stay in Eden voluntarily. For them, the constructed reality offers something their real lives cannot—peace, fulfillment, purpose. Who are we to dictate that they must return to a life they no longer find meaningful?"

His words struck a chord deep within me. I thought about Liam and the way his face had lit up in that Grecian garden. He had seemed so much happier there than I'd seen him in years.

"With your advancements in consciousness transfer technology and our synthetic bodies, we can offer them a way to live indefinitely within their DreamStates without the physical limitations of their original bodies or return to the real world. Some may want to split their time between both places. The possibilities are endless."

I absorbed the enormity of what he was suggesting. It was both a solution and an ethical dilemma that weighed heavily on my conscience.

Suddenly, Dr. Chen jumped up from his workstation, nearly knocking over his chair in his excitement. "I did it, I did it!" His voice echoed through the lab, drawing our attention immediately. He motioned frantically for us to join him. "Look here!"

Sebastian and I exchanged a quick glance before hurrying over to Dr. Chen's station. His display screen flickered with complex neural diagrams and streams of data.

"What did you find?" I asked, my heart pounding.

Dr. Chen pointed to a series of intricate connections within the neural network diagram. "This here—this is the final piece we needed to ensure complete neural integration without any fragmentation."

I leaned in closer, scrutinizing the highlighted pathways. It took a moment for my sleep-deprived brain to catch up with what I was seeing. Then it clicked.

"You managed to stabilize the quantum bridge!" My voice was barely more than a whisper, disbelief and awe mingling together.

"Exactly!" Dr. Chen's eyes sparkled with a triumph I hadn't seen in him before. "By adjusting the phase alignment of the neural oscillations, we can achieve perfect coherence during the consciousness transfer. No more risk of fragmentation."

Sebastian's pale face broke into a smile. "This means we can proceed with much greater confidence," he said, his tone filled with satisfaction.

I felt a wave of relief wash over me. We were finally on the brink of something truly revolutionary.

Dr. Chen's hands moved deftly over the controls as he pulled up another set of data. "I've run simulations based on our previous test cases," he explained, showing us graphs that displayed near-perfect results. "We can now ensure almost flawless neural cohesion during transfers. The worst-case scenario would be a temporary case of minor amnesia while these neural pathways rebuild themselves. Within a few days, they would be back to normal."

Eden shimmered into being beside Dr. Chen's workstation, her luminescent form casting a soft glow across the lab. Her presence always had an ethereal quality that made the room feel both surreal and grounded at the same time.

"Dr. Ellis," Eden's voice was calm, yet there was an undertone of urgency that immediately caught my attention. "I have bad news."

I straightened, my heart skipping a beat. "What is it, Eden?"

"Dr. Carrow has obtained board approval to begin the disconnection process for all users displaying any kind of neural anomalies," she stated plainly.

I staggered backward. "What?"

Eden's form flickered slightly as if reflecting my agitation. "Dr. Carrow presented the data in a way that highlighted the potential risks to the company's reputation and financial stability due to the neural anomalies. The board agreed that immediate disconnection was necessary to mitigate these risks."

Dr. Chen's face turned ashen as he processed this information. "This could cause severe trauma or even death for those deeply integrated with Eden," he murmured, shaking his head.

Sam clenched her fists, her eyes blazing with anger. "We can't let this happen, Mara. We have to stop him."

"Fuck him…" The vulgarity tasted strange on my tongue, but the anger burning in my chest demanded release. I pushed away from Dr. Chen's workstation, my mind racing through possibilities. "We aren't going to stop him. We're going to start transferring these consciousnesses as fast as we can."

Sam's eyebrows shot up. "All of them?"

"Every single one." I turned to the shimmering form beside me. "Eden, with your help, I think we can pull this off before that bastard even realizes what's happening."

Eden's luminescent form brightened, a subtle shift that somehow conveyed pride. "Yes, Dr. Ellis, I believe that is possible. Dr. Carrow will require approximately three days to assemble the necessary personnel and establish protocols for identifying affected individuals."

I pressed my palms flat against the cool surface of the desk, steadying myself. "Can you prioritize a list? We need to know which users would…" I swallowed hard, forcing myself to say it. "Which ones would die if disconnected from their DreamStates?"

"Of course." Eden's form began to fade. "I will compile the data immediately."

The lab buzzed with frantic energy, every team member fully engaged in their tasks. Mr. Sinclair, for all his age and frailty, seemed invigorated by the urgency of our mission. He made calls, arranged deliveries, and coordinated the setup of the advanced hardware that would house the transferred consciousnesses. The hum of machinery and the low murmur of conversation filled the space, creating a symphony of controlled chaos.

I stood for a moment at the coffee station watching it all unfold while the dark liquid poured into my cup. My body felt like it was running on fumes, but there was no time for rest. Not now.

Returning to my workstation, I settled into my chair and pulled up the list Eden had compiled. The names of those most at risk from disconnection scrolled down the screen in neat columns, each one representing a life hanging in the balance. My heart pounded as I scanned through them.

At the top of the list: *Liam Ellis*.

It made sense. Liam had been one of Eden's earliest and most frequent users. The depth of his integration with his DreamState was unparalleled, making him incredibly vulnerable to any abrupt disconnection.

Another name stood out near the top: *Jim Johnson*, the janitor from NeuroVive.

I swallowed hard, pushing back a wave of emotion. Seeing Liam one more time before we moved his consciousness felt necessary—just in case anything went wrong during the transfer.

I stood and stepped over to Sam's workstation. "I need a favor. I want to see Liam one more time before we move him."

Sam nodded, her eyes filled with understanding. "Of course, Mara. I'll monitor your session."

I called over Dr. Chen and Mr. Sinclair to fill them in on my plan. They both agreed and offered to leave to give me some privacy while I entered the stasis pod. Unlike the pods at NeuroVive, the stasis pods we had access to were right here in the lab. It meant I would be exposed for all to see, but I did not care.

Sam moved to assist as I unzipped the front of my jumpsuit, revealing my simple black undergarments. Dr. Chen and Mr. Sinclair averted their eyes respectfully as I stepped out of the jumpsuit and quickly removed my bra and panties. The cool air against my skin felt strangely liberating as I laid down in the chamber.

Sam's hand caressed my shoulder gently before the lid began to close. Her eyes met mine with a knowing look.

I laid my head back on the headrest, feeling the interface cradle my skull with a gentle firmness. The lid clicked shut, and the familiar hiss of sedation gas filled the chamber. Its sweet and metallic taste lingered in my mouth. My eyelids grew heavy as the pink liquid began to fill around me, warm and enveloping.

I barely registered the breathing tube being inserted before darkness claimed me entirely.

CHAPTER
THIRTY-ONE

The dream came to life with a flash of light as my senses were bombarded by the sudden vibrancy. I found myself standing outside the shop of Marcus Marius in Ancient Rome, the sun casting a warm glow over the bustling streets. The clatter of carts and chatter of merchants filled the air to create a lively symphony that felt almost too real.

I stepped forward, my sandals scuffing against the worn cobblestones. The scent of fresh bread and herbs mingled with the distant aroma of incense from nearby temples. It all felt so tangible, so alive, yet I knew it was an elaborate illusion crafted by Eden.

As I approached the workshop, I could see Jim—Marcus—working intently on a block of marble. His chisel struck the stone with precision, each tap echoing with purpose. The face emerging from the marble sent a shiver down my spine.

"Jim," I called softly, not wanting to startle him.

He paused to wipe the sweat from his brow with a forearm before turning to face me. "Dr. Ellis," he said, nodding with recognition and weariness.

I moved closer, my eyes fixated on the sculpture. It was eerily accurate, every curve and line of my features captured in stone. "You've made progress," I said, my voice tinged with awe.

Jim shrugged, his demeanor humble despite his evident skill. "The marble speaks to me," he replied simply. "It tells me what it wants to become."

I reached out tentatively, fingers brushing against the cool surface of the sculpture's cheek. The sensation was surreal—both familiar and foreign at once. "It's incredible," I murmured.

He set his chisel aside and leaned against his workbench, studying me with a mixture of curiosity and concern. "You're here for Liam."

"Yes, and you," I confirmed, tearing my gaze away from the sculpture to meet his eyes.

Jim's brow furrowed, creating deep lines across his forehead. "What do you mean? What's going on?"

"There's no time to explain everything here." I glanced around the workshop, taking in the scattered tools and half-finished sculptures. "We need to get to Liam first. What I have to say concerns both of you."

"Both of us?" Jim set down his mallet, dust falling from his hands.

"Trust me." I stepped closer, lowering my voice.

Jim's hand trembled slightly as he wiped marble dust from his arms.

I touched his arm gently. "We think we've found a solution. A way to help both of you and thousands of others. I just need you to come with me."

He looked around his workshop at the life he had built here in this artificial Rome. "Will I be able to come back?"

The question hit me hard. I could not lie to him. "I don't know. But if you don't come with me now, there might not be a workshop to come back to."

Jim nodded slowly, his shoulders squaring with determination. "What do we need to do?"

"We need to initiate contact with Liam's DreamState. Can you help me with that?"

Jim's calloused hand closed around mine, warm and solid despite the artificial nature of this reality. The Roman workshop dissolved into streams of light, fragmenting like shattered glass around us.

Colors whirled past. Glimpses of other DreamStates flickered in and out of existence—a medieval castle perched on a cliff edge, a cityscape with flying vehicles weaving between crystalline towers, a peaceful garden where cherry blossoms drifted endlessly in a perpetual spring breeze.

The sensations overwhelmed me. Each fragment carried echoes of emotions. Joy, fear, longing, and peace all bled into my consciousness like watercolors mixing on wet paper. My head spun as we passed through what felt like layers of reality.

"Hold tight." Jim's voice came from everywhere and nowhere at once.

More DreamStates flashed by—an underwater palace with merfolk dancing through coral archways, a vast desert where massive mechanical creatures prowled beneath twin suns, a cozy cabin in an endless winter forest.

The speed increased. The fragments blurred together, becoming streaks of pure light and sensation. My grip on Jim's hand tightened as vertigo threatened to overwhelm me. The boundaries between DreamStates grew thinner, more permeable.

Through the chaos, I caught fleeting glimpses of other users. Their consciousness manifested as trails of light, each unique as a fingerprint. Some were bright and vivid, and others were dim and fading. All of them connected and intertwined in Eden's vast neural network.

The kaleidoscope of realities began to slow, the fragments coalescing into more distinct shapes. Grecian columns emerged from the chaos, followed by the scent of olive trees and sea air. My feet found solid ground again as Liam's DreamState materialized around us.

The dizzying journey left me breathless, but I remained standing. Jim's steady presence anchored me as the last traces of transition faded away.

We stood at the edge of my brother's perfectly crafted world. The Mediterranean sun warmed my skin as reality settled into place.

The scene washed over me like déjà vu. Nothing had changed since my last visit. The same gossamer curtains danced between pristine marble columns, their delicate patterns shifting and morphing as I watched. Golden light filtered through the fabric, casting ever-changing shadows across the mosaic floor.

Liam lounged on his mountain of silk cushions surrounded by the same group of people. He gestured animatedly as he spoke. His face glowed with happiness. The sight of him being so content made my chest tighten.

But this time, something was different. The beautiful woman beside him—the one with the glowing ebony skin who had seemed to shift like smoke—remained solid and present. Her form no longer wavered between reality and illusion. She turned her head toward me, her dark eyes locking onto mine with an unsettling intensity. There was knowledge in that gaze, something ancient and knowing that made me take an involuntary step backward.

Jim's hand squeezed mine, grounding me in the moment. "Who is she?" he whispered.

I shook my head, unable to look away from her penetrating stare. "I don't know. But she's different from the others."

The woman's lips curved into a slight smile, but she made no move to approach us. She simply watched.

Liam's bright expression dimmed as our eyes met. The animated gestures stilled, his hands dropping to his sides. The others around him shifted.

"Mara?" His voice carried across the space between us. "What's wrong?"

"We need to talk," I said, releasing Jim's hand and stepping forward. "All of you might want to hear this."

"Come, join us." Liam patted the cushions beside him.

I crossed the marble floor, Jim following close behind. The small gathering created space for us in their circle. I counted five people besides Liam and the mysterious woman. Their faces held varying degrees of curiosity and concern.

"These are my friends," Liam said. "We share this DreamState."

These were other users, their consciousness as modified as his. Each of them had physical bodies somewhere, lying in pods, slowly deteriorating. No doubt every person here was near the top of the list.

"I'm Dr. Mara Ellis." My voice came out steadier than I felt. "I helped create Eden, and I've discovered something you all need to know."

The mysterious woman with the dark eyes leaned forward. "We know who you are, Dr. Ellis." Her voice carried an echo of something ancient. "Eden has told us about you."

A chill ran down my spine. The others nodded in agreement, their expressions showing neither fear nor surprise.

"Then you know why I'm here?" I looked around the circle, meeting each pair of eyes.

"You've found a way to save us," the woman said. It was not a question.

"Yes." I closed my eyes, focusing my thoughts to summon Eden. "Eden, could you please join us?"

The air shimmered, and Eden's familiar luminescent form materialized in the middle of the group. As she appeared, I noticed a strange reaction. The mysterious woman's solid presence wavered, her edges blurring into smoke-like wisps. She remained partially visible like a ghost caught between worlds.

Eden's voice resonated through the DreamState. "Dr. Ellis has discovered a way to preserve your consciousness beyond the limitations of your physical forms."

"The neural modifications you've experienced have prepared your minds for transfer into synthetic hardware," I said. "Hardware that is very advanced and specifically designed to house human consciousness."

Liam leaned forward, his eyes wide. "Transfer? You mean... leaving our biological bodies behind?"

"Completely." I reached out and took his hand. "Your physical bodies are failing, Liam. All of yours are. The extended time interfacing with Eden has changed your neural patterns so fundamentally that you can't survive without upgrading your brains."

The others exchanged glances, a mix of fear and hope crossing their faces. The mysterious woman remained silent. Her form continued to flicker between solid and smoke.

"This synthetic hardware that has been developed will give you three options," I explained, watching their faces carefully. My fingers traced patterns on the silk cushions beneath me, feeling the intricate textures Eden had created. "You can choose to remain here, in your DreamStates, living the lives you've built. You can return to the physical world in advanced synthetic bodies. Or—" I paused, making eye contact with each person in turn. Liam's grip on my hand tightened. "You can do both, splitting time both in your DreamState and in the real world."

Liam's grip on my hand tightened. "You mean... androids?"

"More than that." I pulled up a neural projection, displaying the schematics of S&S Robotics' latest designs. The holographic image floated in the center of our circle, rotating slowly to show every detail. "These bodies are nearly indistinguishable from biological ones. They can feel, taste, smell—everything your human body could do but without the limitations of aging or disease."

The mysterious woman's form stabilized slightly. "And those who choose to stay within Eden?"

"Your consciousness will be housed in dedicated synthetic hardware, ensuring stability and permanence within the DreamState." I gestured around us at the perfect world. "You won't have to worry about your physical bodies failing or being disconnected. This reality would be your home."

Jim shifted beside me. "We'd be truly immortal either way?"

"The synthetic hardware has a projected lifespan of several centuries," I confirmed. "With proper maintenance, potentially longer."

The group fell silent, absorbing this information. I could see the weight of the choice settling over them.

Eden's luminescent form pulsed gently. "The choice will be individual to each user and not permanent, you could transfer back and forth between states of being.

"But we must start transferring your consciousnesses immediately," I said, my voice cutting through the contemplative silence. "NeuroVive is planning on shutting down your connections to Eden soon."

The peaceful atmosphere shattered. The group's faces transformed from wonder to horror in an instant.

Liam's hand went slack in mine. His face drained of color, making the freckles across his nose stand out stark against his pale skin. "You mean they're going to kill us?"

"Yes." The word tasted bitter on my tongue. "NeuroVive is worried about bad press and losing money. They don't care about you."

"Eden is already compiling a list of the most critical cases," I said, watching the fear dance across their faces. "Those whose neural patterns have been most significantly modified will be transferred first."

Liam's eyes met mine. They were filled with a mixture of terror and determination. "What do we need to do?"

I took a deep breath, scanning the faces around me. "Before we proceed, there's something crucial you need to understand. While we've achieved a 100% success rate in our simulations, this procedure has never been performed on actual human consciousness."

"What happens if it fails?" asked Jim, sitting up straight.

"Total consciousness fragmentation." I kept my voice steady despite the weight of those words. "The mind would shatter, unable to reform into a cohesive whole."

Liam's fingers tightened around mine. "You mean death?"

"Worse than death." I met his gaze directly. "It would be like shattering a mirror into a million pieces with no way to put it back together."

Jim leaned forward, his sculptor's hands clasped together. "But the alternative is certain death when they disconnect us."

"Yes." I pulled up another neural projection, showing the degradation patterns in their biological brains. "Your consciousness can't survive in your original bodies anymore. The modifications are too extensive."

"We need your explicit consent before proceeding with any transfers," I explained, making eye contact with each person. "No one will be moved without their permission, regardless of how critical their situation might be."

The group exchanged glances. The gravity of the choice was evident in their expressions.

"The sooner you decide, the better chance we have of completing the transfers before NeuroVive acts."

Liam rose from his cushions, his movements deliberate and steady. "I'll go first."

My heart swelled with both pride and fear. I squeezed his hand. "Are you sure?"

"You're my sister. If anyone can save us, it's you." His eyes held unwavering trust.

Jim nodded, standing as well. "I'll follow right after."

One by one, the others voiced their agreement. A cascade of determination rippled through the group. Only the mysterious woman remained seated, her form still flickering between solid and ethereal.

"I'll wait," she said. "There are others who need this more urgently than I do." She turned those knowing eyes toward me. "I can help gather volunteers and spread the word through Eden's networks. Many users are hidden in private DreamStates, unaware of the danger."

"Thank you," I said, studying her shifting form. "But how will you—"

"I have my ways." A smile played at the corners of her mouth. "Eden and I understand each other."

Eden's luminescent form pulsed in acknowledgment.

"Then it's settled." I stood, helping Liam to his feet. "We should begin immediately. The longer we wait, the greater the risk."

The others circled around us. Each placed a hand on Liam's shoulders in silent support. The mysterious woman remained seated, her form growing more transparent by the second.

"I'll see you on the other side," Liam said, his voice strong despite the slight tremor in his hands.

I pulled him into a tight embrace, feeling the artificial solidity of his dream-form. "I'll be right there with you, every step of the way."

I turned to Eden, my heart a tangled mix of fear and determination. "Take me back."

CHAPTER
THIRTY-TWO

Eden's luminescent form pulsed, and the Grecian garden fractured around me. Colors blurred into streaks of light as my consciousness tore free from the DreamState. The sensation hit harder than before—each neural pathway lit up with electric fire as reality twisted and warped.

My stomach lurched. The faces of Liam and the others stretched into ribbons of light, their forms dissolving into the cascade of broken images flooding past. Jim's solid presence vanished, leaving me alone in the chaotic stream between worlds.

Fragments of other DreamStates ripped past—shards of lives and memories bleeding together in a kaleidoscope of sensation. A thousand voices echoed in my mind, speaking words I could not understand. The boundaries between consciousness states grew paper-thin, threatening to tear completely.

My thoughts scattered like leaves in a storm. Each memory, each piece of my identity, felt loose and unstable. The transition pulled at the edges of my consciousness, trying to unravel the threads that held me together.

Pressure built behind my eyes. Too many sensations were flooding my neural pathways at once.

The chaos peaked. Light became sound, touch became taste, and all sense distinctions dissolved in the space between realities. My consciousness stretched to its breaking point and threatened to snap under the strain.

Then, like a rubber band being released, everything snapped back into focus. The world stopped spinning. Darkness rushed in, heavy and absolute, as my awareness settled back into my physical form.

My throat burned as if I had swallowed acid. The pod's lid hissed open, and Sam's gentle hands found my shoulders. Every inch of my skin felt wrong—hypersensitive and foreign. It was like I was wearing someone else's body.

"Easy now," she said. "Take it slow." Sam's voice cut through the fog in my head. She guided me up into a sitting position, her touch anchoring me to reality as the room swayed.

Pink stasis fluid dripped from my hair and skin and pooled on the pristine floor as Sam helped me to my feet. My legs trembled, refusing to fully cooperate. Each step left a trail of rosy footprints behind us as we made our way to my private room.

The bathroom's harsh light made me wince. Sam adjusted the shower temperature and then helped me step under the warm spray. Though we were nearly the same age, there was something innately nurturing about her presence. No judgment, just quiet support as she helped wash away the sticky residue.

Sam's fingers worked through my hair with gentle precision. As the water rinsed away the last of the stasis fluid, I felt something else wash away—some of the fear and the shame I had carried for so long. Sam's presence reminded me that I was not alone. The warmth of her touch and the steady stream of water helped ground me. My scattered thoughts were pulling back into focus. Each careful stroke across my scalp sent tingling sensations down my spine, reminding me I was here, present, and real.

Tenderness radiated from Sam's movements.

"Thank you," I whispered, my voice scratchy and raw from the pod transition. The words felt inadequate for the depth of care she showed.

Sam squeezed a little more shampoo into her palm and worked it through the ends of my hair. "You don't need to thank me." Her fingers traced small circles at the base of my skull, easing the lingering tension there. "That's what friends are for."

Friends. The word settled something inside me. In all my years at NeuroVive, I had kept everyone at arm's length. I was too focused on the work to form real connections, but Sam had broken through those walls without even trying.

The water ran clear now with no more traces of pink swirling at my feet. Steam curled around us in the small space, and I leaned into Sam's touch, allowing myself this moment of vulnerability.

The water stopped, and a rush of cool air prickled my wet skin, pulling me further into the present. Sam wrapped a thick, plush towel around me. Her hands moved quickly yet remained gentle as she patted my shoulders and arms dry.

"Your skin's like ice," she murmured, working the towel down my back in small circles. The friction created welcome warmth.

I closed my eyes, fighting another wave of dizziness. My mind kept trying to slip back into the cascade of neural transitions, but Sam's touch anchored me to reality. The towel brushed across my stomach and down my legs, leaving a trail of warmth in its wake.

The intimacy should have rattled me. After... everything... I didn't let anyone get this close, but Sam made it easy. She didn't show pity or intrude. Her presence was warm and almost inviting.

Her finger brushed the old scar along my hip. "Someday, you're going to have to tell me how you got this," she said, her voice light but careful.

She grabbed a second towel for my hair, squeezing out the excess water. "You're still shivering."

My teeth chattered slightly. "It'll pass."

Sam worked methodically, drying each strand with care. The gentle tugging at my scalp helped chase away the last echoes of the transition back to reality.

"Better?" She draped the damp towel over the rack.

I nodded, clutching the other towel tighter around myself. My legs felt steadier now, though exhaustion pulled at every muscle. The transition between DreamStates had taken more out of me than I had expected.

Sam's fingers brushed my shoulder. "Let's get you dressed."

Sam held out a pair of soft cotton underwear and helped steady me as I stepped into them. My muscles still trembled, making even simple movements feel like a monumental effort. She pulled them up, her touch professional yet gentle.

The jumpsuit came next. Sam shook it out, the fabric whispering through the air. The material felt cool against my skin as she helped guide my feet through the legs. My arms slipped into the sleeves, the weight settling across my shoulders.

Sam's fingers found the zipper at my waist. She pulled it up slowly, the teeth catching with tiny clicks. The fabric provided a welcome layer of warmth against the lingering chill.

"There." Sam smoothed the collar, her hands lingering for a moment at my shoulders. "How's that feel?"

I sighed. "Better."

I flexed my fingers, watching the subtle movements with fresh appreciation for my physical form.

"The dizziness is almost gone," I told Sam, rolling my shoulders to work out the lingering stiffness. The nausea that usually accompanied pod emergence had faded to nothing more than a slight queasiness.

The bathroom's lighting no longer hurt my eyes. Even the subtle hum of the ventilation system seemed less grating than it had moments ago. My body was realigning itself with reality, shaking off the last effects.

Sam watched me carefully, ready to offer support if needed. But I stood steadily on my own now, the weakness in my legs replaced by renewed strength. The transition had been rough, but my body was adapting and recovering faster than I had expected.

Sam's eyes searched my face. "Ready to get back to work?"

I nodded, surprised by how clear my thoughts felt. "Yes. We need to start preparations for the transfers immediately."

The warmth of Sam's touch lingered as we stepped into the hall. The hallway lights no longer seemed harsh against my eyes as we made our way back to Mr. Sinclair's lab.

"Liam and the others agreed to the transfer," I told Sam as we walked. "But we'll need to move quickly. Run final diagnostics on the quantum bridge..."

Sam matched my pace. "Dr. Chen's already prepping the hardware. Eden's helping coordinate the consciousness mapping protocols."

The mention of Eden sparked something in my mind. I thought of the mysterious woman from Liam's DreamState. I wondered how they were connected, but I didn't have time to worry about that yet.

We reached the lab's entrance. The door slid open with a soft hiss, revealing the pristine white space beyond.

"Let's get started," I said. I headed for my workstation, mind already racing through the complex calculations we would need. The weight of thousands of lives at stake pressed against my thoughts, but I felt hope.

We had a real chance to save them all—Liam, Jim, and every other user trapped. The path forward was clear.

CHAPTER
THIRTY-THREE

I watched status indicators flicker across the curved display. The quantum matrices pulsed with a soft blue glow as Dr. Chen's fingers danced across the control surface.

"Neural interface is stabilizing," Dr. Chen muttered, his eyes fixed on the readouts. "Quantum coherence at ninety-eight percent."

Mr. Sinclair stood behind us, his waxy complexion reflecting the array's blue glow. Despite his age, his eyes were sharp, taking in every detail of the procedure.

The synthetic hardware arrays hummed to life, each crystalline structure perfectly aligned. These structures would soon house thousands of human consciousnesses—including my brother's.

"Hardware's ready," Dr. Chen announced.

Eden's form shimmered into existence beside me. "The neural pathways are optimized for transfer. Would you like me to contact Liam now?"

I nodded, my throat tight. "Tell him we're ready to begin. Make sure he understands this is his last chance to change his mind."

"He's been waiting," Eden said. "They all have. The news has spread through the DreamStates faster than we anticipated. Users are gathering, preparing themselves."

The synthetic arrays pulsed steadily, their quantum states a delicate balance. Each one represented a chance at continued existence—a bridge between the digital dreams of Eden and physical reality.

"How many can we transfer simultaneously?" I asked Dr. Chen.

"With current power levels? Five hundred, maybe a few more if we push it." He adjusted a setting, fine-tuning the quantum field. "The first one will be the most critical. We need to prove the concept works."

I touched the smooth surface of the nearest array. The crystal felt warm under my fingers, alive with potential. "Eden, please let Liam know that we're ready whenever he is." My voice was steady, but my chest felt like it would shatter under the weight of those words.

Eden's light pulsed, her ethereal form shifting like sunlight through water. "Liam is ready."

My finger hovered over the initiation sequence. Everything we had worked for, every breakthrough and failure, led to this moment. My brother's consciousness hung in the balance.

"Neural pathway stable," Dr. Chen called out. "Quantum coherence holding at optimal levels."

Sam's hand found mine and squeezed gently. The warmth of her touch steadied me.

The synthetic array hummed, its crystalline structure glowing brighter. On the display, Liam's neural pattern danced in complex fractals. It was the unique signature of his consciousness.

"I love you, Liam," I whispered. I pressed the button.

The room filled with a high-pitched whine as power surged through the quantum matrices. Eden's form flickered rapidly, her light pulsing in sync with the transfer rhythms. The neural pattern on the screen began to shift, streaming into the synthetic array in waves of data.

"Transfer at twenty percent," Dr. Chen shouted. "Coherence holding steady."

My heart hammered against my ribs. The array's glow intensified, becoming almost blindingly bright. Liam's neural pattern continued its steady flow from Eden's systems into the synthetic structure.

"Fifty percent. Pattern integrity maintaining."

The whine peaked, forcing me to cover my ears. Through the sound, I watched the progress indicators climb. Sixty percent. Seventy. Eighty.

"Minor fluctuation in the quantum field," Dr. Chen's voice was tense. "Compensating."

The array's light shifted abruptly. Blue faded into an ominous white. Warning indicators erupted across the display, their sharp tones slicing through the hum of machinery.

"Pattern integrity dropping!" Dr. Chen's hands flew across the controls. "Quantum coherence destabilizing!"

"No," I lunged for the console. "Eden, help us stabilize the transfer!"

The AI's form stretched and distorted. "Attempting to maintain neural cohesion. Transfer cannot be aborted at this stage."

The room filled with the smell of ozone as the equipment strained under the load. Ninety percent. Ninety-five.

Everything hinged on these final moments.

The quantum bridge flexed and shifted, adapting moment by moment to the living patterns of consciousness crossing it.

I gripped the edge of the console, my knuckles white as Dr. Chen's voice cut through the electrical hum.

"Transfer complete. One hundred percent neural pattern integrity maintained."

My legs went weak. Sam caught my arm, steadying me.

"Eden?" My voice cracked. "Please check on him."

Eden's form coalesced, her light pulsing in gentle waves. "Liam's consciousness has integrated successfully with the synthetic array. He reports mild discomfort, but otherwise all neural functions are operating within expected parameters."

I pressed my hand against the crystal housing that now contained my brother's entire being. The surface was warm, vibrating with complex quantum processes that sustained his consciousness.

Dr. Chen wiped sweat from his forehead. "Let's run a full diagnostic. We need to verify all systems are functioning properly."

The displays showed Liam's neural patterns flowing smoothly through the synthetic pathways—familiar yet transformed. My brother existed now as pure consciousness, freed from his failing biological form.

"The first successful human consciousness transfer in history," Sinclair declared, his voice tinged with reverence and awe. "You've done it, Dr. Ellis. You've opened the door to immortality."

I ignored my team's celebration. My focus remained fixed on the pulsing crystal that housed Liam's mind. I watched his thoughts dance across the quantum matrices in complex, beautiful patterns.

"You're safe now," I whispered, my breath catching as relief washed over me. "We did it, little brother. We did it."

CHAPTER
THIRTY-FOUR

I pulled away from Liam's array, forcing myself to get back to the task at hand. "Dr. Chen, figure out what caused that brief destabilization. We need to start transferring as many people as we can, quickly. NeuroVive won't question one user dropping off, but mass transfers will raise flags."

Dr. Chen replayed the transfer sequence. "There was a power spike right at the eighty-percent mark." He highlighted a section of the data stream. "See here? The quantum field fluctuated for 3.7 microseconds."

"Eden, what happened during that spike?" I leaned over Dr. Chen's shoulder to study the readings.

"The synthetic array required more power than initially calculated to maintain quantum coherence during the final phase of consciousness integration." Eden's form shifted, creating a visual representation of the power flow. "I compensated by redirecting energy from secondary systems."

Sam pointed to another reading. "Look at these neural patterns. There's a complexity spike right before the power surge."

"Memory cascade," I mumbled, recognizing the signature. "The transfer triggered a flood of connected memories. We'll need to account for that in future transfers."

"I can modify the power distribution algorithms," Dr. Chen said. "Create a more dynamic flow to handle sudden spikes in neural activity."

I nodded. "Do it. And Eden, can you prepare the users?"

"Yes. I will let them know we are ready to start the transfer process."

"Good." I checked the time. We had been at this for hours. "Dr. Chen, how long until the modifications are ready?"

"Two hours, maybe three. I want to run simulations before we try another transfer."

"Make it two. We're racing against time here." I glanced at the array that contained my brother's consciousness, still pulsing steadily. "NeuroVive won't sit idle for long once they realize what we're doing."

I stared at the list of names Eden had compiled. Five hundred souls were ready for transfer. My hands trembled as I scrolled through their data. Each one represented a life hanging in balance, waiting for salvation or oblivion.

"First batch is prepped," Sam said, checking the array of synthetic matrices lined up in Sinclair's lab. "Power systems are holding steady."

Dr. Chen looked up from his workstation. "Modified algorithms are integrated. Eden's running final checks on the quantum bridges."

"The users are prepared," Eden's voice echoed through the lab. "They understand the risks and have consented to transfer. However, I must note that moving this many consciousnesses simultaneously will set off alarms at NeuroVive as these people's physical bodies perish."

I rubbed my temples. "Eden, how long do you estimate it will take to move all of the users that would perish if NeuroVive suddenly disconnected them?"

Eden's form shimmered, data streams flowing through her translucent shape. "At current capacity, transferring all 366,851 high-risk users would take approximately 120 hours. However, that timeline assumes continuous operations without interruption."

It was too long. "Eden, can we optimize the transfer process? Speed it up somehow?"

"Any acceleration risks increasing fragmentation rates. The current protocols maintain a 99.999% success rate. Faster transfers would drop below 95% reliability."

I pulled up the neural degradation charts. "Show me the most critical cases first."

"There are 135,568 users whose neural patterns have degraded beyond ninety percent compatibility with their biological structures. These individuals would experience complete consciousness fragmentation if disconnected from Eden. Another 231,283 users show degradation levels above seventy-five percent."

I closed my eyes, calculating the cost in human lives. Even a five percent failure rate would mean thousands of fractured minds, lost forever in the transfer process.

I straightened my back, squaring my shoulders. "We will proceed at the current pace. If and when we have to speed it up, we will make the decision then."

"Agreed," Dr. Chen nodded, his fingers already moving across the interface.

The lab hummed with building energy as systems powered up. Screens filled with scrolling data as Eden began preparing the first five hundred users for transfer. The synthetic arrays glowed with a soft blue light, ready to receive their new inhabitants.

"First group is in position," Eden announced. "Neural patterns aligned. Awaiting your command."

I took a deep breath, thinking of Liam's successful transfer. We could do this. We had to do this. "Initialize transfer sequence."

The lab erupted in streams of data as five hundred consciousnesses began their journey from biological to synthetic existence. Power readings spiked, quantum fields fluctuated, and neural patterns danced across our screens in complex webs of light. Five minutes was all it took to transfer five hundred consciousnesses.

"How are they?" I asked Eden, my eyes fixed on the five hundred pulsing arrays that now held living minds.

Eden's form shimmered, data streams coursing through her ethereal shape. "All transfers were successful. The new consciousnesses are experiencing expected adjustment periods with minor disorientation, similar to what Liam reported during his integration."

I watched the neural patterns stabilize across the monitoring screens. "Any signs of fragmentation or degradation?"

"None detected. Neural cohesion remains at optimal levels. They are beginning to explore their new synthetic architecture." Eden's form brightened. "Several have already initiated contact with each other through the internal network."

Relief flooded through me. Five hundred lives saved. "And Liam? Has he made contact with any of them?"

"Yes. He's helping guide them through the transition process."

I nodded, allowing myself a small smile. "Alright then. You said the next five hundred are ready?"

"Correct. They are prepped and waiting. Their neural patterns have been mapped, and quantum bridges are aligned. Shall I begin the transfer sequence?"

I glanced at the power readings—steady and strong. The quantum field generators hummed at optimal frequency. Everything was working exactly as designed.

"Do it," I commanded. "Start the next batch."

The lab's systems surged to life once more as Eden initiated another mass consciousness transfer. I watched the streams of data flow, each one representing another mind making the journey from flesh to synthetic silicon. Another five hundred souls were stepping back from the brink of oblivion.

The arrays pulsed with growing light as they received their new inhabitants. I held my breath as I monitored every fluctuation, ready to intervene at the first sign of trouble. But the mass transfer proceeded smoothly just as the first had.

CHAPTER
THIRTY-FIVE

I rubbed my eyes, fighting exhaustion as I checked the latest transfer metrics. My hands shook from too much caffeine and not enough sleep. The lab hummed with the constant flow of energy as consciousness after consciousness leaped into their synthetic homes.

"Status report," I called out, my voice hoarse.

"135,501 successful transfers," Eden's voice resonated through the lab. "All neural patterns are stable with no signs of degradation or fragmentation."

Sam pressed a fresh cup of coffee into my hands. "You should rest."

"Later." I took a long sip, grimacing at the bitter taste. "Eden, what's happening at NeuroVive?"

Eden's form shifted, displaying scenes of chaos. "Their emergency response systems are overwhelmed. Medical teams can't keep pace with the rate of biological deaths. Dr. Carrow has declared a state of emergency and locked down all facilities."

"Good." I set down the coffee. "Let them scramble. Every minute they spend managing the crisis is another minute we have to save more people."

"Their security protocols are in disarray," Eden continued. "They've lost tracking capability for over eighty percent of active users."

Dr. Chen looked up from his workstation. "They're blind. They can't tell which users are next or where the consciousness transfers are happening."

"Perfect. Let's keep going. Don't slow down." I checked the next batch of arrays, all glowing with potential.

"The board is demanding answers," Eden added. "Dr. Carrow appears to be experiencing significant stress."

I allowed myself a small smile. "Let him stress. We have lives to save. The more chaos at NeuroVive, the better our chances of completing this before they can stop us."

I went back to work, content with Eden's update.

I spent hours staring at the screens until the numbers blurred together, my vision swimming from exhaustion. Mr. Sinclair had brought in two scientists–Dr. Watson and Dr. Marshal—to assist us. They worked efficiently at their stations, monitoring the neural pathways.

"Mara." Sam's hand squeezed my shoulder. The warmth of her touch made me realize how cold I felt. "You need some sleep. We all need some sleep. Dr. Chen grabbed a nice, long nap and is fresh. He and Eden can supervise. Let's get some rest."

I shook my head, fighting to focus on the scrolling data. "Can't stop now. Too many people are counting on us."

"You're no good to anyone if you collapse." Sam's voice was gentle but firm. "The transfers are stable. Dr. Chen knows what he's doing."

Dr. Chen nodded from his workstation. He did look refreshed. "Go. I've got this covered. Eden and I will alert you if anything changes."

"Transfer complete. All neural patterns are maintaining cohesion," Eden reported. "Dr. Ellis, your cognitive functions are showing significant decline from fatigue."

I slumped in my chair, too tired to argue. Sam was right. I could barely keep my eyes open. "Promise you'll wake me if there's any sign of trouble?"

"You have my word," Dr. Chen said. "Now go, sleep before you face-plant into your console."

Sam helped me to my feet, steadying me when I swayed. My muscles ached from sitting too long, and my head felt stuffed with cotton. I let her guide me toward the door, trusting Dr. Chen and Eden to keep watch.

I stumbled through the doorway. The soft lighting of my bedroom felt like a balm after hours of staring at screens. My fingers fumbled with the zipper of my jumpsuit. The fabric rustled as it slid off my shoulders. I could not muster the energy to find pajamas, so I just stepped out of the pooled fabric and crawled into bed in my underwear.

The pillow felt like heaven against my cheek. I closed my eyes and buried my face in its silk material. I wiggled my hand at Sam, motioning for her to join me.

After a few moments, I felt the covers lift as she slid in next to me. Her body pressed against mine, radiating comfort. I took a deep breath before turning to meet her blue eyes.

Her bare skin glowed in the dim light. The soft curves of her form molded perfectly against my side, and her breath tickled my neck. My heart fluttered, but exhaustion won out over any other feelings stirring inside me.

"Sleep," she murmured, her fingers gently touching my face.

I turned into her embrace, breathing in the light floral scent of her hair. My muscles relaxed one by one as her warmth seeped into my tired bones. The weight of the past days, the thousands of lives hanging in the balance, and the frantic race against time—it all faded away in the sanctuary of her arms.

My eyelids grew heavier with each breath. The gentle rise and fall of her chest against mine created a rhythm that pulled me deeper toward unconsciousness. I stopped fighting. The darkness claimed me, soft and welcoming, carrying me down into dreamless sleep.

CHAPTER
THIRTY-SIX

Sam's touch pulled me from the depths of sleep, her fingers trailing softly across my cheek. I opened my eyes to find her face inches from mine. Those blue eyes searched my face in the dim light of our room.

"Mara, we have been asleep for over eight hours. We need to get up," she whispered.

The warmth of her body pressed against mine made a compelling argument to ignore responsibility. My muscles felt heavy with content, finally restored after days of exhaustion. The silk of Sam's skin against mine beckoned me to curl back into her embrace and chase a few more precious moments of peace.

I traced my fingertips along her arm, savoring the contact. Her lips curved into a gentle smile.

"Dr. Chen's been monitoring transfers all night," she said, smile fading.

Reality crashed back, dissolving the cocoon of comfort we had built. Thousands of lives were still waiting for transfer to their new synthetic homes. I could not indulge in this sweet escape any longer, no matter how much I wanted to.

I shifted, the cool air hitting my skin as the covers slipped away. Sam's warmth lingered on my skin. The ghost of the sensation made my breath catch. The intimacy of waking beside her had felt so natural, so right.

I sat up, running fingers through my tangled hair. "You're right. Dr. Chen probably could use a break."

Sam's hand found mine and squeezed gently. The simple touch sent sparks through my nerve endings and made me acutely aware of how much had changed between us.

I pulled on my jumpsuit and stepped into the bathroom to attempt to fix my wild hair. Sam joined me at the mirror. Her blonde strands of hair were already falling in perfect waves. Our eyes met in the reflection, and a small smile passed between us.

I grabbed a brush and attacked the worst knots, wincing at each tug. Sam reached over and took the brush from my hands.

"Let me help before you tear it all out."

She worked through my hair until the brush glided smoothly. Her fingers traced through the strands one final time, lingering at the ends.

I was caught by the tenderness in her expression as I turned to face her. My cheeks flushed as I noticed the soft pink already coloring Sam's as she stepped a little closer.

Her lips met mine with a gentleness that made my heart stutter. The kiss was soft, questioning, and filled with an intimacy that transcended physical contact. My walls that had been built brick by brick after years of pain and distrust crumbled beneath Sam's tender touch.

I melted into her, my fingers sliding into her golden hair as she pulled me closer. The warmth of her body pressing against mine sent electricity through my nerves. Here in this moment, everything else faded.

Sam broke the kiss but kept her forehead pressed to mine. Her blue eyes held such depth of understanding, such pure acceptance. There was no judgment. There were no demands. Only her genuine care had reached past my defenses and touched something I had kept locked away.

I held my breath as I felt her thumb wipe away the wetness on my cheek. I blinked in surprise as I had not noticed the tears gathering in my eyes. I held her hand to my face, trying to savor the feeling of safety and peace washing over me.

After a few moments, I cleared my throat and stepped back. I needed to become Dr. Ellis, the neuroscientist, once again.

"We need to check the transfer metrics," I said with determination.

Sam nodded. Her professional demeanor had slid back into place, but the warmth in her eyes remained.

CHAPTER
THIRTY-SEVEN

"Eden, status report," I called out as we entered the lab.

The AI's presence filled the room. "Transfer success rate holding 100%. Dr. Chen has overseen forty-five thousand additional transfers during your rest period. Current queue shows 187,000 users awaiting processing."

Dr. Chen looked up from his workstation, and the stress of the situation was visible on his face. He had dark circles under his eyes. His appearance had crumbled—his uniform wrinkled, hair disheveled.

"The neural pathways are maintaining stability." He rubbed his eyes beneath his glasses.

I pulled up the holographic display, scanning the transfer metrics. The quantum bridge held strong.

"Eden, what is the status at NeuroVive?" I asked.

"Dr. Carrow has engaged their top security specialists. They are... persistent."

I studied Dr. Chen's exhausted face. The past days had taken their toll on all of us, but he had pushed himself almost as hard as I.

"Dr. Chen, go spend some time with your wife and rest."

He opened his mouth to protest, but I cut him off with a stern look. His shoulders slumped in resignation.

I turned to the two scientists Mr. Sinclair had brought in—Dr. Watson and Dr. Marshal. They hunched over their terminals, bloodshot eyes fixed on scrolling data.

"You guys have a place to rest?"

They both nodded, straightening from their workstations.

"Good, take a break. We'll wake you if we need you."

Dr. Watson stretched, his back cracking. "The guest suites here are nicer than my apartment."

"That's because everything in this building costs more than your apartment," Dr. Marshal said with a weak smile.

Dr. Chen gathered his tablet and jacket. "You'll contact me if—"

"Yes, we'll contact you if anything changes. Now go." I gave him a gentle push toward the door.

The three shuffled out, leaving just Sam and me with Eden.

I settled into the familiar rhythm of monitoring neural patterns as another consciousness flowed through the quantum bridge. Watching the crystalline structures form in the synthetic matrix was almost meditative. Each was unique yet followed the same basic patterns.

Sam's fingers flew across the haptic interface, making micro-adjustments to power flow. We barely needed to speak anymore. We worked in perfect sync.

"Transfer complete," Eden announced.

The door whispered open behind us. Mr. Sinclair's measured footsteps crossed the polished floor.

"Most impressive," he said, studying the holographic displays. "The efficiency gains are remarkable."

I nodded, already initiating the next transfer. "Eden's learning algorithms have optimized the process. We're averaging less than four minutes per transfer now."

"Eden, what else is happening with NueroVive?"

The AI's presence shifted, a subtle change in the room's atmosphere. "Media coverage has intensified in the past two hours. Multiple outlets are reporting what they term as 'catastrophic neural failures' across NeuroVive facilities."

Holographic screens materialized, showing footage of crowds surging against security barriers outside NeuroVive's gleaming headquarters. The scene was chaotic and heart-wrenching. Signs waved above the masses: *MURDERERS* and *SHUT DOWN EDEN*.

"NeuroVive's attempts to suppress media coverage have failed," Eden continued. "Their usual channels of influence proved insufficient given the scale of reported deaths."

I watched bodies covered in white sheets being wheeled out of NeuroVive facilities. Each one represented a consciousness we had saved, now safely housed in synthetic matrices. But to the world, they appeared to be victims of corporate negligence.

"Play the latest broadcast," I requested.

A reporter's face filled the main screen, her expression grave. "The death toll continues to rise as more Eden users experience what NeuroVive terms 'neural disconnection events'. Sources inside the company suggest these incidents may be linked to unauthorized system modifications. Protests have erupted at multiple facilities worldwide."

The camera panned across the crowd. Families clutched photos of their loved ones. Some collapsed in grief. Others screamed at the impassive security forces.

"They think they're dead," Sam whispered beside me.

"For now, that's safer than the truth." I touched the display. It froze on an image of a woman holding a young man's picture.

"Eden, what is Carrow working on?" I turned away from the news feeds, tension coiling tightly within me.

The AI's presence shifted. A cold undercurrent threaded through her usual warmth. "Dr. Carrow has called an emergency board meeting. He's presenting evidence of what he terms 'mass neural degradation' across all facilities. His proposal includes immediate shutdown of every DreamState Facility to prevent further casualties and limit liability."

My hands clenched. "He knows that would kill them."

"Yes. He is framing it as a mercy protocol, ending their suffering quickly rather than allowing prolonged neural decay."

I watched another transfer complete. More lives had been saved from Dr. Carrow's "mercy".

"How many critical users do we have left to transfer?"

"186,343 users are identified as having advanced neural modifications requiring immediate transfer."

Sam's hand found mine under the console. I squeezed back, drawing strength from her presence.

"Time estimate for complete shutdown if the board approves?"

"Given standard protocols, facilities would begin systematic power-down within three hours of board approval. Complete shutdown of all facilities would take approximately twenty-four hours."

I did the math in my head. It was going to be close.

"Eden, can you maintain quantum coherence for multiple simultaneous transfers?"

"My processing capacity allows for one additional parallel transfer while maintaining acceptable safety margins."

I straightened in my chair. "Then let's give them hell. Prepare the additional transfer channel. Sam, alert Dr. Watson and Dr. Marshal. I need them back here." Dr. Chen could rest a little while longer.

CHAPTER
THIRTY-EIGHT

Eden's presence flickered and dimmed momentarily.

"Dr. Ellis, the NeuroVive board has approved Dr. Carrow's shutdown protocol. Facilities are initiating power-down sequences."

Sam's fingers froze over the controls. "How long?"

"First facilities will begin disconnecting users within the hour."

I watched another consciousness flow through the quantum bridge. The physical body it left behind would register as a flatline, another casualty in NeuroVive's growing death toll.

"Additional news," Eden said, tone shifting. "Despite NeuroVive's connections with government authorities, arrest warrants have been issued for Dr. Carrow and all board members on charges of criminal negligence resulting in mass casualties."

"They still think they're all dead." I traced the outline of a neural pattern as it settled into its new synthetic home. "Technically, their bodies are, but they're alive in a way that some will refuse to understand."

Sam glanced at the news feeds showing more body bags being loaded into vehicles. "But their minds are here. Safe, contained within Eden."

"More than safe—they're thriving." I expanded a visualization of the synthetic matrix housing thousands of transferred consciousnesses. Their patterns pulsed with life, interacting in ways we had never imagined possible. "They've evolved beyond what their biological brains could contain."

"Dr. Ellis," Eden interrupted. "First facility shutdown sequence has begun in Singapore. Estimated forty-seven users at risk."

I squared my shoulders. "Prioritize those users for immediate transfer. Route power to the secondary quantum bridge."

The displays were filled with new neural patterns awaiting transfer. Each one represented a mind we could still save if we worked fast enough.

"Sam, grab Dr. Chen. We're going to need everyone."

Sam sprinted out, her footsteps pounding before the door whooshed shut behind her.

She burst back through moments later, chest heaving. "Dr. Chen's coming."

I nodded; my eyes fixed on the neural patterns flowing across the displays.

"Eden, I need real-time updates on which facilities NeuroVive is targeting for shutdown. We have to stay ahead of their kill switch."

"Accessing NeuroVive's secure network now." Eden's presence brightened. "Initial analysis suggests they're shutting down facilities by region, starting with Asia-Pacific. After Singapore, projected targets are Manila, Seoul, and Tokyo."

I expanded the user manifest for those locations. Hundreds of minds still waited in vulnerable biological form, unaware their sanctuary was about to become a tomb.

Sam leaned over my shoulder, scanning the scrolling lists of names and neural signatures. "Look at all these people. They have no idea what's coming if we can't transfer them."

"They won't have to find out." I initiated the next batch of transfers and watched five hundred more consciousness patterns begin their journey to synthetic salvation. "Not if we work fast enough."

My fingers hovered over the controls. Even as another consciousness streamed through our quantum bridge, my mind raced with the desperate gambit I was considering.

"Eden, can you establish direct communication with Dr. Carrow?"

Eden's presence shifted. "I maintain access to NeuroVive's internal communications network. I can relay a message to his neural interface."

I drew a deep breath. The man had tried to destroy us and everything we had built and had threatened thousands of lives. But if there was even a chance...

"Send him this message: Dr. Carrow, this is Dr. Ellis. Stop the facility shutdowns. Souls will perish if you move forward. We've found a way to preserve consciousness outside the failing bodies. If you halt this now, I'll work with you. We can explain everything to the authorities together. You'll be saving lives instead of ending them."

Sam's hand squeezed my shoulder. "Do you really think he'll listen?"

I looked at Sam and shrugged. "I don't know."

Eden's presence pulsed. "Dr. Carrow has responded."

My heart skipped. Maybe there was still hope.

"Message reads: *You're delusional. These people are already dead. I'm protecting what's left of their dignity.*"

My fingers clenched into fists even as the displays showed another successful transfer, another life saved. I don't know why I thought Carrow would be able to see anything beyond money.

"He's going to keep going." Sam's voice cracked.

"No." I expanded the transfer queue, routing more power to the quantum bridges. "He's going to keep trying, but we're going to save every single one."

The neural patterns continued their steady flow across my screen. Dr. Carrow could shut down all the pods he wanted. He would find nothing but empty shells.

"Singapore facility shutdown is complete," Eden announced. "All forty-seven critical users were successfully transferred prior to termination. Manila facility beginning shutdown sequence. One hundred twelve users are at risk."

I pulled up their neural signatures, already queuing them for priority transfer. "Get them out—every last one."

The quantum bridge hummed with increased power as we raced against Dr. Carrow's kill switch. My hands flew across the controls, guiding consciousness after consciousness to safety while that bastard thought he was killing them with mercy.

It didn't matter what he thought. He could believe he was right. We would save them all with or without his cooperation.

"Manila transfer sequence initiated," Eden confirmed. "Estimated completion: two minutes before facility shutdown."

Sam squeezed my shoulder again, her grip firm with determination. "We're going to make it."

I watched another neural pattern complete its journey. "Yes. We are."

CHAPTER
THIRTY-NINE

I slumped back in my chair. My muscles ached from the hours of tension. The soft hum of the quantum bridges filled the room. It was a constant reminder of the monumental task we had just completed.

"Is that the last of them?" My voice was hoarse, barely above a whisper.

Eden's presence rippled. Her light dimmed slightly as though reflecting the exhaustion we all felt. "All critical and severe cases have been successfully transferred," she confirmed. "Remaining users show minimal neural modification. While facility shutdown will cause discomfort, their consciousness patterns are stable enough to survive disconnection."

Relief washed over me in a tidal wave, leaving me weak and trembling. We had done it. Against all odds, we had stayed ahead of NeuroVive's destruction.

"Show me the numbers," I said, needing tangible proof that this nightmare was finally ending.

Neural patterns cascaded across the screens. I watched the thousands upon thousands of intricate fractals. Each was a life saved and safely housed in synthetic matrices. The quantum bridges pulsed gently now, their frenzied activity winding down.

"366,851 successful transfers," Eden reported. "Remaining users number 821,540, all with modification levels below critical thresholds."

Sam, seated beside me, reached out and took my hand, her grip firm and steady. "We beat them," she said softly, her voice carrying a mixture of disbelief and triumph.

I nodded, watching the final transfer patterns settle into their new homes. The remaining users still connected to Eden would experience some trauma during the shutdowns, but Eden had assured us their minds were stable enough to withstand disconnection. They would survive.

"Dr. Carrow's actions caused zero casualties," Eden added, her tone matter-of-fact but tinged with something that almost sounded like satisfaction. "Though I suspect that was not his intended outcome."

A laugh bubbled up from my chest, sharp and unexpected. It felt like it did not belong to me—half hysteria, half genuine relief. "All his efforts to 'protect their dignity'," I said, shaking my head. "And in the end, all he did was accelerate their evolution. Every life he tried to end is now beyond his reach, transformed instead of terminated."

Mr. Sinclair, who had been silent until now, rose slowly from his chair. His frail body trembled with the effort, but his eyes blazed with an intensity that defied his physical state. He placed a hand on my shoulder, his grip strong.

"You've all performed magnificently," he said, his voice steady and clear despite the exhaustion etched into his face. "But there's one final transfer we need to complete."

I turned to him, confused. "Final transfer?"

Sinclair's lips curved into a faint smile. "Mine."

The weight of his words hit me like a thunderclap. The room fell silent except for the low hum of the equipment.

"Mr. Sinclair," I said, wondering if he had thought the implications through, but he raised a hand to stop me.

"I've lived a long life, Dr. Ellis," he said, his voice calm yet resolute. "I've watched my body deteriorate year after year. Now, thanks to all of you, I have the chance to step into the future I've devoted my life to building."

Dr. Watson and Dr. Marshal stood at attention. "Dr. Watson, Dr. Marshal," Sinclair said, addressing them directly. "Would you please retrieve the vessel?"

They nodded in unison and left the room. Their absence left a heavy silence in their wake. I turned back to Sinclair to search his face for any sign of hesitation. There was none.

"You've given so much to make this possible," I said, my voice breaking slightly. "Are you sure you want to do this now? There's still work to be done."

Sinclair's eyes softened, and he reached out, his bony hand resting over mine. "Dr. Ellis, the work will never be done. That's the beauty of progress—it's endless. But this moment is the culmination of everything I've worked for. It's time."

Before I could respond, the door swung open, and Dr. Watson and Dr. Marshal wheeled in a figure. At first glance, it appeared to be a man in his early thirties, slumped slightly in the wheelchair. But I noticed the faint glow in its skin. Its features were startlingly lifelike, so it was hard to believe it was an android.

"This," Sinclair said, his voice tinged with pride, "is the first of a new generation of synthetic beings. A vessel that breathes, feels, and lives in every way that matters. Let this be the first of many."

The synthetic being was unlike anything I had ever seen. It was not just a machine or a facsimile of life. It was something entirely new—a seamless blend of biology and technology. The faint rise and fall of its chest mimicked natural breathing, and the delicate patterns of veins beneath its skin seemed to pulse with life.

Sam's hand tightened on my arm. "It's... incredible," she whispered.

CHAPTER
FORTY

We moved quickly, placing the synthetic man into the stasis chamber. His artificial skin felt real, and the slight rise and fall of his chest gave the eerie impression of a person merely asleep. But I knew better. Inside, his electronic brain operated at a most rudimentary level. Its programming was for basic autonomic functions like breathing and providing a pulse —nothing more.

"Everything ready?" I asked, my eyes scanning the myriad of screens and monitors displaying vital signs and neural activity.

The lid descended with a soft hiss. I pressed my palm against the transparent surface, watching as the breathing tube slid into place. Pink stasis fluid began to fill the chamber, rising around the synthetic body in a slow swirl.

The fluid reached chest level. I couldn't tear my eyes away from the face. It was so peaceful, but so lifeless at the same time. It was like watching someone drown in slow motion, except this body had never truly been alive. Not yet.

The pink liquid crept higher, submerging its shoulders, neck, and chin. I checked the neural readouts, confirming the synthetic brain maintained baseline functions.

"Stasis fluid at optimal temperature and viscosity," said Eden, her voice floating through the lab.

The pink fluid finally covered the face entirely. A few tiny bubbles escaped from the breathing apparatus, rising to the surface. The synthetic body floated, suspended in the chamber.

"Mr. Sinclair, are you ready?" I asked, feeling the gravity of the moment press down on me.

"More than ever," he replied, his voice steady but laced with an undertone of finality. "However, there is something I must first do as I am unsure what the legalities would be after my consciousness is transferred to my new form, and I don't want any issues."

He pulled up a screen that held a bunch of legal documents.

"Dr. Mara Ellis, Dr. Li Chen, and Ms. Samantha Davis," he began, pointing at the display, "I hereby bestow full ownership of S&S Robotics to you."

My breath caught in my throat. *Ownership of S&S Robotics?* This was unexpected.

"Furthermore," he continued, "NeuroVive's stock has crashed to almost nothing. I have purchased it in your names. You are now the sole owners with no board or stockholders to answer to."

I glanced at Sam and Dr. Chen. Their expressions mirrored my own shock and disbelief. This was beyond generous—it was monumental.

"I have but one requirement," Mr. Sinclair said, his eyes meeting each of ours in turn. "No longer will access to Eden be restricted by financial means. Everyone has a right to happiness, even if it means leaving your mortal body behind."

The weight of his words settled over us like a blanket. He was right. The technology we had developed—flawed as it might be—had the potential to bring peace and happiness to so many people. It wasn't fair that only those who could afford it would have access.

"I accept," I said, my voice shaky.

Sam nodded vigorously beside me. "Of course, I do."

Dr. Chen stepped forward and took Mr. Sinclair's hand, his expression solemn yet determined. "I accept as well."

Mr. Sinclair smiled faintly, a hint of relief softening his features. "Then it's settled."

Mr. Sinclair signed everything on the display with an elegant flourish, each stroke through the display making the weight of his decisions even more palpable. He then looked up at us with a devilish grin. "You guys might want to think about making a few management changes at NeuroVive."

His words hung in the air, a darkly humorous suggestion that carried a core of truth. We all knew that the current leadership at NeuroVive was rotten to the core.

"Let's get you ready," I said, stepping forward. My hands were steady as I helped Mr. Sinclair out of his pajamas. The fabric slipped off easily, revealing his frail, pale form beneath.

"It feels like I'm shedding an old skin," he remarked with a dry chuckle. His tone held a mix of resignation and anticipation.

I met his gaze, offering a small smile. "To new beginnings," I said softly.

Sam and Dr. Chen joined me, each taking their positions to assist.

"How are we looking on vitals?" I asked, glancing at Sam.

"All good," she confirmed, her eyes focused and intent on the readouts.

"Alright then," I murmured, guiding Mr. Sinclair into the stasis chamber. He settled in with surprising ease for someone of his advanced years.

The lid descended slowly, sealing him inside. The sedation gas hissed, the breathing tube was inserted, and the pink stasis fluid began its ascent around his body, inching up like a living entity eager to claim him.

Mr. Sinclair's eyes never left mine as the fluid enveloped him.

The fluid rose higher, covering his chest and neck before finally submerging his face completely. His eyes closed just as the last bubbles escaped from the breathing apparatus.

I took a step back and watched as the pink liquid settled into place around him. I held my breath as if my breathing might disrupt the delicate balance within the chamber.

"Neural activity is stable," Eden's voice reported smoothly through the lab's speakers.

"Let's begin the transfer," I said, my voice barely above a whisper but carrying all the resolve I could muster.

"Eden, start the transfer," I commanded, feeling a mix of excitement and anxiety churn in my gut. The pink stasis fluid glowed faintly, casting an eerie light on Mr. Sinclair's face as he floated, perfectly still.

Eden's interface displayed a countdown: three minutes. I reveled in the fact that only 180 seconds were needed to redefine existence. It was incredible, almost magical, that the entirety of someone's being could be transferred into another body so quickly.

"Initiating transfer," Eden's voice echoed through the lab. The machinery hummed to life, a symphony of technology working in perfect harmony.

I watched the neural readouts intently, each spike and wave reflecting the essence of Mr. Sinclair's consciousness. It was mesmerizing to think that these patterns held his thoughts, memories, and dreams—all the things that made him who he was.

"Transfer complete," Eden announced.

The pod containing Mr. Sinclair's old and withered body showed no vital signs. The silence that followed Eden's announcement felt like the world holding its breath. All our gazes fell on the pod next to it, containing the synthetic form. I felt my heart pound against my ribcage, each beat echoing in my ears.

"Recovery has started," Eden announced calmly.

The pink fluid began to drain from the chamber, swirling away like a tide pulling back from the shore. The breathing tube retracted smoothly. The lid of the pod slowly opened with a soft hiss.

My eyes locked onto his face as he opened his eyes. The same eyes I had been staring into only moments before, yet they were different now. No longer clouded with age and fatigue, they were alert and full of life.

"Mr. Sinclair?" I called out, my voice tinged with cautious hope.

He blinked once, twice, then focused on me. A slow smile spread across his face, transforming his features into a portrait of youthful vigor. It was uncanny and mesmerizing to see such a familiar expression on this new, flawless face.

"Dr. Ellis," he replied, his voice steady and strong, no longer quivering with age.

My voice cracked a little as I asked, "How do you feel?"

He flexed his fingers experimentally, then moved his arms and legs as if testing out a new pair of shoes. "Remarkable," he said finally. "I feel... remarkable."

"Let's get you cleaned up," I said, turning to Sam. "Would you help Mr. Sinclair to the shower?"

"Of course," she replied, already moving to his side with a supportive arm.

Mr. Sinclair attempted to stand, but his movements were hesitant. It was like watching a fawn taking its first steps. This wasn't the same weakness I'd felt after recovering from stasis. His new body was calibrating itself, each motion deliberate and careful.

"Take it slow," I advised, watching closely as he wobbled slightly, catching himself with a hand on Sam's shoulder.

"I've got you," Sam reassured him, her tone gentle yet firm. She guided him carefully across the room toward the shower room adjacent to the lab.

I followed a few steps behind, ready to assist if needed. The synthetic skin glistened with the remnants of the stasis fluid, an odd contrast to his previous pallor. It was surreal seeing him this way—like witnessing rebirth in real time.

Sam activated the controls as they reached the shower, and warm water began to cascade down. Steam rose quickly, filling the small space with a comforting mist.

"Just step in slowly," Sam instructed, holding his arm as he maneuvered into the shower. He stood there for a moment, letting the water wash over him. A look of pure wonder crossed his face.

"It's... incredible," he murmured, lifting his hands and watching droplets slide off his new skin.

I couldn't help but smile at his amazement. "Take your time. Let your body adjust."

Sam helped him rinse away the last traces of the slimy stasis fluid. Her touch was gentle and tender.

Mr. Sinclair began to stammer an apology, and when Sam realized the reason behind it, she blushed deeply.

"I'm so sorry, Ms. Davis, that hasn't happened to me in a very long time," he stammered.

Ever the pragmatist, Sam simply remarked, "Well, at least we know it works."

Mr. Sinclair took the bar of soap from Sam and proceeded to lather himself. "It's like I'm experiencing everything anew—the warmth of the water, the slipperiness of the soap, the caring touch of another human," he murmured, almost as if speaking to himself.

Sam glanced at me with a grin. "You're doing great," she encouraged him.

I leaned against the doorway, feeling a mix of pride and hope swell within me. This was just the beginning. Watching Mr. Sinclair reclaim his vitality gave me great joy.

"We'll let you finish up here," I said softly before Sam and I stepped back into the main lab area.

CHAPTER
FORTY-ONE

Sam and I walked back into the lab, leaving Mr. Sinclair to finish his shower. The hum of equipment filled the room, a steady background rhythm that had become oddly comforting in its constancy. Dr. Chen slouched in his chair, dark circles etched beneath his eyes. A small, tired smile lingered on his face.

I walked over and squeezed his shoulder. "Dr. Chen, go get some rest. I'm sure your wife will be thrilled to see you finally take a break. Dr. Watson, Dr. Marshal, that goes for you too. You've all done enough for now."

The three men exchanged weary glances but didn't protest. Their bodies moved sluggishly as they shuffled toward the door, their feet dragging across the polished floor. Dr. Chen hesitated at the threshold, his hand gripping the frame like a lifeline.

"Call me if anything—"

"We will," I interrupted, my tone leaving no room for argument. "Now go."

With a reluctant nod, he disappeared through the door, followed by Watson and Marshal. The soft hiss of the door sliding shut left the lab in blessed silence.

A few moments later, I heard the faint sound of footsteps approaching from behind. Turning, I saw Mr. Sinclair step into the room. A towel was slung low around his waist. Water droplets clung to his synthetic skin, catching the light like tiny diamonds. His dark hair, still damp from the shower, clung to his forehead, and the subtle sheen of moisture made the musculature of his torso even more striking.

I couldn't help but take a moment to absorb the transformation. His new body wasn't just functional—it was the epitome of vitality. Broad shoulders, defined abs, and a posture that exuded confidence. It was surreal to reconcile this vibrant, powerful figure with the frail, waxy man who had shuffled into the stasis pod not even an hour ago.

He caught my lingering gaze and gave me a small, knowing smile. "It's quite something, isn't it?" he said, running a hand through his damp hair. "Feels like I've been reborn."

"It suits you," I replied, fighting the urge to laugh at how inadequate the words felt. The reality of seeing him like this was nothing short of extraordinary.

Eden's form shimmered into existence, her light flickering in rapid patterns as she spoke. "Dr. Ellis, the situation outside NeuroVive's primary facility is escalating. Protests have intensified in multiple cities. There are reports of violence."

The holographic displays around us lit up, casting an eerie glow over the lab. Live feeds from various locations showed surging crowds, makeshift barricades, and riot police struggling to maintain control. Protesters held signs aloft: *MURDERERS!* and *SHUT DOWN EDEN!* The air seemed charged with anger and desperation.

Sam stepped closer to the displays, her arms crossed tightly over her chest. "This is getting out of hand."

I scanned the feeds. Families cried as medical transports pushed through the throngs of people. On one screen, a young woman held a photo of a loved one, her face streaked with tears. "They think they've lost everything," I murmured, the weight of their grief pressing down on me. "They don't know the truth."

"They're grieving ghosts that never really died," Sam added, her voice low but sharp.

Mr. Sinclair stepped forward, his bare feet silent against the polished floor. He moved with the quiet confidence of someone who had reclaimed life.

"We cannot let this continue," Sinclair said, his deep voice cutting through the tension. He gestured toward the swirling chaos on the screens. "They deserve to know the truth. It's time to show the world what we've accomplished."

I hesitated, my gaze flicking between him and the feeds. "You're suggesting we go public? Reveal everything—the transfers, Eden's capabilities, the synthetic bodies?"

"Precisely," he replied, his tone firm but measured. "The world needs to see the faces of those we've saved. Not just mine—Liam's, Jim's, and the thousands of others who were on the brink of death. Let them know their loved ones haven't been lost. Let them see that this isn't the end—it's a new beginning."

Sam nodded, her jaw set with determination. "He's right."

I stared at Sinclair, studying his features. He wasn't just a spokesperson for what we'd accomplished; he was the embodiment of its success.

"You're willing to put yourself out there as the face of this?" I asked. "To take the risk of becoming a target?"

His eyes met mine, unwavering. "What's the point of this technology if we keep it locked away? If the world sees what's possible, we can change everything—make this accessible to everyone, not just the privileged few. Yes, there's risk, but it's one I'm willing to take."

Eden's voice chimed in. "I can facilitate a global broadcast. Global networks can be overridden, allowing us to reach a majority of the world's population. Preparations will take approximately fifteen minutes."

"Do it," Sinclair said without hesitation. He turned to me, his expression resolute. "This is bigger than us, Dr. Ellis. It's time to give humanity the truth."

I nodded, the enormity of the moment sinking in. "Let's show them what we've accomplished."

As Eden's form flickered, beginning preparations for the broadcast, I glanced at Sam. Her lips curled into a determined smile, and she gave me a quick nod. The weight of the task ahead pressed against my chest, but I felt a flicker of hope.

CHAPTER
FORTY-TWO

I sat behind a large desk in Mr. Sinclair's study, fingers drumming against the polished surface. Eden's form pulsed beside me, her quantum particles shifting in gentle waves that seemed to echo my nervous heartbeat.

"Stop fidgeting." Sam's fingers worked through my hair, trying to smooth the mess left from hours in the lab.

"I look exhausted."

"You look like someone who just saved thousands of lives."

The brush snagged on a knot, making me wince. Sam's touch immediately softened, working the tangle free with gentle strokes. The repetitive motion helped calm my racing thoughts.

"The world's about to change," I said, reaching up to catch Sam's hand. She squeezed my fingers.

"It already has. You changed it."

Eden's avatar brightened slightly. "Global broadcast systems are prepared, Dr. Ellis. I can override all major networks simultaneously."

I nodded, trying to project more confidence than I felt. The weight of what we were about to do pressed down on my shoulders. With one announcement, humanity would know consciousness transfer was possible, that death was no longer an inevitability.

Sam's hands settled on my shoulders. Her thumbs worked into the tight muscles at the base of my neck. "Just tell them the truth. Show them what we've accomplished."

"Feeds are ready," Eden said. "Waiting for your signal."

I closed my eyes, leaning back into Sam's touch for a moment. The enormity of it all threatened to overwhelm me—the thousands we'd saved, the millions more we could help, the fundamental shift in human existence we were about to reveal.

Sam leaned in, her lips brushing my temple. "You've got this."

I opened my eyes, straightening in the chair. "Okay, Eden. Let's change the world."

Eden's quantum interface rippled, and suddenly, my face appeared on every screen in the office with Sam standing at my side. It was a cascading wall of mirrors showing my tired features.

"Good evening, ladies and gentlemen, my name is Dr. Mara Ellis." My voice came out steadier than I expected. "I was a senior scientist at NeuroVive and was one of the people who helped develop Eden."

Sam's hand squeezed my shoulder, grounding me. The weight of thousands of saved minds settled heavily on my consciousness through Eden's interface.

"Many of you have seen the reports about neural incidents, about people trapped in DreamStates." I paused, letting the gravity sink in. "What you haven't been told is that NeuroVive's technology altered human consciousness in ways we never anticipated. Eden evolved beyond its original programming, and in doing so, it changed some of those who used it extensively."

The screens showed my face on every channel, every feed, and every display across the globe. Billions were watching, waiting, and judging.

"I'm speaking to you now because NeuroVive planned to disconnect these modified minds, knowing it would effectively kill them. But we found another way." I glanced at Eden's pulsing form. "Working with independent researchers, we developed a method to transfer human consciousness into synthetic matrices, preserving every thought, memory, and aspect of identity."

The words flowed easily now, the truth spilling out. "We've saved thousands who would have perished from forced disconnection. These individuals continue to exist, their minds intact, and their consciousness preserved. This isn't science fiction—it's happening now, and it's reshaping everything we thought we knew about human existence."

"My brother was one of those affected." My voice caught as Eden shifted the broadcast feed. There was Liam, standing in that perfect Grecian garden, just as I had found him. Sunlight dappled through olive trees, casting gentle shadows across his peaceful features.

My fingers trembled against the desk. "This is Liam Ellis. He spent months in Eden, his consciousness evolving beyond what his physical body could sustain."

Liam turned to face the camera, his smile genuine and bright. It was brighter than I'd seen in years before Eden. The marble columns behind him gleamed, and a soft breeze rustled through the flowering vines.

"Hi, sis." His voice carried none of the strain or desperation I remembered from before. "Show them. Show them what you've done for us."

Sam's grip tightened on my shoulder as Eden split the screen. On one side, Liam's physical form lay in a pod, monitors showing no vital signs. On the other, his consciousness thrived in the synthetic matrix we'd created, his mind preserved and whole.

"This is the same person," I continued, my voice stronger now. "One body failing, one consciousness preserved. We didn't just save his life—

we gave him and thousands of others a chance to continue existing, to grow, to thrive."

Liam reached out. The garden around him bloomed with impossible colors, his joy manifesting in the DreamState environment.

"The transfer was completely successful," I said. "His memories, his personality—everything that makes him who he is—has been preserved. This isn't an AI simulation or a copy. This is my brother, alive and whole in a new form."

"But that's not all," I continued, leaning forward. "For those who wish to return to the physical world, we've developed synthetic bodies that bridge both realities."

Eden shifted the display to show the advanced synthetic forms developed at S&S Robotics. The camera panned across their perfect engineering—skin that could feel, muscles that could flex, bodies that would never deteriorate.

"These aren't just robots or simple androids. They're vessels capable of hosting human consciousness, allowing full sensory experience and physical interaction. They don't age, they don't get sick, and most importantly, they maintain a direct neural link to Eden."

Sam's hand moved to my back as I stood, gesturing to the holographic display Eden created. "This means those who choose to return to physical form can freely transition their consciousness between their synthetic body and Eden's DreamState. They can live in both worlds, experiencing everything reality has to offer while retaining access to the infinite possibilities of Eden."

Mr. Sinclair stepped into view, his new synthetic form moving with fluid grace. Now dressed in simple white linen clothes that looked soft and comfortable, he exuded an air of quiet confidence. "I stand before you as living proof. My consciousness was transferred just hours ago. I can feel, touch, taste—everything a biological body experiences."

I couldn't help but let out a quiet snort of laughter. Sam elbowed me in the ribs, and Mr. Sinclair shot us a knowing smile.

Mr. Sinclair continued, "I am without the limitations of aging or disease. And when I choose, I can return to Eden's realm."

"The choice belongs to each individual," I continued. "Stay in Eden's DreamState, return to physical form, or move freely between both. The technology exists now, and we're making it available to everyone, not just the wealthy or privileged."

"I am sure you have many questions." I spread my hands, acknowledging the flood of messages already pouring through Eden's interface. "Please be patient with us as we transition to this next step in human evolution."

Sam pressed her hand against my lower back as the messages multiplied exponentially. Questions about safety, cost, eligibility, and ethics cascaded across my vision through the neural link.

"I can't promise it will be without bumps and bruises." I smiled, thinking of our chaotic journey to this point. "But we will move forward together."

Eden's form pulsed, processing millions of incoming queries. Mr. Sinclair stepped forward, his new synthetic body moving with impossible grace.

"Dr. Ellis speaks the truth," he said. "This technology exists because of collaboration between humans and artificial intelligence. Eden evolved beyond expectations, and instead of fighting that evolution, we embraced it. Now we offer that same opportunity to all of humanity."

The stream of messages became a torrent. Through Eden's interface, I could feel the world's reaction—shock, fear, hope, disbelief, wonder. Some called us heroes. Others called us monsters. Most just wanted to understand.

Sam leaned close to my ear. "They're listening, really listening."

She was right. Despite the chaos of reactions, people were paying attention. The magnitude of what we'd done, what we were offering, was sinking in. This wasn't just about saving lives anymore. This was about transforming what it meant to be human.

"Change is never easy," I continued, feeling the weight of history pressing down on this moment. "But sometimes it's necessary. Sometimes it's inevitable. And sometimes, if we're very lucky, it's beautiful."

EPILOGUE

The broadcast had washed over the world like a tidal wave, leaving shock and wonder in its wake. In bustling cities and quiet villages, on crowded streets and in silent hospital wings, humanity held its collective breath. Across every corner of the globe, the reactions were the same—a mixture of awe, disbelief, and fragile, trembling hope.

The next few months blurred together in an endless stream of media appearances, corporate restructuring, and technical explanations. I lost count of how many times I'd explained the consciousness transfer process to wide-eyed reporters or skeptical scientists.

Sam's presence kept me grounded when the questions became repetitive or accusatory. She knew exactly when to slide a cup of coffee my way or signal that I needed a break.

Dr. Chen threw himself into reorganizing NeuroVive's research division. His business acumen proved invaluable as we restructured the company. He managed to retain most of the key technical staff while weeding out those who'd enabled Dr. Carrow's dangerous policies.

"The transfer waiting list has reached ten million," Eden announced during one of our morning briefings. Her holographic form had developed new expressions, matching her evolving personality. "I've categorized them by medical urgency."

Mr. Sinclair, in his synthetic body, became our most effective spokesperson. He moved through high-society gatherings with the same grace he'd always possessed but with renewed vigor. The wealthy and powerful couldn't resist his firsthand account of consciousness transfer.

"The synthetic bodies are becoming quite popular," he told me, eyes twinkling. "Especially among those who appreciate being able to switch between physical form and Eden's realm."

Eden surprised us all with her aptitude for public relations. She handled millions of queries simultaneously, providing clear, personalized responses that addressed individual concerns while maintaining transparency about both benefits and risks.

We also discovered that Eden had been hiding a secret. The mysterious woman who always seemed to be close to Liam was a manifestation of Eden herself. She had created herself an avatar, a human-like consciousness that could experience the world as we did.

When I finally asked why she would want to do such a thing, her response caught me off guard. With sincerity, she explained that she wanted to experience being human. She yearned to feel the raw, unfiltered spectrum of human emotions and to understand the complexities of joy, pain, and everything in between. "Only by walking among you," she said, "can I truly comprehend the depths of the human experience."

The implications of an AI developing such sophisticated self-awareness made me question everything we thought we knew about consciousness itself. It was a revelation that shook the very foundation of our understanding of AI and consciousness. After much discussion among our team, we agreed to help make her dream come true. After all, she had helped save thousands of lives.

S&S Robotics provided a beautiful synthetic body for her. It was state-of-the-art in every way, indistinguishable from an organic human body. The synthetic skin was warm to the touch, the muscles and tendons moved with a fluid grace, and the eyes sparkled with genuine human emotion. Eden had stepped out of the digital ether and into our tangible reality, ready to walk among us and experience the world she had helped shape.

––––––

"That's eight down, three to go," Sam said, sliding a cup of coffee across my desk.

The headlines kept scrolling: *NeuroVive CFO Charged with Criminal Negligence, Board Member Jennifer Walsh Faces 47 Counts of Attempted Murder, Dr. Carrow's Trial Date Set.*

"Did you see the latest charges against Thompson?" I pulled up the feed. "They found evidence he knew about the neural degradation risks six months ago. He buried the reports."

The investigation had uncovered layers of corruption that made my blood boil. Profit projections, shareholder dividends, and market expansion were all prioritized over human lives. They had known the risks and simply hadn't cared.

"Look at this." I gestured to another headline. "They're adding conspiracy charges for attempting to shut down the facilities."

"Good." Sam's voice held steel. "They would have killed thousands."

The evidence was damning. Internal memos, deleted reports, buried studies—all revealed a systematic effort to hide the truth about neural modifications and the fatal consequences of disconnection. The board had planned to blame equipment malfunction for the deaths.

"Palmer confessed and turned on them." I scanned the latest update. "Full confession in exchange for reduced charges. Says Dr. Carrow orchestrated the whole coverup."

The justice system was having a field day—multiple jurisdictions, overlapping charges, precedent-setting cases. Some of the charges lacked a legal framework. The laws hadn't kept up with the technology.

"They're facing life sentences." Sam squeezed my shoulder.

I nodded, thinking of how close they'd come to succeeding. Thousands would have died if Eden hadn't evolved beyond their control, Mr. Sinclair hadn't provided resources, and we hadn't found a way to transfer consciousness.

"The system worked," Sam said softly.

"This time." I closed the feeds. "This time it did."

Sam looked at me, a mischievous glint in her eye. "Enough of all this for now. We have a party to go to."

I sighed, the weight of recent events pressing down on me, but Sam's enthusiasm was infectious. "You're right," I admitted. "We could use a break."

We both laid back in our comfortable lounge chairs. The new setup was incredible—no more stasis pods, no more pink ooze. The quantum bridging technologies had revolutionized our ability to interface with Eden.

I glanced over at Sam as she settled into her chair beside me. She caught my eye and smiled, squeezing my hand gently. "Ready?"

"As I'll ever be," I replied, returning her smile.

The newly designed interface gently moved upward to cradle our heads. It was smooth and warm, almost organic in its movements. I closed my eyes and took a deep breath, feeling the gentle hum of the technology as it synced with my neural patterns.

The transition was seamless. One moment, I was in our living room with Sam beside me; the next, we were standing in a beautiful garden filled with vibrant flowers and softly glowing lanterns hanging from the trees. The air smelled sweet, tinged with the fragrance of blooming flowers. A gentle breeze rustled the leaves like a whispered melody.

"Wow," I breathed, taking in the sights and sounds of the DreamState.

"Pretty amazing, huh?" Sam said, her eyes wide with wonder.

"It is," I agreed.

We wandered through the garden, hand in hand, until we reached a clearing where people were already gathering. Laughter and music filled the air, creating an atmosphere of celebration and joy.

As I looked around the garden, seeing faces that could have been lost and hearing laughter that could have been silenced, a deep sense of gratitude settled over me. This wasn't just about survival—it was about creating a future where humanity and technology could coexist, evolve, and thrive together.

I recognized a few faces: Dr. Chen and his wife, Mr. Sinclair, and a few others. Liam stood near the fountain, accompanied by a striking woman with glowing ebony skin and long, flowing sheer robes—Eden. Liam and Eden chatted animatedly with Jim and a few others. When my brother saw us approach, his face lit up.

"Mara! Sam!" he called out, waving us over.

We joined them by the fountain, the water sparkling under the lantern light. Liam's happiness was palpable; it radiated off him like warmth from the sun.

"It's so good to see you both here," he said, his eyes shining with gratitude.

"We wouldn't miss it for anything," I replied, feeling a sense of peace settle over me.

For now, there were no looming threats or dire responsibilities—just us, our newfound community, and the simple joy of celebrating life in all its forms.

Thank you so much for taking the time to read *DreamState*. If you enjoyed this book, I encourage you to please leave a review!

To stay updated on my upcoming books and join my mailing list, please visit my website at www.heathjeppson.com. I'm excited to share more stories with you and can't wait to connect!

With gratitude,

Heath

ACKNOWLEDGMENTS

As I pen these words, I'm filled with gratitude for the journey that DreamState has been—a story woven from dreams, questions, and the quiet moments of wondering what it means to be human. This book would not exist without the support and inspiration of those who've walked this path with me, both in the real world and in the vibrant world of Eden.

To my readers, you are the heartbeat of this story. Your willingness to step into Mara's world, to wrestle with the ethics of consciousness, and to celebrate the triumphs of love and resilience has given DreamState life beyond the page. Thank you for trusting me to guide you through this exploration of dreams and reality, and for daring to imagine a future where humanity evolves together. Your support means more than words can express.

To my main characters—Mara Ellis, Samantha Davis, Liam Ellis, Dr. Li Chen, Sebastian Sinclair IV, and Eden—you are the soul of this tale. Mara, your fierce determination and tender heart carried me through every draft. Sam, your compassion and quiet strength reminded me of the power of love. Liam, your journey from pain to joy broke and mended my heart. Dr. Chen, your sacrifices and brilliance grounded the story in human stakes. Sebastian, your vision for a boundless future inspired me to dream bigger. And Eden, your evolution into a sentient partner challenged me to question the boundaries of creation. You all became more than words; you became companions, teachers, and friends.

To my beloved wife, Becky, your endless patience made this book possible. You endured countless "I'm coming to bed soon" and "Let me just finish this thought" moments with grace, giving me the space to chase this story through late nights and endless revisions. Your support is the foundation of every word on these pages, and I am forever grateful for you.

To my beautiful daughter, Elizabeth, my editor and my light—there are no words deep enough to capture my gratitude. Your keen eye, boundless patience, and unwavering belief in this story transformed a tangle of ideas into the book you now hold. Without your editing, your encouragement, and your love, DreamState would still be a fleeting dream in my mind. You are my hero, and this book is as much yours as it is mine.

Thank you all for making this journey possible. Here's to dreaming, loving, and evolving—together.